THE VICAR'S DAUGHTER

George MacDonald

EDITED BY DAN HAMILTON

A Quiet Neighborhood
The Seaboard Parish
The Vicar's Daughter

VICTOR BOOKS a division of SP Publications, Inc.
WHEATON, ILLINOIS 60187

Offices also in
Whitby, Ontario, Canada
Amersham-on-the-Hill, Bucks, England

Second printing, 1985

The Vicar's Daughter was first published in England in 1872.

Library of Congress Catalog Card Number: 84-52362
ISBN: 0-89693-330-X

VICTOR BOOKS
A division of SP Publications, Inc.
Wheaton, Illinois 60187

CONTENTS

INTRODUCTION

George MacDonald (1824-1905), a Scottish preacher, poet, novelist, fantasist, expositor, and public figure, is most well known today for his children's books—*At the Back of the North Wind, The Princess and the Goblin, The Princess and Curdie,* and his fantasies, *Lilith* and *Phantastes.*

But his fame is based on far more than his fantasies. His lifetime output of more than fifty popular books placed him in the same literary realm as Charles Dickens, Wilkie Collins, William Thackeray, and Thomas Carlyle. He numbered among his friends and acquaintances Lewis Carroll, Mark Twain, Lady Byron, and John Ruskin.

Among his later admirers were G.K. Chesterton, W.H. Auden, and C.S. Lewis. MacDonald's fantasy *Phantastes* was a turning point in Lewis' conversion; Lewis acknowledged MacDonald as his spiritual master and declared that he had never written a book without quoting from MacDonald.

PROLOGUE

My name is Ethelwyn, and my father is the Vicar Walton who wrote *A Quiet Neighborhood* and *The Seaboard Parish*. Ten days ago he came up to London from Marshmallows to pay us a visit, and brought with him Mr. Sutton, his publisher. Mr. Blackstone, a clergyman and friend, was also present.

Mr. Sutton looked at me with a twinkle in his eye, and asked, "Do you keep a diary?"

"I would rather keep a rag and bottle shop," I answered, at which Mr. Blackstone burst into one of his splendid infectious roars of laughter. If ever a man could laugh like a Christian who believed the world was in a fair way after all, that man was Mr. Blackstone.

"I mean," I continued, "that it would be a more profitable employment to keep the one than the other."

"I suppose you think," said Mr. Blackstone, "that the lady who keeps a diary is in the same danger as the old woman who prided herself in keeping a strict account of her personal expenses. It was always correct. Whenever she could not make it balance, she brought it right by putting the remainder down as *charity*."

"That's just what I mean."

"But," resumed Mr. Sutton, "I did not mean a diary of your feelings, but of the events of the days and hours."

"Which are never in themselves worth putting down," I said. "All that is worth remembering will find for itself some convenient cranny to sleep in till it is wanted, without being made a poor mummy of in a diary."

"If you have such a memory, that is even better for my purpose."

"For your purpose!" I repeated in surprise. "I beg your pardon, but what designs can you have upon my memory?"

"I will be straightforward: I want you to make up the sum of words your father owes me. He has provided me two books, but another story is required to complete the trilogy. He has left me in the lurch with an unfinished story, not to say an incomplete series. I have waited for the third for many years, and pressed him many times—but all I receive in return are excuses about the difficulties of growing older through the years, and failing judgments and all that. The upshot of it is that now he says I will have to get the third book from you."

I laughed, for the very notion of writing a book seemed preposterous. "You don't say you mean it! The thing is perfectly impossible. I never wrote a book in my life."

"Nor had I, my dear," said my father, "before I wrote my first one."

"But you grew up to it by degrees!"

"That will make it easier for you."

"It is perfectly absurd to suppose me capable of finishing anything my father has begun."

"I think, Wynnie, as everyone appears to wish it, you might as well try."

"If you will write a dozen pages or so," said Mr. Sutton, "I shall be able to judge by those well enough, and I will take the responsibility after that. Besides, my readers want to know about you and your sisters, and little Theodora."

They were all silent, and I began to feel as if I had behaved ungraciously. There was more talk, and in the end I agreed to try.

So I must start somewhere, and I will look at *The Seaboard Parish* to see how it ends. We had just returned from Kilkhaven to Marshmallows, but that was ten years ago. Can it be so long? So many things have happened, and I will try to give them in their right order.

ONE

AFTER KILKHAVEN

In the year after our return from Kilkhaven, my mother and father had a good many talks about me and Percivale, and sometimes they took different sides. One conversation, as I have since been told, went like this:

"But Harry," my mother said, "I am afraid they are too like each other to make a suitable match. For instance, Mr. Percivale does not seem, by all I can make out, a bit nearer believing in anything than poor Wynnie herself."

"Well," continued my father, "at least he doesn't fancy he believes when he does not, as so many do—and consider themselves superior persons in consequence. I don't know that it did you any great harm, Miss Ethelwyn, to have made my acquaintance when I was in the worst of my doubts concerning the truth of things. Allow me to tell you that I was nearer making shipwreck of my faith at a certain period than I ever was before or have been since."

"What period was that?"

"Just the little while when I had lost all hope of ever marrying you—unbeliever as you counted yourself."

"You don't mean to say you would have ceased to believe in God, if He hadn't given you your own way?"

"No, my dear. I firmly believe that had I never married you, I should have come in the end to say, 'Thy will be done,' and to believe that it must be all right, however hard to bear. But, oh, what a terrible thing it would have been, and what a frightful

9

valley I should have had to go through first!"

My mother said nothing more just then, but let my father have it all his own way for a while.

"You see," continued my father, "Percivale attributes to Christianity doctrines which, if I supposed they actually belonged to it, would make me reject it at once as ungodly and bad. This may be the case with him. I think his difficulty comes mainly from seeing so much suffering in the world, so that he cannot imagine the presence and rule of a good God. Therefore he sides with religion rather than with Christianity as yet. The only thing that will ever make him able to believe in a God at all is meditation on the Christian idea of God—I mean the idea of God *in* Christ reconciling the world to Himself—not that pagan corruption of Christ in God reconciling Him to the world. He will then see that suffering is neither wrath nor neglect, but purehearted love and tenderness. But we must give Percivale time.

"And as to trusting him with Wynnie, he seems to be as good as she is. I should have more apprehension in giving her to one who might be called a thoroughly religious man, for not only would the unfitness be greater, but such a man would be more likely to confirm her in doubt. How should they be able to love one another if they were not fit to be married to each other? The fitness seems inherent to the fact."

"But," interposed my mother, "many a two love each other, who would have loved each other a good deal more if they hadn't been married."

"Then it was most desirable they should find out that what they thought a grand affection was not worthy of the name. But I don't think there is much fear of that between those two. And love is the one great instructor. When Wynnie sees the troubled face of Percivale, she will know that he is suffering, and sympathy being thus established between them, the least word of the one will do more to help the other than oceans of argument."

"But I don't like her going from home for the help that lies at her very door. And then," added my mother, "if you will have them married, will you say how on earth you expect them to live? He just makes both ends meet now."

"Ah, yes!" agreed my father, "That is a consideration. There will be difficulty there, for Percivale is far too independent to let us do anything for him."

"And you couldn't do much, if he would. Really, they oughtn't to marry yet."

"We must leave it to them. When Percivale considers himself prepared to marry, and Wynnie thinks he is right, you may be sure they will have seen their way to a livelihood without running in hopeless debt to their tradespeople. And a little poverty and struggling would be a most healthy and healing thing for Wynnie. It hasn't done Percivale much good yet, for he is far too indifferent to his own comforts to mind it. But it will be quite another thing when he has a young wife and perhaps children depending upon him."

It may seem odd that my parents should be taking such opposite sides to those they had taken when we were in Kilkhaven, and Percivale and I had just met. But engagement and marriage are two different things, and although my mother was the first to recognize the possible good of our being engaged, she became frightened when it came time to consider marriage.

But then Percivale began to have what his artist friends called a run of luck, and sold one picture after another in a very extraordinary and hopeful manner. Percivale said it was his love for me which enabled him not only to see more deeply into things, but also to see much better the bloom that hangs about everything, and so to paint better pictures than before. He said he felt he now had a hold, where before he had only a sight. My mother, however, believed it was my father's good advice to Percivale (concerning the sort of pictures he painted) that brought his increased sales—and in consequence our marriage—about.

At any rate, he got on very well through the winter. In the very early spring he wrote, at last, that if I was willing to share his poverty, it would not be absolute starvation.

I, of course, was perfectly content. My father and mother made no objection. They had worked their way through many discussions, on one side or the other, had come to be of one mind about Mr. Percivale and me, and at last were quite agreed that marriage would be the best thing for both of us.

We fixed a date in early summer. In the spring, my mother went up to London— at Percivale's request—to help him get together a few things absolutely needful for the barest housekeeping.

She came back satisfied with the little house he had taken. It had not been easy to get one to suit us, for he required a large room to paint in, with a good north light.

"You will find things very different from what you have been

11

used to, Wynnie," said my mother.

"Of course, Mamma," I answered. "I hope I am prepared to meet it. If I don't like it, I shall have no one to blame but myself, and I don't see what right people have to expect what they have been used to."

"There is just this advantage," said my father, "in having been used to nice things, that it ought to be easier to keep from sinking into sordid circumstances."

In the days after that, I found that leaving the place where I had been born was like forsaking the laws and order of the nature I knew. How could one who has been used to our bright sun and our pale modest moon, with our soft twilights, and far, mysterious skies of night, be willing to fall in with the order of things in a different planet with three or four suns, one red and another green and another yellow? I found it a great wrench to leave the dear old place, and of course loved it more than I ever had. But I would get all my crying about that over beforehand. It would be bad enough afterward to have to part with my father and mother and Connie and the rest. Only it wasn't like leaving them, for you can't leave hearts like you do rooms. Those you love only come nearer to you when you go away from them.

The night before my wedding, my last to spend in my father's house as just his daughter and not as Mrs. Percivale, my father had taken me and my mother into the octagon room, and there knelt down with us, and prayed for me in such a wonderful way that I was perfectly astonished and overcome. He was not favorable to extemporaneous prayer in public, or even in the family, and indeed had often seemed willing to omit prayers for what I could not always count sufficient reason. He had a horror of their getting to be a matter of course and form, for then, he said, they ceased to be worship at all, and were a mere pagan rite and far better left alone.

The first thing I did the morning of my wedding was to have a good cry. And after that it became very hard to get up and dress. I seemed to have grown very fond of my own bed and the queer old crows—as I had called them from my babyhood—on the chintz curtains, and the Chinese paper on the walls with the strangest birds and creeping things on it. It was a lovely spring morning and the sun was shining gloriously. I knew that the rain of the last night must be glittering on the grass and the young leaves, and I heard the birds singing as if they knew far more than mere human beings, and believed a great deal more than they knew.

Dora and the boys were making a great chatter under my window, like a whole colony of sparrows. Still, I felt as if I had twenty questions to settle before I could get up comfortably, and so lay on and on till the breakfast bell rang; and I was not more than half dressed when my mother came to see why I was late. She comforted me as nobody but a mother can comfort her child. And indeed, that morning, I felt more like her child than a woman about to become a man's wife.

TWO

THE WEDDING

My father, of course, gave me away, and my uncle, Mr. Weir, married us. We decided we should have no wedding journey, for we all liked the old-fashioned plan of the bride going straight from her father's house to her husband's.

After the wedding we spent the time as we should have done any other day, wandering about in groups, or sitting and reading, only that we were more smartly dressed. Then it was time for an early dinner, after which we drove to the station, accompanied only by my father and mother.

After our train left, my husband did not speak to me for nearly an hour. I knew why, and I was very grateful. He would not show his new face in the midst of my old loves, but would give me time to accustom myself to the new arrangement and bring him in when all was ready for him. When at last I had things a little tidier inside me, I held out my hand to him, and then I knew that I was his wife.

In London, instead of my father's nice carriage, we got into a jolting, lumbering, horrid cab, with my five boxes and Percivale's little portmanteau perched on the top of it, and drove away to Camden Town, a part of it near Regent's Park. It was indeed a change from a fine old house in the country; but, after what I had been told to expect, I was surprised at the prettiness of the little house. It was stuck like a swallow's nest onto the end of a great row of commonplace houses, nearly a quarter of a mile in length, though our nest itself was not the work of one of those wretched

14

builders. It had been built by a painter for himself, in the Tudor style, and though Percivale said the idea was not very well carried out, I liked it.

It was, however, dreary and empty inside. The sitting room had just a table and two or three old-fashioned chairs, and not even a carpet on the floor. The bedroom and dressing room were as scantily furnished.

"Don't be dismayed, my darling," said my husband. "Look here," he continued, showing me a bunch of bank notes, "we shall go out tomorrow and buy all we want—as far as this will go—and then wait for the rest. It will be such a pleasure to buy the things with you, and see them come home, and have you appoint their places. You will make the carpets, won't you? And I will put them down, and we shall be like birds building their nest."

"We have only to line it—the nest is built already."

"Well, neither do the birds build the tree," he replied. "It is the only pretty house I know in all London," he went on, "with a studio at the back of it. I have had my eye on it for a long time, but there seemed no sign of a migratory disposition in the bird who had occupied it for three years past. All at once he spread his wings and flew. I count myself very fortunate."

"So do I. But now you must let me see your studio," I said, "I hope I may sit in it when you've got nobody there."

"As much as ever you like, my love," he answered. "Only I don't want to paint all my women like you, as I've been doing for the last two years."

He led me to the back of the little hall where he opened a small cloth-covered door. There yawned before me, below me, and above me, a great wide lofty room. Down into it led an almost perpendicular stair.

"So you keep a little private precipice here," I said.

"No, my dear," he returned. "It is a Jacob's ladder—or will be in one moment more."

He gave me his hand, and led me down.

"This is quite a banqueting hall, Percivale!" I cried, looking round me.

"It shall be, the first time I get a thousand pounds for a picture," he returned.

"How grand you talk!" I said, looking up at him with some wonder, for big words rarely came out of his mouth.

"Well," he answered merrily, "I had two hundred and seventy

five for the last."

"That's a long way off a thousand," I returned, with a silly sigh.

"Quite right. And, therefore, this study is a long way off a banqueting hall."

There was literally nothing inside the seventeen-foot cube except one chair, one easel, a horrible thing like a huge doll with no end of joints (called a lay-figure, but Percivale called it his bishop), a number of pictures leaning their faces against the walls in attitudes of grief that their beauty was despised and no man would buy them, a few casts of legs and arms and faces, a half dozen murderous-looking weapons, and a couple of yards square of the most exquisite tapestry I ever saw.

"Will you shut your eyes for one minute," he went on, "and whatever I do, not open them till I tell you?"

"You mustn't hurt me then, or I may open them without being able to help it, you know," I said, closing my eyes tight.

"Hurt you!" he repeated, with a tone I would not put on paper if I could, and the same moment I found myself in his arms, being carried like a baby.

But it was only for a few yards, and he laid me down somewhere and told me to open my eyes.

I was lying on a couch in a room, small, indeed, but beyond exception the loveliest I had ever seen. At first I was only aware of an exquisite harmony of color. Light came from a soft lamp hung in the middle, and when my eyes went up to see where it was fastened, I found the ceiling marvelous in deep blue, with a suspicion of green—just like some of the shades of a peacock's feathers—with a multitude of gold and red stars upon it. The walls were covered with pictures and sketches, and against one wall was a lovely little set of bookshelves filled with books. On a little carved table stood a vase of white hothouse flowers, with one red camellia. One picture had a curtain of green silk before it, and by its side hung the picture of the wounded knight whom his friends were carrying home to die

"O my Percivale!" I cried, and could not say more.

"Do you like it?" he asked quietly, but with shining eyes.

"Like it?" I repeated. "Shall I like Paradise when I get there? But what a lot of money it must have cost you!"

"Not much," he answered. "Not more than thirty pounds or so. Every spot of paint there is from my own brush."

"O Percivale!"

"The carpet was the only expensive thing. That must be as thick as I could get it, for the floor is of stone and must not come near your pretty feet. You would never guess that the place was a shed before, in which the sculptor used to keep his wet clay and blocks of marble."

"Seeing is hardly believing," I said. "Is it to be my room? I know you mean it for my room, where I can ask you to come when I please, and where I can hide when anyone comes you don't want me to see."

"That is just what I meant it for, and to let you know what I *would* do for you if I could."

He made me shut my eyes again, and carried me into the study.

"Now," he said, "find your way to your own room."

I looked about me, but could see no sign of a door. He took up a tall stretcher with a canvas on it, and revealed the door. The canvas, as he turned it over, showed a likeness of myself at the top of the Jacob's ladder, as he called it, with one foot on the first step, and the other half way to the second. The light came from the window on my left, which he had turned into a western window, in order to get certain effects from a supposed sunset. I was represented in a white dress, tinged with the rose of the west—and he had managed to suggest one rosy wing behind me, with just the shoulder-root of another wing visible.

"There!" he said. "It is not finished yet, but that is how I saw you one evening as I was sitting here all alone in the twilight."

"But you didn't really see me like that!" I said.

"I was dreaming about you, and there I saw you, standing at the top of the stair, smiling to me as if to say, 'Have patience. My foot is on the first step. I'm coming.' I turned at once to my easel, and before the twilight was gone had sketched the vision."

The next morning we set out on our furniture hunt. We did not agree about the merits of everything by which one or the other was attracted; but an objection by the one always turned the other, and we bought nothing we were not agreed about. Yet that evening the hall was piled with things sent home to line our nest. Percivale, as I have said, had saved up some money for the purpose, and I had a hundred pounds my father had given me before we started, which, never having had more than ten of my own at one time, I was eager enough to spend. So we found plenty to do for the fortnight, during which time my mother had promised to say nothing to her friends in London of our arrival. Percivale also kept out of the way of his friends, and so everybody thought we were on the Continent, or somewhere else, and left us to ourselves. And as he had sent in his pictures to the Academy, he was able to take a rest—which consisted in working hard at all sorts of uphol- stery, not to mention painters' and carpenters' work, so that we soon got the little house made into a very warm and very pretty nest.

Percivale was particularly pleased with a cabinet I bought for him on the sly, to stand in his study and hold his paints and brushes and sketches. There were all sorts of drawers in it, and some that it took us a good deal of trouble to find out, though he was more clever than I, and suspected them from the first. That cabinet is just like him, for I have been going on finding out things in him that I had no idea were there when I married him.

THREE

MRS. MORLEY'S VISIT

The very first morning after the expiry of the fortnight, when I was in the kitchen with our cook and housekeeper, Sarah, giving her instructions about a certain dish as if I had made it twenty times, whereas I had only just learned how from a shilling cookery book, there came a double knock at the door. I guessed who it must be.

"Run, Sarah," I said, "and show Mrs. Morley into the drawing room."

When I entered, there she was—Mrs. Morley, alias Cousin Judy.

"Well, Cozzie!" she cried, as she kissed me three or four times, "I'm glad to see you gone the way of womankind—wooed and married and a'! Fate, child! Inscrutable fate!" And she kissed me again.

She always calls me Little Coz, though I am a head taller than herself. She was as good as ever, quite as brusque, and at the first word apparently more overbearing. After a little trifling talk, which is sure to come first when people are more than ordinarily glad to meet, I asked after her children. I forget how many there were, but they were then pretty far into the plural number. All the little Morleys were full of life and eagerness. The fault in them was that they wouldn't take petting, and what's the good of a child that won't be petted? They lacked that something which makes a woman feel motherly.

"When did you arrive, Cozzie?" she asked.

"A fortnight ago yesterday."

"Ah, you sly thing! What have you been doing with yourself a' the time?"

"Furnishing."

"What? You came to an empty house?"

"Not quite that, but nearly."

"It is very odd that I should never have seen your husband."

"Not so *very* odd, seeing he has been my husband only a fortnight."

"What is he like?"

"Like nothing but himself."

"Is he tall?"

"Yes."

"Is he stout?"

"No."

"Very clever, I believe."

"Not at all." (For my father had taught me to look down on that word.)

"Why did you marry him then?"

"I didn't. He married me."

"What did you marry him for then?"

"For love."

"What did you love him for?"

"Because he was a philosopher."

"That's the oddest reason I ever heard for marrying a man."

"I said for loving him, Judy."

Her bright eyes were twinkling with fun. "Come, Cozzie," she said, "give me a proper reason for falling in love with this husband of yours."

"Well, I'll tell you, then," I said, "only you mustn't tell anybody: he has such a big shaggy head, just like a lion's."

"And such a big foot, just like a bear's?"

"Yes, and such great huge hands! Why, the two of them go quite around my waist! And such big eyes, that they look right through me. And such a big heart, that if he saw me doing anything wrong, he would kill me, and bury me in it."

"Well, I must say, it is the most extraordinary description of a husband I have ever heard. It sounds to me very like an ogre."

"The description is rather ogrish. But then he's poor, and that makes up for a good deal."

"How does that make up for anything?"

"Because if he is a poor man, he isn't a rich man, and therefore not so likely to be a stupid."

"How do you make that out?"

"Because, first of all, the rich man doesn't know what to do with his money, whereas my ogre knows what to do without it. Then the rich man wonders in the morning which waistcoat he shall put on, while my ogre has but one, besides his Sunday one. Then supposing the rich man has slept well, and has done a fair stroke or two of business, he wants nothing but a well-dressed wife, a well-dressed dinner, a few glasses of his favorite wine, and the evening paper, all well-diluted with a sleep in his easy chair, to be perfectly satisfied that this world is the best of all possible worlds. Now my ogre, on the other hand—"

She interrupted me, saying with an odd tone of voice, "You are satirical, Cozzie. He's not the worst sort of man you've just described. A woman might be very happy with him."

It flashed upon me that, without the least intention, I had been giving a very fair portrait of Mr. Morley. I felt my face grow as red as fire.

"I had no intention of being satirical, Judy," I replied. "I was only describing a man the very opposite of my husband."

"You don't know mine yet," she said. "You may think—"

She actually broke down and cried. I had never in my life seen her cry, and I was miserable at what I had done. Here was a nice beginning of social relations in my married life!

I knelt down, put my arms round her, and looked up in her face.

"Dear Judy," I said. "I never thought of Mr. Morley when I said that. How should I have dared to say such things if I had? He is a most kind, good man, and Papa and everyone are glad when he comes to see us. I dare say he does like to sleep well—I know Percivale does—and I don't doubt he likes to get on with what he's at. Percivale does, for he's ever so much better company when he has got on with his picture, and I know he likes to see me well-dressed. I wish Percivale cared a little more for his dinner, for then it would be easier to do something for him. As to the newspaper, there I fear I must give him up, for I have never yet seen him with one in his hand. He's *so* stupid about some things!"

"Oh, you've found that out, have you? Men *are* stupid there's no doubt of that. But you don't know my Walter yet."

I looked up, and, behold, Percivale was in the room! His face wore such a curious expression that I could hardly help laughing. And no wonder. For here was I on my knees, clasping my first visitor, and to all appearances pouring out the woes of my wedded life in her lap, woes so deep that they drew tears from her as she listened. All this flashed upon me as I started to my feet, but I could give no explanation: I could only make haste to introduce my husband to my cousin Judy.

He behaved, of course, as if he had heard nothing. But I fancy Judy caught a glimpse of the awkward position, for she plunged into the affair at once.

"Here is my cousin, Mr. Percivale—abusing my husband to my face, calling him rich and stupid, and I don't know what all. I confess he is so stupid as to be very fond of me, but that's all I know against him." And her handkerchief went once more to her eyes.

"Dear Judy!" I expostulated, "you know I didn't say one word about him."

"Of course I do, you silly coz!" she cried, and burst out laughing. "But I won't forgive you except you make amends by dining with us tomorrow."

Thus for the time she carried it off; but I believe that she had really mistaken me at first, and been much annoyed. And as glad as I had been to see her, how I longed to see the last of her! The moment she was gone, I threw myself into Percivale's arms, and told him how it came about. He laughed heartily.

"I *was* a little puzzled," he said, "to hear you informing a lady I had never seen that I was so very stupid."

"But I wasn't telling a story, either, for you know you are ve-e-e-ry stupid, Percivale. You don't know a leg from a shoulder of mutton, and you can't carve a bit. How you draw as you do is a marvel to me, when you know nothing about the shapes of things. It was very wrong to say it, even for the sake of covering poor Morley, but it was quite true."

"Perfectly true, my love," he said (with something else where I've only put commas), "and I mean to remain so, in order that you may always have something to fall back upon when you get yourself into a scrape by forgetting that other people have husbands too."

FOUR

GOOD SOCIETY

We had agreed, rather against our inclinations, to dine the next evening with the Morleys. We should have preferred our own society, but could not refuse.

"They will be talking to me about my pictures," said my husband, "and that is just what I hate. People who know nothing of art, who can't distinguish purple from black, will yet parade their ignorance, and expect me to be pleased."

"Mr. Morley is a well-bred man, Percivale," I said.

"That's the worst of it—they do it for good manners. I know the kind of people perfectly. I hate to have my pictures praised. It is as bad as talking to one's face about the nose upon it."

I wonder if all ladies keep their husbands waiting. I did that night, I know, and, I am afraid, a good many times after; but not since Percivale told me very seriously that being late for dinner was the only fault of mine the blame of which he would not take on his own shoulders.

When we reached Bolivar Square, we found the company waiting; and, as if for a rebuke to us, the butler announced dinner the moment we entered. I was seated between Mr. Morley and a friend of his, Mr. Baddeley, a portly gentleman with an expanse of snowy shirt from which flashed three diamond studs. A huge gold chain reposed upon his front, and on his finger shone a brilliant of great size. Everything about him seemed to say, "Look how rich I am! Nothing shoddy about me!" His hands were plump and white, and looked as if they did not know what dust was. His talk

23

sounded very rich, and yet there was no pretense in it. His wife looked less of a lady than he a gentleman, for she betrayed conscious importance. I found afterwards that he was the only son of a railway contractor, who had himself handled the spade, but at last had died enormously rich. He spoke blandly, but with a certain authority which I disliked.

"Are you fond of the opera, Mrs. Percivale?" he asked me in order to make talk.

"I have never been to the opera," I answered.

"Never been to the opera? Are you not fond of music?"

"Did you ever know a lady that wasn't?"

"Then you must go to the opera."

"But it is just because I fancy myself fond of music that I don't think I should like the opera."

"You can't hear such music anywhere else."

"An artist's wife must do without such expensive amusements, except her husband's pictures be very popular indeed. I might as well cry for the moon. The cost of a box at the opera for a single night would keep my little household for a fortnight."

"Ah, well! But you should see *The Barber*," he said.

"Perhaps if I could hear without seeing, I should like it better," I answered.

He fell silent, busying himself with his fish, and when he spoke again turned to the lady on his left. I went on with my dinner. I knew that our host had heard what I said, for I saw him turn rather hastily to his butler.

Mr. Morley is a man difficult to describe, stiff in the back, and long and loose in the neck, reminding me of those toy birds that bob head and tail up and down alternately. When he agrees with anything you say, down comes his head with a rectangular nod. When he does not agree with you, he is so silent and motionless that he leaves you in doubt whether he has heard a word of what you have been saying. His face is hard, and was to me then inscrutable, while what he said always seemed to have little or nothing to do with what he was thinking. I had not then learned whether he had a heart or not. His features were well formed, but they and his head and face were too small for his body. He had been very successful in business, and always looked full of schemes.

"Have you been to the Academy yet?" he asked.

"No. This is only the first day of it."

"Are your husband's pictures well hung?"

24

GOOD SOCIETY

"As high as Haman," I answered, "skied, in fact."

"I would advise you to avoid slang, my dear cousin, *professional* slang especially, and to remember that in London there are no professions after six o'clock."

"Indeed!" I returned. "As we came along in the carriage I saw no end of shops open."

"I mean in society—at dinner—amongst friends."

"My dear Mr. Morley, you have just done asking me about my husband's pictures. And, if you will listen a moment, you will hear that lady next to my husband talking to him about Leslie and Turner, and I don't know who more, all in the trade."

"Hush! Hush! I beg you," he almost whispered, looking agonized. "That's Mrs. Baddeley. Her husband, next to you, is a great picture buyer. That's why I asked him to meet you."

"I thought there were no professions in London after six o'clock."

"I am afraid I have not made my meaning quite clear to you. We'll have a talk about it another time."

"With pleasure."

It rather irritated me that he should talk to me, a married woman, as to a little girl who did not know how to behave herself, but his patronage of my husband displeased me far more. I was on the point of committing the terrible blunder of asking Mr. Baddeley if he had any poor relations, but I checked myself in time, and prayed to know whether he was a member of Parliament. He answered that he was not at present, and asked in return why I had wished to know. I answered that I wanted a bill brought in for the punishment of fraudulent milkmen, for I couldn't get a decent pennyworth of milk in all Camden Town. He laughed, and said it would be a very desirable measure, only too great an interference with the liberty of the subject. I told him that kind of liberty was just what the law in general owed its existence to, and was there on purpose to interfere with, but he did not seem to see it.

The fact is, I was very silly. Proud of being the wife of an artist, I resented the social injustice which I thought gave artists no place but one of sufferance. Proud also of being poor for Percivale's sake, I made a show of my poverty before people whom I supposed, rightly enough in many cases, to be proud of their riches. But I knew nothing of what poverty really meant, and was as yet only playing at being poor. I was thus wronging the dignity of my

25

husband's position, and complimenting wealth by making so much of its absence. Poverty or wealth ought to have been in my eyes such a trifle that I never thought of publishing, whether I was rich or poor.

I suspect also, now that I think of it, that I looked down on my cousin Judy because she had a mere man of business for her husband, forgetting that our Lord had found a collector of conquered taxes—a man, I presume, with little enough of the artistic about him—one of the fittest in his nation to bear the message of redemption to the hearts of his countrymen. It is his loves and his hopes, not his visions and intentions, by which a man is to be judged.

"Is Mrs. Percivale a lady of fortune?" asked Mr. Baddeley of my cousin Judy when we were gone, for we were the first to leave.

"Certainly not. Why do you ask?"

"Because, from her talk, I thought she must be."

Cousin Judy told me this the next day, and I could see she thought I had been bragging of my family. So I recounted all the conversation I had had with him, as nearly as I could recollect, and set down the question to an impertinent irony. But I have since changed my mind; I now judge that he could not believe any poor person would joke about poverty.

FIVE

A REFUGE FROM THE HEAT

Our house boasted a little garden by the studio. One side was enclosed by the house, another by the studio, and the remaining two by walls, evidently built for the nightly convenience of promenading cats. One pear tree in a grass plot occupied the center, and a few small fruit trees (which, I may now safely say, never bore anything) around the walls. The last occupant had cared for his garden, but if you stop thinking about a garden, it begins at once to go bad.

Although I had been used to great wide lawns and parks and gardens and wilderness, the tiny enclosure soon became to me the type of the boundless universe. The streets roared about me with ugly omnibuses and uglier cabs, fine carriages, huge earthshaking drays, and (worse far) the cries of all the tribe of costermongers. Suburban London was roaring about me, and I was confined to a few square yards of grass and gravel walk and flower plot. But above was the depth of the sky, and at night the hosts of heaven looked in upon me with a calm assured glance, and there the moon would come, and cast her lovely shadows. There was room enough to feel alone and to try to pray.

And, strangely, the space seemed greater (for the loneliness was gone) when my husband walked up and down in it with me. True, the greater part of the walk seemed to be the turnings, for they always came just when you wanted to go on and on. But even with the scope of the world for your walk, you must turn and come back some time. At first, when he was smoking his great brown meer-

27

schaum, he and I would walk in opposite directions, passing each other in the middle, and so make the space double the size, for he had all the garden to himself, and I had it all to myself. That is how by degrees I grew able to bear the smoke of tobacco, for I had never been used to it, and found it a small trial at first. But now I like it, and greet a stray whiff from the study like a message from my husband.

There was in the garden a little summer house. Knowing my passion for the flower, Percivale had surrounded it with a multitude of sweet peas, which he had trailed over the trelliswork of its sides. To sit there in a warm evening, when the moth-airs just woke and gave two or three wafts of their wings and ceased, was like sitting in the midst of a small gospel.

The summer had come and the days were very hot, so hot and changeless, with their unclouded skies and their glowing center, that they seemed to grow stupid with their own heat. Like a hen brooding over her chickens, the day, brooding over its coming harvests, grew dull and sleepy, living only in what was to come. I began to long for a wider horizon, whence some wind might come and blow upon me, and wake me up, not merely to live, but to know that I lived.

One afternoon I left my little summer seat, where I had been sitting at work, and went through the house, and down the precipice into my husband's study.

"It is so hot," I said, "I will try my little grotto. It may be cooler."

He opened the door for me, and, with his palette on his thumb, and a brush in his hand, sat down for a moment beside me.

"This heat is too much for you, Darling," he said.

"I do feel it. I wish I could get from the garden into my nest without going up through the house and down the Jacob's ladder," I said. "It is so hot! I never felt heat like it before."

He sat silent for a while, and then said, "I've been thinking I must get you into the country for a few weeks. It would do you no end of good."

"I suppose the wind does blow somewhere," I returned. "But—"

"You don't want to leave me?"

"I don't. And with that ugly portrait on hand you can't go with me."

He happened to be painting a portrait of a plain red-faced lady

28

in a delicate lace cap (a very unfit subject for art) much needing to be made over again first, it seemed to me. Only there she was, with a right to have her portrait painted if she wished it. And there was Percivale, with time on his hands and room in his pockets, and the faith that whatever God had thought worth making could not be unworthy of representation. Hence he had willingly undertaken her likeness, to be finished within a certain time, and was now working at it as conscientiously as if it had been the portrait of a lovely young duchess or peasant girl. (I was only afraid he would make it too like her to please the lady herself!) His time was now getting short, and he could not leave home before fulfilling his engagement.

"But," he returned, "why shouldn't you go to the Hall for a week or two without me? I will take you down, and come and fetch you."

"You want to get rid of me!" I said. I did not in the least believe it, and yet I was on the edge of crying.

"You know better than that, my Wynnie," he answered gravely. "You want your mother to comfort you. And there must be some air in the country. So tell Sarah to put up your things, and I'll take you down tomorrow evening. When I get this portrait done, I will come and stay a few days, if they will have me, and then take you home."

The thought of seeing my mother and my father and the old place came over me with a rush, and I felt all at once as if I had been absent for years instead of weeks. I cried in earnest now, with delight though, and there is no shame in that. So it was all arranged, and the next evening I was lying on a couch in the yellow drawing room, with my mother seated beside me. Connie sat in an easy chair by the open window, through which came every now and then such a sweet wave of air as bathed me with hope, and seemed to wash all the noises from my brain.

Yet, glad as I was to be once more at home, I felt, when Percivale left me the next morning to return by a third-class train to his ugly portrait, that the idea of home was already leaving Oldcastle Hall, and flitting back to the suburb of London.

But soon I felt better, for here there was plenty of shadow and in the hottest days my father could always tell where any wind would be stirring, for he knew every out and in of the place like his own pockets.

One forenoon in particular was most oppressive. I was sitting under a tree, trying to read, when he came up to me. There was a wooden gate, with open bars near. He went and set it wide, saying, "There, my love! You will fancy yourself cooler if I leave the gate open."

His words went deep to my heart, and I seemed to know God better for it ever after. A father is a great and marvelous truth, and one you can never get at the depth of, try how you may.

My mother was, if possible, yet more to me than my father. I could tell her anything and everything without fear, while I confess to a little dread of my father still. He is too like my conscience for me to be quite confident with him.

SIX

CONNIE

The worst of some illnesses (especially some small ones) is that they make you think a great deal too much about yourself. My sister Connie's illness (which was a great and terrible one) never made her do so.

She was now a thin, pale, delicate-looking girl, not handsome, but lovely. Some people said her eyes were too big for her face. She had been early ripened by the hot sun of suffering, and by the self-restraint which pain had taught her. Patience had mossed her over, and made her warm and soft and sweet. She never looked for attention, but accepted all that was offered with a smile. She was not confined to her sofa now, though she needed to lie down often, but could walk about pretty well—only you had to give her time. You could always make her merry by saying she walked like an old woman, and it was the only way we could get rid of the sadness of seeing it. And so we laughed her sadness away from us.

She was always forgetting herself in her interest about others, and now she would watch me with her gentle, dovelike eyes, and seemed to know at once, without being told, what was the matter with me. She never asked me what I should like, but went and brought something—and, if she saw that I didn't care for it, she wouldn't press me or offer anything instead, but chat for a minute or two, carry it away, and return with something else. My heart was like to break at times with the swelling of the love that was in it.

Once, as I lay on a couch on the lawn, she came toward me

carrying a bunch of grapes from the greenhouse—a great bunch, each individual grape ready to burst with the sunlight bottled up in its swollen purple skin.

"They are too heavy for you, old lady," I cried.

"Yes, I *am* an old lady," she answered. "Think what good use of my time I have made compared with you! I have gone ever so far before you—I've nearly forgotten how to walk!"

The tears gathered in my eyes as she left the bunch with me—for how could one help being sad to think of the time when she used to bound like a slender fawn over the grass? She turned to say something and, perceiving my emotion, came slowly back.

"Dear Wynnie," she said, "you wouldn't have me back with my old foolishness, would you? Believe me, life is ten times more precious than it was before. I feel and enjoy and love so much more! I often thank God for what befell me."

And I believe she had a special affection for poor Sprite, the pony which threw her, regarding him as in some sense the angel which had driven her out of paradise into a better world. If ever he got loose and Connie was anywhere about, he was sure to find her. He was an omnivorous animal, and she always had something he would eat when his favorite apples were unobtainable. More than once she had been roused from her sleep on the lawn by the lips and the breath of Sprite on her face. Although she usually started at the least noise or sudden discovery of a presence, she never started at the most unexpected intrusion of Sprite, any more than at the voice of my father or mother.

There was one more whose voice or presence never startled her. The relation between that one and her was lovely to see. Turner was a fine, healthy, broad-shouldered fellow, of bold carriage and frank manners, above the middle height, with rather large features, keen black eyes, and great personal strength. Yet to such a man, poor little wan-faced, big-eyed Connie assumed imperious airs, mostly—but perhaps not entirely—for the fun of it, while he looked only enchanted every time she honored him with a little tyranny.

"There! I'm tired," she would say, holding out her arms like a baby. "Carry me in."

And he would stoop, and take her carefully, and carry her in as lightly and gently and steadily as if she had been but the baby whose manners she had for the moment assumed. This began, of course, when she was unable to walk, but it did not stop then, for she would occasionally tell him to carry her after she was quite capable of crawling at least. They had now been engaged for some months, and in front of me—a newly married woman—they did not mind talking a little.

One day she was lying on a rug on the lawn, with him on the grass beside her, leaning on his elbow, and looking down into her sky-like eyes. She lifted her hand, and stroked his mustache with a forefinger.

"Poor, poor man!" she said, and from the tone I knew the tears had begun to gather in those eyes.

"Why do you pity me, Connie?" he asked.

"Because you will have such a wretched little creature for a wife someday—or perhaps never."

"If you will allow me my choice," he answered cheerily, "I prefer just such a wretched little creature to anyone else in the world."

"And why, pray? Give a good reason, and I will forgive your bad taste."

"Because she won't be able to hurt me much when she beats me."

"A better reason, or she will."

"Because I can punish her if she isn't good by taking her up in my arms, and carrying her about until she gives in."

"A better reason, or I shall be naughty directly."

"Because I shall always know where to find her."

"Ah, yes! She must leave you to find her. But that's a silly reason. If you don't give me a better, I'll get up and walk into the house."

"Because there won't be any waste of me. Will that do?"

"What do you mean?" she asked.

"I mean that I shall be able to lay not only my heart but my brute strength at her feet. I shall be her beast of burden, to carry her whither she would."

"There! Take me, take me!" she said, stretching up her arms to him. "How good you are! I don't deserve such a great man one bit. But I will love him. Take me directly, for there's Wynnie listening and laughing at us."

I was crying, and the creature knew it. Turner brought her to me, and held her down for me to kiss, then carried her in.

I believe the country people round considered our family far gone on the inclined plane of degeneracy. First my mother, the heiress, had married a clergyman of no high family, and they had given their eldest daughter to a poor artist. And now Connie was engaged to a country practitioner, a man who made up his own prescriptions. Connie and I talked and laughed over certain remarks of the kind that reached us, and compared our two with the gentlemen about us—in no way to the advantage of any of the latter, you may be sure. It was silly work, but we were only two loving girls, with the best possible reasons for being proud of the men who had honored us with their love.

SEVEN
CONNIE'S BABY

Theodora, our orphan, was now nearly four years old and a very pretty, dark-skinned, lithe-limbed, wild little creature. She was not like a lady's child, and neither did she look like the child of working people. She had a certain tinge of the savage about her, specially manifest in a certain furtive look of her black eyes, with which she seemed now and then to be measuring you, and her prospects in relation to you.

I have seen children stare at a stranger in the most persistent manner, never withdrawing their eyes, as if they would pierce to his soul. I have also seen their sidelong glance of sly merriment, or loving shyness, or small coquetry. But I have never, in any other child, seen *that* look of self-protective speculation; and it used to make me uneasy, for of course, like everyone else in the house, I loved Theodora. She was a wayward, often unmanageable creature, but affectionate. She would take an unaccountable preference for some one of the family or household, at one time for the housekeeper, at another for the stableboy, at another for one of us. In these fits of partiality she would always turn a blind and deaf side on everyone else, actually seeming to imagine she showed the strength of her love to the one by the paraded exclusion of the others.

I cannot tell how much of this was natural to her, and how much the result of the foolish and injurious jealousy of the servants. I say servants, because I know such an influencing was all but impossible in the family itself. If my father heard anyone utter

35

such a phrase as, "Don't you love me best?" or, "better than such a one?" or, "Ain't I your favorite?"—well, you would have been astonished, and perhaps at first bewildered as well, by the look of indignation that flashed from his eyes. He was not the gentle, all-excusing man some fancy him. He was gentle even to tenderness when he had time to think a moment, and in any quiet judgment he always took as much the side of the offender as was possible with any likelihood of justice.

Theodora was subject to attacks of the most furious passion, especially when anything occurred to thwart the indulgence of her partiality. Then, wherever she was, she would throw herself down on the floor, on the walk or lawn, or, as happened on one occasion, in the water, and kick and scream. At such times she cared nothing even for my father, of whom generally she stood in considerable awe—a feeling he rather encouraged.

"She has plenty of people about her to represent the Gospel," he said once. "I will keep the department of the law, without which she will never appreciate the Gospel. My part will, I trust, vanish in due time, and the law turn out to have been, after all, only the imperfect Gospel, just as the leaf is the imperfect flower. But the Gospel is no Gospel till it gets into the heart, and it sometimes wants a torpedo to blow the gates of that open."

For no torpedo, however, did Theodora care at such times. After repeated experience, my father gave orders that when a fit occurred, everyone, without exception, should not merely leave her alone, but go out of sight and out of her hearing, that she might know she had driven her friends far from her, and be brought to a sense of loneliness and need. I am pretty sure that if she had been one of his own, he would have taken sharper measures with her. But he said we must never attempt to treat other people's children as our own, for they are not. We did not love them enough, he said, to make severity safe either for them or for us.

The plan worked so far well that, after a time, varied in length according to causes inscrutable, she would always reappear smiling. But, as to any conscience of wrong, she seemed to have no more than Nature herself, who looks out with her smiling face after hours of thunder, lightning, and rain. Although this treatment brought her out of her attacks sooner, the fits themselves came quite as frequently as before.

But she had another habit, more alarming, and more troublesome as well—she would vanish and have to be long sought, for in such cases she never reappeared of herself. What made it so alarming was that there were dangerous places about our house. Yet she would generally be found seated, perfectly quiet, in some out-of-the-way nook where she had never been before, playing not with any of her toys, but with something she had picked up and appropriated, finding in it some shadowy amusement which no one understood but herself.

She was very fond of bright colors, especially in dress. If she found a brilliant or gorgeous fragment of any substance, she would be sure to hide it away in some hole or corner. Her love of approbation was strong, and her affection demonstrative, but she had not yet learned to speak the truth. She must, we thought, have come of wild parentage, for so many of her ways were like those of a forest animal.

In our design of training her for a maid to Connie, we seemed already likely enough to be frustrated. She had some sort of aversion to Connie, amounting almost to dread, and we could rarely persuade her to go near her. Perhaps it was a dislike to her helplessness—some vague impression that lying all day on the sofa indicated an unnatural condition of being. Those of us who had the highest spirits, the greatest exuberance of animal life, were evidently those whose society was most attractive to her. Connie tried all she could to conquer Theodora's dislike and entice the wayward thing to her heart, but nothing would do. Sometimes she would seem to soften for a moment—but all at once, with a wriggle and a backward spasm in the arms of the person who carried her, she would manifest a fresh access of repulsion, and wailing, would be borne off hurriedly. I have seen Connie cry because the child treated her so.

You could not interest Theodora so much in a story that if the buzzing of a fly or the flutter of a bird reached her eye or ear, away she would dart on the instant, leaving the discomfited narrator in lonely disgrace. External nature and almost nothing else had free access to her mind; at any sudden sight or sound, she was alive on the instant. She was a most amusing and sometimes almost bewitching little companion, but the delight in her would be not unfrequently quenched by some altogether unforeseen outbreak of heartless petulance or turbulent rebellion.

Her resistance to authority grew as she grew older, and occasioned all of us no little anxiety. Even Charley and Harry would stand with open mouths, contemplating aghast the unheard-of atrocity of resistance to the will of the unquestioned authorities. Such resistance was almost always accompanied by storm and tempest, and the treatment which carried away the latter, generally carried away the former with it. After the passion had come and gone, she would obey. Had it been otherwise—had she been sullen and obstinate as well—I do not know what would have come of it, or how we could have got on at all. Miss Bowdler would have had a very satisfactory crow over Papa.

I have seen him sit in silent contemplation of the little puzzle, trying, no doubt, to fit her into his theories or, as my mother said, to find her a three-legged stool and a corner somewhere in the kingdom of heaven. We were certain something or other would come out of that pondering, though whether the same night or a twelvemonth after, no one could tell. I believe the main result of his thinking was that he did less and less with her.

"Why do you take so little notice of the child?" my mother said to him one evening. "It is all your doing that she is here, you know. You mustn't cast her off now."

"Cast her off!" exclaimed my father. "What *do* you mean, Ethel?"

"You never speak to her now."

"Oh, yes I do, sometimes!"

"Why only sometimes?"

"I believe I am a little afraid of her. I don't know how to attack the small enemy. She seems to be bombproof, and generally impregnable."

"But you mustn't therefore make *her* afraid of you."

"I suspect that is my only chance with her. She wants a little of Mount Sinai, in order that she may know where the manna comes from. But indeed I am laying myself out only to catch the little soul. I am watching and pondering how to reach her. I am biding my time to come in with my small stone for the building up of this temple of the Holy Ghost."

The moon was rising in the last fold of the twilight, and at that moment the nurse came through the darkening air, her figure hardly distinguishable from the dusk, saying, "Please, Ma'am, have you seen Miss Theodora?"

"I don't want you to call her *Miss*," said my father.

"I beg your pardon, Sir," said the nurse, "I forgot."

"I have not seen her for an hour or more," said my mother.

"I declare," said my father, "I'll get a retriever pup and train him to find Theodora. He will be capable in a few months, and she will be foolish for years."

On that occasion the truant was found in the apple-loft, sitting in a dark corner upon a heap of straw. She was discovered only by the munching of her little teeth—she had found some wizened apples, and was busily devouring them.

My father actually did what he had said—a favorite spaniel had pups a few days after, and he took one of them in hand. Soon the long-drawn nose of Wagtail had learned to track Theodora to whatever retreat she might have chosen, and it was very amusing to watch the course of the proceedings. Someone would come running to my father with the news that Theo was hiding. Then my father would give a peculiar whistle, and Wagtail would come bounding to his side. My father himself would lay him on the scent, for he would heed directions from no one else. It was not necessary to follow him, however; after his tortuous and fatiguing pursuit, a joyous barking would be heard, always kept up until the ready pursuers were guided by the sound to the place. There Theo was certain to be found, hugging the animal, without the least notion of the traitorous character of his blandishments. It was long before she began to discover that there was danger in that dog's nose.

EIGHT

THE FOUNDLING
AND WAGTAIL

One evening during this first visit to my home, we had gone to take tea with the widow of an old servant—Connie and I in the pony carriage, and my father and mother on foot. It was quite dark when we returned, for the moon was late. Connie and I got home first, though we had a good round to make, and the path across the fields was but a third of the distance. My father and mother were lovers, and sure to be late when left out by themselves. When we arrived, there was no one to take the pony, and when I rang the bell, no one answered. I could not leave Connie in the carriage to go and look, so we waited and waited till we were getting very tired, and were glad indeed to hear the voices of my father and mother as they came through the shrubbery. My mother went to the rear to make inquiry, and came back with the news that Theo was missing, and that they had been searching for her in vain for nearly an hour. My father instantly called Wagtail, and sent him after her. We then got Connie in and laid her on the sofa, where I kept her company while the rest went in different directions, listening from what quarter would come the welcome voice of the dog. This was so long delayed, however, that my father began to get alarmed. At last he whistled very loudly, and in a little while Wagtail came creeping to his feet, with his tail between his legs—no wag left in it—clearly ashamed of himself.

My father was now thoroughly frightened, and began questioning the household. One of the servants then remembered that

40

a strange-looking woman had been seen about the place in the morning, a tall, dark woman, with a gypsy look. She had come begging, but nothing had been given her, and she had gone away in anger. As soon as he heard this, my father ordered his horse, and told two of the men to get ready to accompany him. In the meantime, he came to us in the little drawing room, trying to look calm but evidently in much perturbation. He said he had little doubt that the woman had taken her.

"Could it be her mother?" said my mother.

"Who can tell?" returned my father. "It is less likely that the deed was prompted by revenge."

"If she be a gypsy's child—" said my mother.

"The gypsies," interrupted my father, "have always been more given to taking other people's children than forsaking their own. But one of them might have had reason for being ashamed of her child, and, dreading the severity of her family, abandoned it, with the intention of repossessing it herself, and passing it off as the child of gentlefolks. If we should fail in finding her tonight, the police all over the country can be apprised of the fact in a few hours, and the thief can hardly escape."

"But if she *should* be the mother?" suggested my mother.

"She would have to *prove* that."

"And then?"

"What then?" returned my father, and began pacing up and down the room, stopping now and then to listen for the horses.

'Would you give her up?" persisted my mother.

Still my father made no reply. He was evidently much agitated—more, I fancied, by my mother's question than by the present trouble. He left the room, and presently his whistle for Wagtail pierced the still air. A moment more, and we heard them all ride out of the paved yard. I had never known him to leave my mother without an answer.

There was not a dry eye amongst the women. Harry was in floods of tears and Charley was howling. We could not send them to bed in such a state, so we kept them with us in the drawing room. They soon fell fast asleep, one in an easy chair, the other on a sheepskin mat. Connie lay quite still, and my mother talked so sweetly and gently that she soon made me quiet and drowsy too. But I was haunted with the idea that it was somehow a child of my own lost out in the dark night, and that I could not anyhow reach her. I cannot explain the odd feeling—as if a dream

41

had wandered out of the region of sleep, and half-possessed my waking brain. Every now and then my mother's voice would bring me back to my senses, and I would understand it all perfectly; but in a few moments I would be involved once more in a hazy search after my own child. Mother sought to quiet our hearts, helping us to trust in the great love of God that never ceases to watch. And she did make us quiet. But the time glided so slowly past that it seemed immobile.

When twelve struck, we heard in the stillness every clock in the house, and it seemed as if they would never have done.

Still the time went on, and there was no sound of horses or anything to break the silence, except the faint murmur which now and then the trees will make in the quietest night, as if they are dreaming and talking in their sleep. Only this and the occasional cry of an owl broke the silent flow of the undivided moments. We seldom spoke, and at length the house within seemed possessed by the silence from without, but we were all ears.

My mother at length started up, saying, "I hear them! They're coming!" Then we too heard the sound of horses, and my mother hurried down to the hall. I would have stayed with Connie, but she begged me to go, and come back as soon as I knew the result. As I descended the stairs, I could see the dim light of the low-burning lamp on the heads of the listening, anxious groups—my mother at the open door with the housekeeper and her maid, and the menservants visible through the door in the moonlight beyond.

The first news that reached me was my father's shout the moment he rounded the sweep that brought him in sight of the house. "All right! Here she is!" he cried.

And, ere I could reach the stair to run up to Connie, Wagtail was jumping on me and barking furiously. He rushed up before me with the scramble of twenty feet, licked Connie's face all over in spite of her efforts at self-defense, then rushed at Dora and the boys one after the other, and woke them all up. He was satisfied enough with himself now, and his tail was doing the wagging of forty. There was no tucking it away now, no drooping of the head in mute confession of conscious worthlessness; he was a dog self-satisfied because his master was well pleased with him.

My father cantered up to the door, followed by the two men. My mother hurried to meet him and only then saw the lost little lamb asleep in his bosom. He gave her up, and my mother ran in with her. He dismounted, and walked merrily but wearily up the stair after her. The first thing he did was to quiet the dog; the next to sit down beside Connie; the third to say, "Thank God!" and the next, "God bless Wagtail!" My mother was already undressing the little darling, and the maid was gone to fetch her night things. Tumbled hither and thither, she did not wake, but was carried off stone-sleeping to her crib.

As soon as he had had a bit of supper, my father began to tell us the whole story.

As they had ridden out of the gate, one of the menservants— Burton—rode up alongside of my father, and told him that there was an encampment of gypsies on the moor about five miles away. My father thought, in the absence of other indication, they ought to follow that direction and told Burton to guide them to the place as rapidly as possible. After half an hour's sharp riding, they came to the rising ground behind which lay the camp.

The other servant, Sim, was an old man who had been whipper-in to a baronet in the next county, and knew much of the ways of wild animals. It was his turn now to address my father, who had halted for a moment to think what ought to be done next.

"She can't well have got here before us, Sir, with that child to carry, but I think I had better have a peep over the brow first. She may be there already, or she may not; but, if we find out, we shall know better what to do."

"I'll go with you," said my father.

"No, Sir—excuse me—that won't do. You can't creep like a serpent. I can. They'll never know I'm stalking them. No more you couldn't show fight if need was, you know, Sir."

"How did you find that out, Sim?" asked my father, a little amused, notwithstanding the weight at his heart.

"Why, Sir, they do say a clergyman mustn't show fight."

"Who told you that, Sim?" he persisted.

"Well, I can't say, Sir. Only it wouldn't be respectable, would it, Sir?"

"There's nothing respectable but what's right, Sim, and what's right always is respectable, though it mayn't *look* so one bit."

"Suppose you was to get a black eye, Sir?"

"Did you ever hear of the martyrs, Sim?"

"Yes, Sir. I've heard you talk on 'em in the pulpit, Sir."

"Well, they didn't get black eyes only, they got black all over, you know—burnt black. And what for, do you think, now?"

"Don't know, Sir, except it was for doing right."

"That's just it. Was it any disgrace to them?"

"No, sure, Sir."

"Well, if I were to get a black eye for the sake of the child, would that be any disgrace to me, Sim?"

"None that I knows on, Sir. Only it'd *look* bad."

"Yes, no doubt. People might think I had got into a row at the Griffin. And yet I shouldn't be ashamed of it. I should count my black eye the more respectable of the two. I should also regard the evil judgment much as another black eye, and wait till they both came round again. Lead on, Sim."

They left their horses with Burton, and went toward the camp. But when they reached the slope behind which it lay, my father— much to Sim's discomfiture—my father, instead of lying down at the foot of it and creeping up the side of it, walked right up over the brow and straight into the camp with Wagtail.

There was nothing going on, neither tinkering nor cooking, and all seemed asleep. But presently, out of two or three of the tents— the dingy squalor of which no moonshine could silver over—came three or four men, half undressed, demanding of my father in no gentle tones what he wanted there.

"I'll tell you all about it," he answered. "I'm the parson of this parish, and therefore you're my own people, you see."

"We don't go to *your* church, Parson," said one of them.

"I don't care. You're my own people, for all that, and I want your help."

"Well, what's the matter? Whose cow's dead?" said the man.

"This evening," returned my father, "one of my children is missing; and a woman who might be one of your clan—mind, I say *might be*—I don't know, and I mean no offense, but such a woman was seen about the place. All I want is the child, and if I don't find her, I shall have to raise the county. I should be very sorry to disturb you, but I am afraid, in that case, whether the woman be one of you or not, the place will be too hot for you. I'm no enemy to honest gypsies; but you know there is a set of tramps that call themselves gypsies, who are nothing of the sort, only thieves. Tell me what I had better do to find my child. You know all about such things."

The men turned to each other, and began talking in undertones in a language my father could not understand. At length the spokesman of the party addressed him again.

"We'll give you our word, Sir, if that will satisfy you," he said more respectfully than he had spoken before, "to send the child home directly if anyone should bring her to our camp. That's all we can say."

My father saw that his best chance lay in accepting the offer. "Thank you," he said. "Perhaps I may have an opportunity of serving you someday."

They in their turn thanked him politely enough, and my father and Sim left the camp.

Upon this side the moor was bordered by a deep trench, the bottom of which was full of young firs. As the moon was now up, my father resolved to halt for a time, and watch the moor from the shelter of the firs, on the chance of the woman making her appearance.

They had lain in the firs for about half an hour when suddenly Wagtail rushed into the underwood and vanished. In a few moments they heard his joyous bark, followed, however, by a howl of pain. Before they had gained many yards in pursuit, Wagtail came cowering to my father's feet, who, patting his side, found it bleeding. He bound his handkerchief round him, and, fastening the lash of Sim's whip to his collar that he might not go too fast for them, told him to find Theodora. Instantly he pulled away through the brushwood, giving a little yelp now and then as some broken twig or stem hurt his wounded side.

Before he reached the spot for which he was making, however, my father heard a rustling nearer to the outskirts of the wood, and the same moment Wagtail turned and tugged fiercely in that direction. The figure of a woman rose up against the sky, and began to run for the open space beyond.

"Mount and head her, Sim. Mount, Burton. Ride over everything," cried my father, as he slipped Wagtail, who shot through the underwood like a bird. Wagtail reached her just as she reached the trench, and in an instant had her by the gown. My father saw something gleam in the moonlight, and again a howl broke from Wagtail, who was evidently once more wounded. But he held on. And now the horsemen were approaching her in front, and my father was hard upon her from behind. She gave a peculiar cry— half a shriek, and half a howl—clasped the child to her bosom, and stood rooted like a tree, evidently in the hope that her friends, hearing her signal, would come to her rescue.

But it was too late. The dog held her by the poor ragged skirt, and the horses snorted on the bank above her. She heaved the child over her head, either in appeal to Heaven, or to dash her to the earth. Then my father caught both her uplifted arms with his, so that she could not lower them, and Burton flung himself from his horse and took Theodora from them. Then my father called off Wagtail, and the poor woman sunk down in the bottom of the trench amongst the young firs without a sound, and there lay. My father went up to her, but she only stared at him with big blank black eyes, and yet such a lost look on her young, handsome, yet gaunt face, as almost convinced him she was the mother of the child. But, whatever might be her rights, she could not be allowed to recover possession, without those who had saved and tended the child having a word in the matter.

As he was thinking what he could say to her, Sim's voice reached his ear. "They're coming up over the brow, Sir—five or six from the camp. We'd better be off."

"The child is safe," he said, as he turned to leave her.

"From *me*," she rejoined, in a pitiful tone, and this ambiguous utterance was all that fell from her.

My father mounted, took the child from Burton, and rode away, followed by the two men and Wagtail. Through the green rides they galloped in the moonlight, and were soon beyond all danger of pursuit. When they slackened pace, my father instructed Sim to find out all he could about the gypsies, to learn their names and to what tribe or community they belonged. Sim promised to do what was in his power, but said he did not expect much success.

The children had listened to the story wide awake. Wagtail was lying at my father's feet, licking his wounds which were not very serious, and had stopped bleeding.

"It is all your doing, Wagtail," said Harry, patting the dog.

"I think he deserves to be called *Mr.* Wagtail," said Charley.

And from that day he was Mr. Wagtail, much to the amusement of visitors, who, hearing the name gravely uttered, saw the owner of it approach on all fours with a tireless pendulum in his rear.

NINE

HOME AGAIN

My father took every means in his power to find out something about the woman and the gang of gypsies. But, the very next day, he heard that they had already vanished, and all his inquiries were of no avail. I believe he was dissatisfied with himself in what had occurred, thinking he ought to have discovered at the time whether she was indeed the mother, and, in that case, to do for her what he could. Had he done so, he might only have heaped difficulty upon difficulty. As it was, if he was saved from trouble, he was not delivered from uneasiness. Clearly, however, the child must not be exposed to the danger of the repetition of the attempt. By now the whole household was so fully alive to the necessity of not losing sight of her for a moment, that her danger was far less than it had been at any time before.

I continued at the hall for six weeks, during which my husband came several times to see me, and, at the close of that period, took me back with him to my dear little home. The rooms, all but the study, looked very small after those I had left, but I felt, notwithstanding, that the place was my home. I was at first a little ashamed of the feeling—for why should I be anywhere more at home than in the little house of parents such as mine? There is a certain amount of the queenly element in every woman, so that she cannot feel perfectly at ease without something to govern, however small and however troublesome her queendom may be. At my father's, I had every ministration and all comforts, but no responsibilities and no rule. I could not help feeling idle.

47

Besides, I could not be at all sure that my big bear was properly attended to. He was most independent of personal comforts, and should not be left to his own neglect. I still have to rack my brains for weeks before my bear's birthday comes round, to think of something that will in itself have a chance of giving him pleasure. Of course, it would be comparatively easy if I had plenty of money to spare, and hadn't "to muddle it all away" in paying butchers and bakers and such.

So home I went, to be queen again.

My father often used to say that the commonest things in the world were the loveliest—like the sky and water and grass. Now I found that the commonest feelings of humanity—for what feelings could be commoner than those which now made me blessed amongst women?—are those that are fullest of the divine. For simply because the life of the world was moving on toward its unseen goal, and I knew it and had a helpless share in it, I felt as if God was with me.

The winter passed slowly away, fog, rain, frost, snow, thaw, succeeding one another in all the seeming disorder of the season. A good many things happened, I believe, but I don't remember any of them. My mother wrote, offering me Dora for a companion in my growing need, but somehow I preferred being without her.

My father came to see me several times, and was all himself to me, but I could not feel quite comfortable with him: it indicates something very wrong in me somewhere. But he seemed to understand me, and always, the moment he left me, the tide of confidence began to flow afresh in the ocean that lay about the little island of my troubles. Then I knew he was my own *father*—something that even my husband could not be, and would not wish to be to me.

In the month of March, my mother came to see me, and that was all pleasure. My father did not always see when I was not able to listen to him, though he was most considerate when he did. But my mother—why, there is nothing better for a woman than to be with her own mother when she is awaiting a child. She brought with her a young Irish woman to take Sarah's place as cook for Sarah was now to be the child's nurse. Jemima had been kitchen-maid in a small family of my mother's acquaintance, and had a good character for honesty and plain cooking. I should have been perfectly satisfied with my mother's choice, even if I had not been so indifferent at the time to all that was going on in the lower regions of the house. But while my mother was there, I knew well enough that nothing could go wrong, and my housekeeping mind had never been so much at ease since we were married. It was very delightful not to be accountable; for the present, I felt exonerated from all responsibilities.

I woke one morning, after a sound sleep, recalling a very odd dream. I thought I was a hen, strutting about amongst ricks of corn, picking and scratching, followed by a whole brood of chickens, toward which I felt exceedingly benevolent and attentive. Suddenly I heard the scream of a hawk in the air above me, and tried to fetch the little creatures under my wings. They came scurrying to me as fast as their legs could carry them—all but one, which wouldn't mind my cry, although I kept repeating it again and again. Meantime the hawk kept screaming—and I felt as if I didn't care for any of those that were safe under my wings, but only for the solitary creature that kept pecking away as if nothing was the matter. I grew so terribly anxious that I woke with a cry of misery and terror.

I opened my eyes, and there was my mother standing beside me. The room was so dark that I thought for a moment what a fog there must be—but the next, I forgot everything at hearing a little cry, which I verily believe, in my stupid dream, I had taken for the voice of the hawk. It was the cry of my first chicken, which I had not yet seen, but which my mother now held in her grandmotherly arms, ready to hand her to me. I dared not speak for I felt very weak, and was afraid of crying from delight. I looked in my mother's face, and she folded back the clothes, and laid the baby down beside me, with its little head resting on my arm.

"Draw back the curtain a little bit, Mother dear," I whispered, "and let me see what it is like."

I believe I said *it,* for I was not quite a mother yet. My mother did as I requested, and a ray of clear spring light fell upon the face of the little white thing by my side—for white she was, though most babies are red—and if I dared not speak before, I could not now. My mother went away, and sat down by the fireside, leaving me with my baby. Never shall I forget the unutterable content of that hour. It was not gladness, nor was it thankfulness that filled my heart, but a certain absolute contentment—just on the point (but for my want of strength) of blossoming into unspeakable gladness and thankfulness. Somehow, too, there was mingled with it a sense of dignity, as if I had vindicated for myself a right to a part

in the creation. Besides, the state of perfect repose after what had
passed was in itself bliss. The very sense of weakness was delightful, for I had earned the right to be weak, to rest as much as I
pleased, to be important, and to be congratulated.

I was listening to the gentle talk about me in the darkened
room—not listening, indeed, only aware that loving words were
spoken. Whether I was dozing, I do not know, but something
touched my lips. I only opened my eyes, and there was my great
big huge bear looking down on me, with something in his eyes I
had never seen there before. But even his presence could not ripple
the waters of my deep rest. I gave him a half-smile—I knew it was
but a half-smile, but I thought it would do—closed my eyes and
sank again, not into sleep, but into that same blessed repose. I
remember wondering if I should feel anything like that for the first
hour or two after I was dead.

This was all but the beginning of endlessly varied pleasures.
First I began to wash and dress my baby myself. One who has not
tried that kind of amusement cannot know what endless pleasure it
affords. I do not doubt that to the paternal spectator it appears
monotonous, unproductive, and unprogressive. But then he, looking on it from the outside, and regarding the process with a specu-
lative compassion and not with sympathy, cannot know the communion with the baby into which it brings you.

Next I began to order the dinners, and the very day in which I
first ordered the dinner, I took my place at the head of the table. I
saw it all through the rose mists of my motherhood, but I am
nevertheless bold to assert that my husband was happy, and that
my mother was happy. And if there was one more guest at the
table concerning whom I am not prepared to assert that he was
happy, I can confidently affirm that he was merry and gracious
and talkative, originating three parts of the laughter of the
evening.

To watch him with the baby was a pleasure even to the heart of
a mother, anxious as she must be when anyone, especially a gentleman, more especially a bachelor, and most especially a young
bachelor, takes her precious little doll in his arms, and pretends to
know all about the management of such. It was he indeed who
introduced her to the dining room; leaving the table during des-
sert, he returned bearing her in his arms, to my astonishment, and
even mild maternal indignation at the liberty. Resuming his seat,
and pouring out for his charge, as he pretended, a glass of old

port, he said, in the soberest voice:

"Charles Percivale, with all the solemnity suitable to the occasion, I, the old moon, with the new moon in my arms, propose the health of Miss Percivale on her first visit to this boring bullet of a world. By the way, what a mercy it is that she carries her atmosphere with her!"

Here I, stupidly thinking he reflected on the atmosphere of baby, rose to take her from him with supressed indignation—for why should a man, who assumes a baby unbidden, be so very much nicer than a woman who accepts her as given, and makes the best of it? But he declined giving her up.

"I'm not pinching her," he said.

"No, but I am afraid that you find her disagreeable."

"On the contrary, she is the nicest of little ladies, for she lets you talk all the nonsense you like, and never takes the least offense."

I sat down again directly.

"I propose her health," he repeated, "coupled with that of her mother, to whom I, for one, am more obliged than I can explain, for at length convincing me that I belong no more to the youth of my country, but am an uncle with a homuncle in his arms."

"Wifie, your health! Baby, yours too!" said my husband, and the ladies drank the toast in silence.

It is time I explained who this fourth—or should I say fifth?—person in our family party was. He was the younger brother of my Percivale, by name, Roger, and still more unsuccessful than he. He was of similar trustworthiness, but less equanimity, for he was subject to sudden elevations and depressions of the inner barometer. And so my daughter began her acquaintance with him.

TEN

MY FIRST DINNER PARTY

We had not yet seen much company in our little house. My husband disliked parties, eschewed evening parties utterly, and never accepted an invitation to dinner except to the house of a friend, and there were not many, even among his artist acquaintances, whom he cared to visit. Altogether, I feared he passed for an unsociable man. I am certain he would have sold more pictures if he had accepted what invitations came his way. But to hint at such a thing would, I knew, crystallize his dislike into a resolve.

One day after I had got quite strong again, I proposed that we should ask some friends to dinner. Instead of objecting to the procedure upon general principles, which I confess I had half anticipated, he only asked me whom I thought of inviting. When I mentioned the Morleys, he made no reply, but went on with his painting as if he had not heard me. I knew then, of course, that the proposal was disagreeable to him.

"You see, we have been twice to dine with them," I said.

"Well, don't you think that enough for a while?"

"I'm talking of asking them here now."

"Couldn't you go and see your cousin some morning instead?"

"It's not that I want to see my cousin particularly. I want to ask them to dinner."

"Oh!" he said, as if he couldn't in the least make out what I was after. "I thought people asked people because they desired their company."

"But, you see, we owe them a dinner.'

"Owe them a dinner! Did you borrow one, then?"

"Do you consider yourself under no obligation to people who ask you to dinner?"

"None in the least—if I accept the invitation. That is the natural acknowledgment of their kindness. Surely my company is worth my dinner. It is far more trouble to me to put on black clothes and a white choker and go to their house, than it is for them to ask me or, in a house like theirs, to have the necessary preparations made for receiving me in a manner befitting their dignity. I do violence to my own feelings in going—is not that enough? You know how much I prefer a chop alone with my wife to the grandest dinner the grandest of her grand relations could give me."

"Now, don't you make game of my grand relations. I'm not sure that you haven't far grander relations yourself, only you say so little about them, they might all have been jailed for housebreaking. Don't you think it natural, if a friend asks you to dinner, that you should ask him again?"

"Yes, if it would give him any pleasure. But just imagine your Cousin Morley dining at our table. Do you think he would enjoy it?"

"Of course, we must have somebody in to help Jemima."

"And somebody to wait, I suppose?"

"Yes, of course, Percivale."

"And what Thackeray calls cold balls handed about?"

"Well, I wouldn't have them cold."

"But they would be."

I was by this time so nearly crying, that I said nothing here.

"My love," he continued, "I object to the whole thing. It's all false. I have not the least disinclination to asking a few friends who would enjoy being received in the same style as your father or my brother—namely, to one of our better dinners, and perhaps something better to drink than I can afford every day. But just think with what uneasy compassion Mr. Morley would regard our poor ambitions, even if you had an occasional cook and an undertaker's man. And what would he do without his glass of dry sherry after his soup, and his hock and champagne later, not to mention his fine claret or tawny port afterwards? I don't know how to get things good enough for him without laying in a stock. And that, you know, would be as absurd as it is impossible."

"Oh, you gentlemen always think so much of the wine!"

53

"Believe me, it is as necessary to Mr. Morley's comfort as the dainties you would provide him with. Indeed, it would be cruelty to ask him. He would not and could not enjoy it."

"If he didn't like it, he needn't come again," I said, cross with the objections of which I could not but see the justice.

"Well, I must say you have an odd notion of hospitality," said my bear. "You may be certain that a man so well aware of his own importance will take it far more as a compliment that you do not presume to invite him to your house, but are content to enjoy his society when he asks you to his."

"I don't choose to take such an inferior position," I said.

"You can't help it, my dear," he returned. "Socially considered, you *are* his inferior. You cannot give dinners he would regard with anything better than a friendly contempt, combined with a certain mild indignation at your having presumed to ask him. It is far more graceful to accept the small fact, and let him have his whim, which is not a subversive one or at all dangerous to the community, being of a sort easy to cure. Ha! Ha! Ha!"

"May I ask what you are laughing at?" I said with severity.

"I was only fancying how such a man must feel—if what your blessed father believes is true—when he is stripped all at once of every possible source of consequence. Stripped of position, funds, house, including cellar, clothes, body, including stomach—"

"There, there! Don't be vulgar. It is not like you, Percivale."

"Don't be vexed with me, Wynnie," he said.

"I don't like not to be allowed to pay my debts."

"Back to the starting point, like a hunted hare! A woman's way," he said merrily, hoping to make me laugh, for he could not doubt I should see the absurdity of my position with a moment's reflection. But I was out of temper, and chose to pounce upon the liberty taken with my sex, and regard it as an insult. Without a word I rose, pressed my baby to my bosom as if her mother had been left a widow, and swept away. Percivale started to his feet. I did not see, but I knew he gazed after me for a moment. Then I heard him sit down to his painting as if nothing had happened—but, I knew, with a sharp pain inside his great chest. For me, I found the ladder very subversive of my dignity—for when a woman has to hold a baby in one arm, and with the hand of the other lift up the front of her skirt in order to walk up an almost perpendicular staircase, it is quite impossible for her to *sweep* anymore.

When I reached the top, the picture he had made of me (with

the sunset coming through the window) flashed upon my memory. All dignity forgotten, I bolted through the door at the top, flung my baby into the arms of her nurse, turned, almost tumbled headlong down the precipice, and altogether tumbled down at my husband's chair. I couldn't speak, but could only lay my head on his knees.

"Darling," he said, "you shall ask the great Pan Jan with his button atop, if you like. I'll do my best for him."

Between crying and laughing, I nearly lost my composure altogether. "I was very naughty, Percivale," I said. "I will give a dinner party, and it shall be such as you shall enjoy, and I won't ask Mr. Morley."

"Thank you, my love," he said, "and the next time Mr. Morley asks us I will go without a grumble, and make myself as agreeable as I can."

Now I have had a good many servants, but Jemima seems a fixture. How this has come about, it would be impossible to say in ever so many words. She has by turns every fault under the sun—I say *faults*. She will struggle with one for a day, and succumb to it for a month, while the smallest amount of praise is sufficient to render her incapable of deserving a word of commendation for a week. It was long an impossibility to make her see, or at least own, that she was to blame for anything. If the dish she had last cooked to perfection made its appearance the next time inedible, she would lay it all to the silly oven, which was too hot or too cold, or the silly pepper pot, the top of which fell off as she was using it. She had no sense of the value of proportion and would insist, for instance, that she had made the cake precisely as she had been told, but suddenly betray that she had not weighed the flour, which *could* be of no consequence, seeing she had weighed everything else.

"Please, 'm, could you eat your dinner now? It's all ready," she came saying an hour before dinnertime, the very first day after my mother left. Even now her desire to be punctual is chiefly evidenced by absurd precipitancy, to the danger of doing everything to either a pulp or a cinder. Yet here she is, and here she is likely to remain, so far as I see, till death or some other catastrophe do us part. The reason of it is that with all her faults—and they are innumerable—she has some heart. Yes, after deducting all that can be laid to the account of a certain cunning perception that she is well off, she has yet a good deal of genuine attachment left, and is a jealous partisan to her master and mistress.

There was nothing more said about the dinner party until my father came to see us in July, commissioned by my mother to arrange for my going to Marshmallows the next month.

As soon as I had shown my father to his little room, I ran down to Percivale. "Papa is come," I said.

"I am delighted to hear it," he answered, laying down his palette and brushes. "Where is he?"

"Gone upstairs," I answered. "I wouldn't disturb you till he came down again."

'I haven't quite finished my pipe—I will go on till he comes down."

Although he laid it on his pipe, I knew well enough it was just that little bit of paint he wanted to finish, and not the residue of tobacco in the black and red bowl.

"And now we'll have our dinner party," I said.

I do believe that, for all the nonsense I had talked about returning invitations, the real thing at my heart even then was an impulse toward hospitable entertainment, and the desire to see my husband merry with his friends, under the protecting wing of his wife. For, as mother of the family, the wife has to mother her husband also, to consider him as her firstborn, and look out for what will not only give him pleasure but be good for him. My bear has fully given in to this.

"And who are you going to ask?" he said. "Mr. and Mrs. Morley to begin with, and—"

"No, no," I answered. "We are going to have a jolly evening of it, with nobody present who will make you either anxious or annoyed. Mr. Blackstone—and Miss Clare, I think, for I must have one lady to keep me in countenance with so many gentlemen, you know.

"Mr. Blackstone I know. And being a clergyman, he would get on well with your father. But who is Miss Clare?"

"I met her at Cousin Judy's. I have a reason for asking her, which I would rather you should find out by yourself. Do you mind?"

"Not in the least, if you don't think she will spoil the fun."

"I am sure she won't. Then there's your brother Roger."

"Of course. Who more?"

"I think that will do. There will be six of us then—quite a large enough party for our little dining room."

"Why shouldn't we dine here in the studio? It wouldn't be so hot, and we should have more room."

I liked the idea. So the night before the dinner, Percivale arranged not only his paintings but all his properties to be accessory to a picturesque effect. And when the table was laid and adorned with flowers, the bird's-eye from the top of the Jacob's ladder was a very pretty one indeed.

Resolved that Percivale should have no cause of complaint as regarded the simplicity of my arrangements, I gave orders that our little Ethel (who at that time of the evening was always asleep) should be laid on the couch in my room off the study, with the door ajar, so that Sarah, who was now her nurse, might wait with an easy mind. The dinner was brought in by the outer door of the study, to avoid the awkwardness and possible disaster of the private precipice.

The principal dish, a small sirloin of beef, was at the foot of the table and a couple of boiled fowls were (I thought) before me. But when the covers were removed, to my surprise I found they were roasted.

"What have you got there, Percivale?" I asked. "Isn't it a sirloin?"

"I'm not an adept in such matters," he replied. "I should say it was."

My father gave a glance at the joint. Something seemed to be wrong. I rose and went to my husband's side. Powers of cuisine! Jemima had roasted the fowls and boiled the sirloin. My exclamation was the signal for an outbreak of laughter, led by my father. I was trembling in the balance between mortification on my own account and sympathy with the evident amusement of my father and Mr. Blackstone. But the thought that Mr. Morley might have been and was not of the party came with such a pang and such a relief as to settle the point, and I burst out laughing.

"I dare say it's all right," said Roger. "Why shouldn't a sirloin be boiled as well as roasted? I venture to assert that it is all a whim, and we are on the verge of a new discovery to swell the number of those which already owe their being to blunders."

"Let us all try a slice, then," said Mr. Blackstone, "and compare results."

This was agreed to—and a solemn silence followed, during which each sought acquaintance with the new dish.

"I am sorry to say," remarked my father, finally, "that Roger is all wrong, and we have only made the discovery that custom is right. It is plain enough why sirloin is always roasted."

"I yield myself convinced," said Roger.

"And I am certain," said Mr. Blackstone, "that if the loin set before the king, whoever he was, had been boiled, he would never have knighted it."

Thanks to the loin, the last possible touch of constraint had vanished, and the party grew a very merry one. The apple pudding which followed was declared perfect and eaten up, and Percivale produced some good wine from somewhere. But a tiny whimper called me away, and Miss Clare accompanied me. The gentlemen insisted that we should return as soon as possible, and bring the homuncle, as Roger called the baby, with us.

When we returned, the two clergymen were in close conversation, and the other two gentlemen were chiefly listening. My father was saying, "My dear sir, I don't see how any man can do his duty as a clergyman who doesn't visit his parishioners."

"In London it is simply impossible," returned Mr. Blackstone. "In the country *you* are welcome wherever you go. Any visit I might pay would most likely be regarded either as an intrusion or as giving the right to pecuniary aid, of which evils the latter is worse. There are portions of every London parish which clergymen and their coadjutors have so degraded, by the practical teaching of beggary, that they have blocked up every possible door to a healthy spiritual relation between them and the pastor."

"Would you not give alms at all, then?"

"One thing, at least, I have made up my mind on—alms from any hand but the hand of a personal friendship tend to evil, and will, in the long run, increase misery."

"What, then, do you suppose the proper relation between a London clergyman and his parishioners?"

"One, I am afraid, which does not at present exist—one which it is his first business perhaps to bring about. I confess I regard with a repulsion amounting to horror the idea of walking into a poor man's house, except either I have business with him, or desire his personal acquaintance."

"But if our office—"

"My business is to serve, not to force service upon them. I will not say how far intimacy may justify you in immediate assault upon a man's conscience, but I shrink from any plan that seems to take it for granted that the poor are more wicked then the rich.

Why don't we send missionaries to Belgravia? The outside of the cup and platter may sometimes be dirtier than the inside."

"Your missionary could hardly force his way through the servants to the boudoir or drawing room."

"And the poor have no servants to defend them."

"Don't you think, Sir," Miss Clare said, addressing my father, "that the help one can give to another must always depend on the measure in which one is free oneself?"

My father was silent, thinking. We were all silent. With marked deference and solemnity he answered at length, "I have little doubt you are right, Miss Clare. That puts the question upon its own eternal foundation. The mode used must be of infinitely less importance than the person who uses it."

As he spoke, he looked at her with attentive regard. Indeed, the eyes of all the company seemed to be scanning the small woman. But she bore the scrutiny well, if indeed she was not unconscious of it, and my husband began to find out one of my reasons for asking her, which was simply that he might see her face. At this moment it was in one of its higher phases. It was, at its best, a grand face; at its worst, a suffering face. It was a little too large, perhaps, for the small body which it crowned with a flame of soul, but while you saw her face you never thought of the rest of her.

"But," my father went on, looking at Mr. Blackstone, "I am anxious, from the clergyman's point of view, to know what my friend here thinks he must try to do in his very difficult position."

"I think the best thing I could do," returned Mr. Blackstone, laughing, "would be to go to school under Miss Clare."

"I shouldn't wonder," my father responded.

"But, in the meantime, I should prefer the chaplaincy of a suburban cemetery."

"Certainly your charge would be a less troublesome one. Your congregation would be quiet enough, at least," said Roger.

"Then are they glad because they be quiet," said my father, as if unconsciously uttering his own reflections. But he was a little cunning, and would say things like that when, fearful of irreverence, he wanted to turn the current of the conversation.

"But surely," said Miss Clare, "a more active congregation would be quite desirable."

She had one fault—no—defect; she was slow to enter into the humor of a thing. It seemed almost as if the first aspect of any bit of fun presented to her was that of something wrong. A moment's reflection, however, almost always ended in a sunny laugh, partly at her own stupidity, as she called it.

"You mistake my meaning," said Mr. Blackstone. "My chief, almost sole, attraction to the regions of the grave is the sexton, and not the placidity of the inhabitants—though perhaps Miss Clare might value that more highly if she had more experience of how noisy human nature can be."

Miss Clare gave a little smile, but she said nothing.

"My first inquiry," he went on, "before accepting such an appointment, would be as to the character and mental habits of the sexton. If I found him a man capable of regarding human nature from a standpoint of his own, I should close with the offer at once If, on the contrary, he was a commonplace man, who made faultless responses, and cherished the friendship of the undertaker, I should decline. In fact, I should regard the sexton as my proposed master, and whether I should accept the place or not would depend altogether on whether I liked him or not. Think what revelations of human nature a real man in such a position could give me: 'Hand me the shovel. You stop a bit—you're out of breath. Sit down on that stone there, and light your pipe—here's some tobacco. Now tell me the rest of the story. How did the old fellow get on after he had buried his termagent wife?' That's how I should treat him, and I should get, in return, such a succession of peeps into human life and intent and aspirations as, in the course of a few years, would send me to the next vicarage a sadder and wiser man, Mr. Walton."

"I don't doubt it," said my father. But whether in sympathy with Mr. Blackstone, or in latent disapproval of a tone judged unbecoming to a clergyman, I could not tell.

Miss Clare was the first to leave.

"What a lovely countenance that is!" said my husband, the moment she was out of hearing.

"She is a very remarkable woman," said my father.

"I suspect she knows a good deal more than most of us," said Mr. Blackstone. "Did you see how her face always lighted up before she said anything? You can never come nearer to seeing a thought than in her face just before she speaks."

"What is she?" asked Roger.

"Can't you see what she is?" returned his brother. "She's a saint—Saint Clare."

"But what does she do?"

"Why should you think that she does anything?" I asked.

"She looks as if she had to earn her own living."

"She does. She teaches music."

"Why didn't you ask her to play?"

"Because this is the first time she has been to the house."

"Does she go to church, do you suppose?"

"I have no doubt of it, but why do you ask?"

"Because she looks as if she didn't want it. I never saw such an angelic expression upon a countenance."

"You must take me to call upon her," said my father.

"I will with pleasure," I answered.

This was easier promised than performed, for I had asked her by word of mouth at Cousin Judy's, and had not the slightest idea where she lived. Of course I applied to Judy, but she had mislaid her address, and, promising to ask her for it, forgot more than once. So my father had to return home without seeing Miss Clare again.

ELEVEN

PICTURES AND RUMORS

For some time I was fully occupied with a new life to tend and cultivate. I marveled that God should entrust me with such a charge, that He did not keep the lovely creature in His own arms, and refuse her to any others. Then I would realize that He had not sent her out of His own arms, for I too was a child in His arms, holding and tending my live doll, until she should grow something like me, only ever so much better.

But I feared lest my love for my baby should make me neglect my husband. The fear first arose in me one morning as I sat with her half-dressed on my knees. I was dawdling over her in my fondness (as I used to dawdle over the dressing of my doll) when suddenly I became aware that never once since her arrival had I sat with my husband in his study. A pang of dismay shot through me. "Is this to be a wife?" I said to myself, "to play with a live love like a dead doll, and forget her husband!" I caught up a blanket from the cradle, wrapped it round the treasure, which was shooting its arms and legs in every direction like a polypus feeling after its food, and rushed downstairs and down the precipice into the study. Percivale started up in terror, thinking something fearful had happened, and I was bringing him all that was left of the child.

"What—what—what's the matter?" he gasped.

"I've brought you the baby to kiss," I said, unfolding the blanket and holding up the sprawling little goddess toward the face that towered above me.

"Was it dying for a kiss, then?" he asked, taking her, blanket and all, from my arms.

The end of the blanket swept across his easel, and smeared the face of the baby in his picture of "The Three Kings."

"O Percivale!" I cried. "You've smeared your baby!"

"But this is a real live baby—she may smear anything she likes."

"Except her own face and hands, please, then, Percivale."

"Or her blessed frock," said Percivale. "She hasn't got one, though. Why hasn't the little angel got her feathers on yet?"

"I was in such a hurry to bring her."

"To be kissed?"

"No, not exactly. It wasn't her I was in a hurry to bring—it was myself."

"Ah! You wanted to be kissed, did you?"

"No, I didn't want to be kissed, but I did so want to kiss you, Percivale."

"Isn't it all the same, though, Darling?"

"Sometimes, Percivale, you are so very stupid! It's not the same at all. There's a world of difference between the two, and you ought to know it, or be told it, if you don't."

"I shall think it over as soon as you leave me," he said.

"But I'm not going to leave you for a long time. I haven't seen you paint for weeks and weeks, not since this little troublesome thing came poking in between us."

"But she's not dressed yet."

"That doesn't signify. She's well wrapped up, and quite warm." He put me in a chair where I could see his picture without catching the shine of the paint. I took the baby from him, and he went on with his work.

"You don't think I am going to sacrifice all my privileges to this little tyrant, do you?" I asked.

"It would be rather hard for me, at least," he rejoined.

"You did think I was neglecting you, then, Percivale?"

"Not for a moment."

"Then you didn't miss me?"

"I did, very much."

"And you didn't grumble?"

"No."

"Do I disturb you?" I asked, after a little pause. "Can you

paint just as well when I am here as when you are alone?"

"Better. I feel warmer to my work somehow."

I was satisfied, and held my peace. When I am best pleased, I don't want to talk. But Percivale, perhaps not having found this out yet, looked anxiously in my face. As at the moment my eyes were fixed on his picture, I thought he wanted to find out whether I liked the design.

"I see it now!" I cried. "I could not make out where the Magi were."

He had taken for the scene of his picture an old farm kitchen, or yeoman's hall, with its rich brown rafters, its fire on the hearth, and its red brick floor. A tub half full of bright water stood on one side, and the mother was bending over her baby which, undressed for the bath, she was holding out for the admiration of the Magi. Immediately behind the mother stood, in the garb of a shepherd, my father, leaning upon the ordinary shepherd's crook. My mother, like a peasant woman in her Sunday best, with a white handkerchief crossed upon her bosom, stood beside him, and both were gazing with a chastened yet profound pleasure on the lovely child.

In front stood two boys and a girl, between the ages of five and nine, each gazing with a peculiar wondering delight. The youngest boy, with a great spotted wooden horse in his hand, was approaching to embrace the infant in such a fashion as made the toy look dangerous, and the left hand of the mother was lifted with a motion of warning and defense. The little girl, the next youngest, had, in her absorption, dropped her gaudily dressed doll at her feet, and stood sucking her thumb, her big blue eyes wide with contemplation. The eldest boy had brought his white rabbit to give to the baby, but had forgotten all about it, so full was his heart of his new brother. An expression of mingled love and wonder and perplexity had already begun to dawn on the face, but it was yet far from finished. He stood behind the other two peeping over their heads.

"Were you thinking of that Titian in the Louvre, with the white rabbit in it?" I asked Percivale.

"I did not think of it until after I had put in the rabbit," he replied. "And it shall remain, for it suits my purpose, and Titian would not claim all the white rabbits because of that one."

"Did you think of the black lamb in it, then, when you laid that black kitten on the hearth?" I asked.

"Black lamb?" he returned.

64

"Yes," I insisted. "A black lamb, in the dark background—such a very black lamb, and in such a dark background, that it seems you never discovered it."

"Are you sure?" he persisted.

"Absolutely certain," I replied. "I pointed it out to Papa in the picture itself in the Louvre. He had not observed it before either."

"I am very glad to know there is such a thing there. I need not answer your question, you see. It is odd enough I should have put in the black cat. Upon some grounds I might argue that it is better than Titian's lamb."

"What grounds? Tell me."

"If the painter wanted a contrast, a lamb—be he as black as ever paint could make him—must still be a more Christian animal than a cat as white as snow. Under what pretense could a cat be used as a Christian symbol?"

"What do you make of her playfulness?"

"I should count that a virtue, were it not for the fatal objection that it is always exercised at the expense of other creatures."

"A ball of string, or a reel, or a bit of paper is enough for an uncorrupted kitten."

"But you must not forget that it serves only in virtue of the creature's imagination representing it as alive. If you do not make it move, she will herself set it in motion as the initiative of the game. If she cannot do that, she will take no notice of it."

"Yes, I see. I give in."

All this time he had been painting diligently. But then a knock came to the study door and, remembering baby's unpresentable condition, I cuddled her up, climbed the stair again, and finished the fledging of my little angel in a very happy frame of mind.

I descended with the baby to find that Cousin Judy had called and was waiting for me. I remembered that I must again ask her for Miss Clare's address, so, as soon as she had kissed and admired the baby, I said, "Have you found out yet where Miss Clare lives, Judy?"

"I don't choose to find out," she answered. "I am sorry to say I have had to give her up. It is a disappointment, I confess."

"What do you mean?" I said. "I thought you considered her a very good teacher."

"I have no fault to find with her on that score. She was always punctual, and I must allow she played well and taught the children delightfully. But I have heard such questionable things about

65

her! Very strange things indeed!"

"What are they?"

"I can't say I've been able to fix on more than one thing directly against her character, but—"

"Against her character!" I exclaimed.

"Yes, indeed. She lives by herself in lodgings, and the house is not at all a respectable one."

"But have you made no further inquiry?"

"I consider that quite enough. I had already met more than one person, however, who seemed to think it very odd that I should have her teach music in my family."

"Did they give any reason for thinking her unfit?"

"I did not choose to ask them. One was Miss Clarke—you know her. She smiled in her usual supercilious manner, but in her case I believe it was only because Miss Clare looks so dowdy. But nobody knows anything about her except what I've just told you."

"And who told you that?"

"Mrs. Jefferson."

"She is a great gossip."

"Else she wouldn't have heard it. But that doesn't make it untrue. In fact, she convinced me of its truth, for she knows the place she lives in, and assured me it was at great risk of infection to the children that I allowed her to enter the house. So, of course, I felt compelled to let Miss Clare know that I didn't require her services any longer."

"There must be some mistake, surely!" I said.

"Oh, no! Not in the least, I am sorry to say."

"How did she take it?"

"Very sweetly indeed. She didn't even ask me why, which was just as well, seeing I should have found it awkward to tell her. But I suppose she knew too many grounds herself to dare the question."

I was dreadfully sorry, but I could not say much more then. I only expressed my conviction that there could not be any charge to bring against Miss Clare herself. Judy, however, insisted that what she had heard was reason enough for at least ending the engagement—indeed, that no one was fit for such a situation of whom such things could be said, whether they were true or not.

When she left me, I gave the baby to her nurse, and went straight to the studio, peeping in to see if Percivale was alone, for I had heard another voice.

He caught sight of me, and called to me to come down. "It's only Roger," he said.

I was always pleased to see Roger. He was a strange creature, one of those gifted men who are capable of anything, if not everything, and yet carry nothing within sight of proficiency. He whistled like a starling, and accompanied his whistling on the piano, but never played. He could copy a drawing to a hair's breadth, but never drew. He could engrave well on wood and, although he had often been employed in that way, he had always got tired of it after a few weeks. He was forever wanting to do something other than what he was at, and the moment he tired of a thing, he would work at it no longer, for he had never learned to drive himself. He would come everyday to the study for a week to paint in backgrounds, or make a duplicate and then, perhaps, we wouldn't see him for a fortnight. At other times he would work, say, for a month, modeling or carving marble for a sculptor friend, from whom he might have had constant employment if he had pleased. He had given lessons in various branches, for he was an excellent scholar, and had the finest ear for verse, as well as the keenest appreciation of the loveliest of poetry.

I could not help liking him. There was a half-plaintive playfulness about him, alternated with gloom, and occasionally wild merriment, which made him interesting even when one felt most inclined to quarrel with him. The worst was that he considered himself a generally misunderstood—if not ill-used—man, who could not only distinguish himself but render valuable service to society, if only society would do him the justice to give him a chance. Were it only, however, for his love to my baby, I could not but be ready to take up his defense. When I mentioned what I had just heard about Miss Clare, Percivale looked both astonished and troubled. But before he could speak, Roger, with the air of a man of the world whom experience enabled to come at once to a decision, said, "Depend upon it, Wynnie, there is falsehood there somewhere. You will always be nearer the truth if you believe nothing, than if you believe the half of what you hear."

"That's very much what Papa says," I answered. "He affirms that he never searched into an injurious report in his own parish without finding it so nearly false as to deprive it of all right to go about."

"Besides," said Roger, "look at that face! How I should like to model it. She's a good woman that, depend upon it."

I was delighted with his enthusiasm.

"I wish you would ask her again, as soon as you can," said Percivale, who always tended to embody his conclusions in acts rather than in words. "Your cousin Judy is a jolly good creature, but from your father's description of her as a girl, she must have grown a good deal more worldly since her marriage. Respectability is an awful snare."

"I should be very glad to," I said, "but how can I? I haven't learned where she lives. It was asking Judy for her address that brought it all out. I certainly didn't insist, but if she didn't remember it before, you may be sure she could not have given it to me then."

"It's very odd," said Roger, stroking his long mustache, the sole ornament of the kind he wore. "It's very odd," he repeated thoughtfully, and then paused again.

"What's so very odd, Roger?" asked Percivale.

"The other evening," answered Roger, "happening to be in Tottenham Court Road, I walked for some distance behind a young woman carrying a brown beer jug in her hand. You understand that I sometimes amuse myself in the street by walking persistently behind someone, devising the unseen face in my mind, until the person looks round and gives me the opportunity of comparing the two—I mean the face I had devised and the real one. When the young woman at length turned her head, it was only my astonishment that kept me from addressing her as Miss Clare. My surprise, however, gave me the time to see how absurd it would have been. Presently she turned down a yard and disappeared."

"Don't tell my cousin Judy," I said. "She would believe it *was* Miss Clare."

"There isn't much danger," he returned. "Even if I knew your cousin, I should not be likely to mention such an incident in her hearing."

"Could it have been she?" said Percivale thoughtfully.

"Absurd!" said Roger. "Miss Clare is a lady, wherever she may live."

"I don't know," said his brother thoughtfully. "Who can tell? It mightn't have been beer she was carrying."

"I didn't say it was beer," returned Roger. "I only said it was a beer-jug—one of those brown, squat, stone jugs, with a dash of gray."

"Brown jug or not, I wish I could get a few sittings from her.

She would make a lovely St. Cecilia," said my husband.

"Brown jug and all?" asked Roger.

"If only she were a little taller," I objected.

"And had an aureole," said my husband. "But I might succeed in omitting the jug as well as adding the aureole and another half-foot of stature, if only I could get that lovely countenance on the canvas, so full of life and yet of repose."

"Don't you think it a little hard?" I ventured to say.

"I think so," said Roger.

"I don't," said my husband. "I know what in it looks like hardness, but I think it comes of the repression of feeling."

"You have studied her well for your opportunities," I said.

"I have. And I am sure, whatever Mrs. Morley may say, if there be any truth at all in those reports, there is some satisfactory explanation. I wish we knew anybody else who knew her. Do try to find one who does, Wynnie."

"I should be only too glad, but I don't know how to set about it."

"I will try," said Roger.

And try he did. One evening he came in late from a dinner at Lady Bernard's.

"Whom do you think I took down to dinner?" he asked, almost before he was seated.

"Lady Bernard?" I said, flying high.

"Her dowager aunt?" said Percivale.

"No, no—Miss Clare."

"Miss Clare!" we both repeated.

"Yes, Miss Clare."

"Did you ask her if it was she you saw carrying the jug of beer in Tottenham Court Road?" said Percivale.

"Did you ask her address?" I said. "That is a question more worthy of an answer."

"Yes, I did. I believe I did. I think I did."

"What is it, then?"

"Upon my word, I haven't the slightest idea."

"So, Mr. Roger! You have had a perfect opportunity, and have let it slip! You are a man to be trusted indeed!"

"I don't know how it could have been. I distinctly remember approaching the subject more than once or twice, and now I discover that I never asked the question. Or if I did, I am certain I got no answer."

"Bewitched!"

"Yes, I suppose so."

"Or," suggested Percivale, "she did not choose to tell you. She saw the question coming, and led you away from it, never let you ask it."

"I have heard that ladies can keep one from saying what they don't want to hear. But she shan't escape me so a second time."

"Indeed, you don't deserve another chance," I said. "You're not half so clever as I took you to be, Roger."

"When I think of it, though, it wasn't a question so easy to ask, or one you would like to be overheard asking."

"Clearly bewitched," I said. "But for that I forgive you. Did she sing?"

"No. I don't suppose anyone there ever thought of asking such a dingy-feathered bird to sing."

"You had some music?"

"Oh, yes! Pretty good, and very bad. Miss Clare's forehead was crossed by no end of flickering shadows as she listened."

"It wasn't for want of interest in her you forgot to find out where she lived! You had better take care, Master Roger."

"Take care of what?"

"Why, you don't know her address."

"What has that to do with taking care?"

"That you won't know where to find your heart if you should happen to want it."

"Oh! I am past that kind of thing long ago. You've made an uncle of me."

And so on, with a good deal more nonsense, but no news of Miss Clare's retreat.

I had before this remarked to my husband that it was odd she had never called since dining with us. But he made little of it, saying that people who gained their own livelihood ought to be excused from attending to rules which had their origin with another class. I thought no more about it, save in disappointment that she had not given me that opportunity of improving my acquaintance with her.

TWELVE

A DISCOVERY

One Saturday night when my husband happened to be out (an event of rare occurrence), Roger called. I asked him to go with me to Tottenham Court Road. It was not far from the region where we lived, and I did a great part of my small shopping there. Several of the shops were shut, and we walked a long way down the street, looking for some place likely to supply what I required.

"It was just here I came up with the girl and the brown jug," said Roger, as we reached the large dissenting chapel. "She was so like Miss Clare! I can't get the one face clear of the other. When I met her at Lady Bernard's, the first thing I thought of was the brown jug."

"Were you as much pleased with her conversation as at our house?" I asked.

"Even more," he answered. "I found her ideas of art so wide, as well as just and accurate, that I was puzzled to think where she had had opportunity of developing them. I questioned her about it, and found she was in the habit of going, as often as she could spare time, to the National Gallery. Her custom was, she said, not to pass from picture to picture, but keep to one until it formed itself in her mind, until she seemed to know what the painter had set himself to do, and why this was and that was—which she could not at first understand. Clearly, without ever having taken a pencil in her hand, she has educated herself to a keen perception of what is demanded of a true picture. Of course the root of it lies in her musical development— There!" he cried suddenly, as we came

71

opposite a paved passage. "That is the place I saw her go down."

"Then you do think the girl with the beer jug was Miss Clare, after all?"

"Not in the least."

"But where, then, does Miss Clare live? Nobody seems to know."

"You never asked any one but Mrs. Morley."

"You have yourself, however, given me reason to think she avoids the subject. If she did live anywhere hereabout, she would have some cause to avoid it."

I stopped to look down the passage.

"Suppose," said Roger, "some one were to come past now, and see Mrs. Percivale, the wife of the celebrated painter, standing in Tottenham Court Road beside the swing door of a corner public-house, talking to a young man."

"Yes, it might give occasion for scandal," I said. "To avoid it, let us go down the court and see what it is like."

"It's not a fit place for you to go into."

"If it were in my father's parish, I should have known every-body in it. Come, and let us see what the place is like," I insisted.

He gave me his arm and down the court we went, past the flaring gin shop, and into the gloom beyond. The houses had once been occupied by people in better circumstances than their present inhabitants. Indeed, they all looked decent enough until, turning two right angles, we came upon another sort. They were still as large, and had plenty of windows but, in the light of a single lamp at the corner, they looked very dirty and wretched and dreary. A little shop, with dried herrings and bull's-eyes in the window, was lighted by a tallow candle set in a ginger beer bottle, with a card of "Kinahan's LL Whiskey" for a reflector.

The houses had sunken areas, just wide enough for a stair, and the basements seemed full of tenants. There was a little wind blowing, so that the atmosphere was tolerable, notwithstanding a few stray leaves of cabbage, suggestive of others in a more objec-tionable condition not so far off.

A confused noise of loud voices, calling and scolding, now reached our ears. The place took one turn more, and at the farther end of the passage a lamp shone upon a group of men and women in altercation which had not yet come to blows. It might, includ-ing children, have numbered twenty, of which some seemed drunk, and all more or less excited. Roger turned to go back the moment he caught sight of them, but I felt inclined to linger a little. Should any danger offer, it would be easy to gain the open thoroughfare.

"It's not at all a fit place for a lady," he said.

"Certainly not," I answered. "It hardly seems a fit place for human beings. These are human beings, though. Let us go through it."

He still hesitated, but as I went on, he could only follow me. I wanted to see what the attracting center of the little crowd was. A good many superterrestrial spectators looked down from the windows upon the disputants, whose voices now and then lulled for a moment only to break out in fresh dispute.

A slight parting of the crowd revealed its core to us. It was a little woman, without bonnet or shawl, whose back was toward us. She turned from side to side, now talking to one, and now to another of the surrounding circle. At first I thought she was setting forth her grievances in hope of sympathy or justice, but her motions were too calm for that. Sometimes the crowd would speak altogether, sometimes keep silent for a full minute while she went on talking. When she turned her face toward us, Roger and I turned ours and stared at each other. The face was disfigured by a swollen eye, evidently from a blow; but clearly enough, if it was not Miss Clare, it was the young woman of the beer jug.

Neither of us spoke, but turned once more to watch as the argument settled down to an almost amicable conference. After a few more grumbles and protestations, the group began to break up into twos and threes. These the young woman set herself to break up again. Here, however, an ill-looking fellow like a costermonger, with a broken nose, came up to us; and with a strong Irish accent and offensive manner, but still with a touch of Irish breeding, requested to know what our business was. Roger asked if the place wasn't a thoroughfare.

"Not for the likes o' you," he answered, "as comes pryin' after the likes of us. We manage our own affairs down here, we do. You'd better be off, my lady."

I have my doubts what sort of reply Roger might have returned if he had been alone, but he certainly spoke in a very conciliatory manner which, however, the man did not seem to appreciate, for he called it blarney. The young woman caught sight of our little group and approached us. She had come within a yard of us, when suddenly her face brightened, and she exclaimed, in a tone of surprise, "Mrs. Percivale! You here?"

It was indeed Miss Clare. Without the least embarrassment, she held out her hand to me, but I am afraid I did not take it very cordially. Roger, however, behaved to her as if they stood in a drawing room, and this brought me to a sense of propriety.

"I don't look very respectable, I fear," she said, putting her hand over her eye. "I have had a blow, and it will look worse tomorrow. Were you coming to find me?"

I forget what lame answer either of us gave.

"Will you come in?" she said.

I declined. For all my fine talk to Roger, I shrunk from the idea of entering one of those houses. I can only say, in excuse, that I was bewildered.

"Can I do anything for you, then?" she asked, in a tone slightly marked with disappointment, I thought.

"Thank you, no," I answered, hardly knowing what my words were.

"Then good night," she said, and, nodding kindly, turned and entered one of the houses.

We also turned in silence, and walked out of the court.

"Why didn't you go with her?" said Roger, as soon as we were in the street.

"I didn't think you wanted to go, Roger, but—"

"I think you might have gone, seeing I was with you," he said.

"I don't think it would have been at all a proper thing to do, without knowing more about her," I answered, a little hurt. "You can't tell what sort of a place it may be."

"It's a good place wherever she is, or I am much mistaken," he returned.

"You would have gone if I hadn't been with you?"

"Certainly, if she had asked me, which is not very likely."

"And you lay the disappointment of missing a glimpse into the sweet privacy of such a home to my charge?"

It was a spiteful speech, and Roger's silence made me feel it was. With the rather patronizing opinion I had of Roger, I found it not a little galling. So I too kept silence, and nothing beyond a platitude had passed between us when I found myself at my own door, my shopping utterly forgotten, and something acid on my mind.

"Don't you mean to come in?" I said. "My husband will be home soon, if he has not come already. You needn't be bored with my company—you can sit in the study."

"I think I had better not," he answered.

"I am very sorry, Roger, if I was rude to you," I said, "but how could you wish me to be hand-in-glove with a woman who visits people who she is well aware would not think of inviting her if they had a notion of her surroundings. That can't be right, I am certain. I protest I feel just as if I had been reading an ill-invented story, an unnatural fiction."

"There must be some accounting for it," said Roger. "You may be wrong in supposing that the people at whose houses she visits know nothing about her habits."

"My cousin dispensed with her services as soon as she came to the knowledge of certain facts concerning these very points."

"Excuse me—certain rumors—very uncertain facts."

When you are cross, the slightest play upon words is an offense. I knocked at the door in dudgeon, then turned and said, "My cousin Judy, Mr. Roger—"

But here I paused, for I had nothing ready. Anger makes people cleverer for the moment, but when I am angry I am always stupid. Roger finished the sentence for me.

"Your cousin Judy is, you must allow, a very conventional woman," he said.

"She is very good-natured, anyhow. And what do you say to Lady Bernard?"

"She hasn't repudiated Miss Clare's acquaintance."

"But, answer me, do you believe Lady Bernard would invite her to meet her friends if she knew at all?"

"Depend upon it, Lady Bernard knows what she is about. People of her rank can afford to be unconventional."

This irritated me yet more, for it implied that I was influenced by the conventionality which both he and my husband despised. Sarah opened the door, and I stepped in without even saying good-night. Before she closed it, however, I heard my husband's voice and ran out again to welcome him.

He and Roger had already met in the little front garden. They did not shake hands—they never did—they always met as if they had just parted only an hour ago.

"What were you and my wife quarreling about, Roger?" I heard Percivale ask. I paused on the middle of the stair to hear his answer.

"How do you know we were quarreling?" returned Roger gloomily.

"I heard you from the very end of the street," said my husband. "That's not so far," said Roger.

"Too far to hear a wife and brother, though," returned Percivale jocosely.

It stung me to the quick. Here I had been regarding, not even with contempt, only with disgust, the quarrel in which Miss Clare was mixed up. And yet half an hour after, my own voice was heard in dispute with my husband's brother from the other end of our own street!

I rushed down the steps, and kissed Roger before I kissed my husband.

"Come in," interposed Percivale, "and refer the cause in dispute to me."

We did go in, and we did refer the matter to him. By the time he had the facts of the case, however, the point in dispute between us appeared to have grown hazy, and neither of us cared to say anything more about it. Percivale insisted that there was no question before the court.

At length Roger, turning from me to his brother, said, "It's not worth mentioning, Charley, but what led to our quarrel was this: I thought Wynnie might have accepted Miss Clare's invitation to walk in and pay her a visit. Wynnie thought me, I suppose, too ready to sacrifice her dignity to the pleasure of seeing a little more of Miss Clare."

My husband turned to me and said, "Mrs. Percivale, do you accept this as a correct representation of your difference?"

"Well," I answered, hesitating, "yes, on the whole. All I object to is the word *dignity*."

"I retract it," cried Roger, "and accept any substitute you prefer."

"Let it stand," I returned. "It will do as well as a better. I only wish to say that it was not exactly my dignity—"

"No, no, your sense of propriety," said my husband, who then sat silent for a minute or two, pondering like a judge. At length he said, "Wife, you might have gone with your brother, I think, but I understand your disinclination. At the same time, a more generous judgment of Miss Clare might have prevented any difference of feeling in the matter."

"But," I said, greatly inclined to cry, "I only postponed my judgment concerning her." And I only postponed my crying, for I was very much ashamed of myself.

Later, of course, my husband and I talked a good deal more about what I ought to have done, and I saw clearly enough that I ought to have run any risk there might be in accepting her invitation. I had been foolishly taking more care of myself than was necessary. I told him I would write to Roger, and ask him when he could take me there again.

"I will tell you a better plan," he said. "I will go with you myself."

"But would that be fair to Roger? Miss Clare would think I didn't like going with him, and I would go with Roger anywhere. It was I who did not want to go. He did."

"My plan, however, will pave the way for a full explanation or confession. The next time you can go with Roger, and then you will be able to set him right in her eyes."

The plan seemed unobjectionable. But just then Percivale was very busy, and I was as much occupied with my baby, so day after day and week after week passed, during which our duty to Miss Clare was not forgotten, but only unfulfilled.

One afternoon I was surprised by a visit from my father. He not unfrequently surprised us.

"Why didn't you let us know, Papa?" I said. "A surprise is very nice, but an expectation is much nicer, and lasts so much longer."

"I might have disappointed you."

"Even if you had, I should have already enjoyed the expectation. That would be safe."

"There's a good deal to be said in excuse of surprises," he rejoined, "but in the present case, I have a special one to offer. I was taken with a sudden desire to see you. It was very foolish no doubt, and you are quite right in wishing I weren't here, only going to come tomorrow."

"Don't be so cruel, Papa. Scarcely a day passes in which *I* do not long to see *you*. My baby makes me think more about my home than ever."

"Then she's a very healthy baby, if one may judge her influences. But you know, if I had had to give you warning I could not have been here before tomorrow. And surely you will acknowledge, that, however nice expectation may be, presence is better."

"Yes, Papa. We will make a compromise, if you please. Every time you think of coming to me, you must either come at once, or let me know you are coming. Do you agree to that?"

"I agree," he said.

So I have the pleasure of a constant expectation. Any day he may walk in unheralded, or by any post I may receive a letter with the news that he is coming at such a time.

As we sat at dinner that evening, he asked if we had lately seen Miss Clare.

"I've seen her only once, and Percivale not at all, since you were here last, Papa," I answered.

"How's that?" he asked again, a little surprised. "Haven't you got her address yet? I want very much to know more of her."

"So do we. I haven't got her address, but I know where she lives."

"What do you mean, Wynnie? Has she taken to dark sayings of late, Percivale?"

I told him the whole story of my adventure with Roger, and the reports by which Judy had prejudiced my judgment. He heard me through in silence, for it was a rule with him never to interrupt a narrator. He used to say, "You will generally get at more, and in better fashion, if you let any narrative take its own devious course, without the interruption of requested explanations. By the time it is over, you will find the questions you wanted to ask mostly vanished."

"Describe the place to me, Wynnie," he said, when I had ended. "I must go and see her. I have a suspicion—almost a conviction—that she is one whose acquaintance ought to be cultivated at any cost."

"I don't think I could describe the place to you so that you would find it. But if Percivale wouldn't mind my going with you instead of with him, I should be only too happy to accompany you. May I, Percivale?"

"Certainly. It will do just as well to go with your father as with me. I only stipulate that, if you are both satisfied, you take Roger with you next time."

"Of course I will."

"Then we'll go tomorrow evening," said my father.

So it was arranged. My father went about some business in the morning. We dined early, and set out about six o'clock.

My father was getting an old man, and if any protection had been required, he could not have been half so active as Roger, and yet I felt twice as safe with him. I am satisfied that the deepest sense of safety, even in respect of physical dangers, can spring only from moral causes. I believe what made me so courageous was the undeveloped forefeeling that if any evil should overtake me in my father's company, I should not care; it would be all right then, anyhow. The repose was in my father himself, and not in his strength nor his wisdom. The former might fail, the latter might mistake; but so long as I was with him in what I did, no harm worth counting harm could come to me.

It was a cold evening in the middle of November. The light, which had been scanty enough all day, had vanished in a thin penetrating fog. Round every lamp in the street was a colored halo. The shops gleamed like jewel caverns of Alladin hollowed out of the darkness, and the people who hurried or sauntered along looked inscrutable. Where could they live? Had they anybody to love them? Were their hearts quiet under their dingy cloaks and shabby coats?

"Yes," returned my father, to whom I had said something to this effect, "what would not one give for a peep into the mysteries of all these worlds that go crowding past us. If we could but see through the opaque husk of them, some would glitter and glow like diamond mines. Others perhaps would look mere earthy holes, some of them forsaken quarries, with a great pool of stagnant water in the bottom, some like vast coalpits of gloom, into which you dared not carry a lighted lamp for fear of explosion. Some would be mere lumber rooms, and others ill-arranged libraries, without a poet's corner anywhere. But what a wealth of creation they show, and what infinite room for hope it affords!"

"But don't you think, Papa, there may be something of worth lying even in the earth-pit, or at the bottom of the stagnant water in the forsaken quarry?"

"Indeed I do, though I *have* met more than one in my lifetime concerning whom I felt compelled to say that it wanted keener eyes than mine to discover the hidden jewel. But then there *are* keener eyes than mine, for there are more loving eyes. I have myself been able to see good very clearly where some could see none, and shall I doubt that God can see good where my mole eyes can see none? Just as He is keen-eyed for the evil in His creatures in order to destroy it, He would, if it were possible, be yet keener-eyed for the good to nourish and cherish it. If men would only side with the good that is in them, and that the seed should grow and bring forth fruit!"

THIRTEEN
MISS CLARE'S HOME

We arrived at the passage where the gin shop flared through the fog. A man in a fustian jacket came out of the shop and walked slowly down before us, with brickfield clay clinging to him as high as the leather straps which confined his trousers, garterwise, under the knee. The place was quiet. We and the brickmaker seemed the only people in it. When we turned the last corner, he was walking in at the very door where Miss Clare had disappeared. When I told my father that was the house, he called after the man, who came out again and, standing on the pavement, waited until we came up.

"Does Miss Clare live in this house?" my father asked.

"She do," answered the man curtly.

"First floor?"

"No. Nor yet the second, nor the third. She live nearer heaven then 'ere another in the house 'cep' myself. I live in the attic, and so do she."

He was a rough, lumpish young man, with good but dull features—only his blue eyes were clear. He looked my father full in the face, and I thought I saw a dim smile about his mouth.

"You know her, then, I suppose?"

"Everybody in the house knows *her*. There ain't many the likes o' her as lives wi' the likes of us. You go right up to the top. I don't know if she's in, but a'most any one'll be able to tell you. I ain't been home yet."

My father thanked him, and we entered the house, and began to ascend. The stair was very much worn and rather dirty, and some of the bannisters were broken away, but the walls were tolerably clean. Halfway up we met a little girl with tangled hair and tattered garments, carrying a bottle.

"Do you know, my dear," said my father to her, "whether Miss Clare is at home?"

"I dunno," she answered. "I dunno who you mean. I been mindin' the baby. He ain't well. Mother says his head's bad. She's a-going up to tell Grannie, and see if she can't do suthin' for him. You better ast mother—Mother!" she called out—"Here's a lady an' a gen'lem."

"You go about yer business, and be back direckly," cried a gruff voice from somewhere above.

"That's Mother," said the child, and ran down the stair.

When we reached the second floor, there stood a big fat woman on the landing, with her face red, and her hair looking like that of a doll poorly stuck on. She did not speak, but stood waiting to see what we wanted.

"I'm told Miss Clare lives here," said my father. "Can you tell me, my good woman, whether she's at home?"

"I'm neither a good nor bad woman," she returned in an insolent tone.

"I beg your pardon," said my father, "but you see I didn't know your name."

"An' ye don't know it yet."

"All I wanted to trouble you about was whether Miss Clare was at home or not."

"I don't know on one o' that name. If it's Grannie you mean, she's at home, I know, though it's not much reason I've got to care whether she's at home or not. I don't care what you call her. I dare say it'll be all one, come judgment. You'd better go up till you can't go no further, an' knocks yer head agin the tiles, and then you may feel about for a door, and knock at that, and see if the party as opens is the party you wants."

So saying, she turned in at a door behind her, and shut it. But we could hear her still growling and grumbling.

"It's very odd," said my father, with a bewildered smile. "I think we'd better do as she says, and go up till we knock our heads against the tiles."

We climbed two stairs more—the last one very steep and so dark that when we reached the top we found it necessary to follow the woman's directions literally and feel about for a door. But we had not to feel long or far, for there was one close to the top of the stair. My father knocked. There was no reply, but we heard the sound of a chair and presently someone opened it. The only light being behind her, I could not see her face, but the size and shape were those of Miss Clare.

She did not leave us in doubt, however; for, without a moment's hesitation, she held out her hand, saying to me, "This *is* kind of you, Mrs. Percivale," then to my father, "I'm very glad to see you, Mr. Walton. Will you walk in?"

We followed her into the room. It was not very small, for it occupied nearly the breadth of the house. On one side the roof sloped so nearly to the floor that there was not height enough to stand erect. On the other side the sloping part was partitioned off, evidently for a bedroom. But what a change it was from the lower part of the house! By the light of a single candle, I saw that the floor was as clean as old boards could be scrubbed. The two dormer windows were hung with white dimity curtains. Back in the angle of the roof, between the windows, stood an old bureau. There was little more than room between the top of it and the ceiling for a little plaster statuette with bound hands and a strangely crowned head. A few books on hanging shelves were on the opposite side by the door to the other room, and the white-washed walls were a good deal covered with engravings or etchings or lithographs, none of them framed.

There was a fire cheerfully burning in the gable, and opposite that a tall old-fashioned cabinet piano, in faded red silk. On the music rest lay Handel's "Verdi Prati." A few wooden chairs, and one very old-fashioned easy chair covered with striped chintz, from which not glaze only but color had almost disappeared, with an oblong table of deal, completed the furniture of the room. She made my father sit down in the easy chair, placed me one in front of the fire, and took another at the corner opposite my father. A moment of awkward silence followed. But my father never allowed awkwardness to accumulate.

"I had hoped to have been able to call upon you long ago, Miss Clare, but there was some difficulty in finding out where you lived."

"You are no longer surprised at that difficulty, I presume," she returned with a smile.

"But," said my father, "if you will allow an old man to speak to you freely—"

"Say what you please, Mr. Walton. I promise to answer *any* question *you* think proper to ask me."

"My dear Miss Clare, I had not the slightest intention of catechising you. What I meant to say might indeed have taken the form of a question, but as such could have been intended only for you to answer to yourself whether, namely, it was wise to place yourself at such a disadvantage as living in this quarter must be to you."

"If you were acquainted with my history, you would perhaps hesitate, Mr. Walton, before you said I *placed myself* at such disadvantage."

Here a thought struck me. "I fancy, Papa, it is not for her own sake Miss Clare lives here."

"I hope not," she interposed.

"I believe," I went on, "she has a grandmother, who probably has grown accustomed to the place, and is unwilling to leave it."

She looked puzzled for a moment, then burst into a merry laugh. "I see!" she exclaimed. "How stupid I am! You have heard some of the people in this house talk about *Grannie:* That's me! I am known in the house as Grannie, and have been for a good many years now—I can hardly, without thinking, tell for how many."

Again she laughed heartily, and my father and I shared her merriment.

"How many grandchildren have you then, pray, Miss Clare?"

"Let me see." She thought for a while. "There are about thirty-five in this house, but unfortunately the name has been caught up in the neighboring houses, and I cannot with certainty say how many grandchildren I have. I think I know them all, however, and I fancy that is more than many an English grandmother, with children in America, India, or Australia, can say for herself."

Certainly she was not older than I was. While hearing her merry laugh, and seeing her young face overflowing with smiles, which appeared to come sparkling out of her eyes as out of two well-springs, one could not help feeling puzzled how, even in jest, she could have got the name of Grannie.

"Would you like to hear," she said, when our merriment had a little subsided, "how I have so easily arrived at the honorable name of Grannie?"

"I should be delighted," said my father.

"You don't know what you are pledging yourself to when you say so," she rejoined, again laughing. "You will have to hear the whole of my story from the beginning."

"Again I say I shall be delighted," returned my father, confident that her history could be the source of nothing but pleasure to him.

FOURTEEN

MISS CLARE'S STORY

Thereupon Miss Clare began.

"My mother died when I was very young, and I was left alone with my father, for I was his only child. He was a studious and thoughtful man. He supported us by literary work of, I presume, a secondary order. He would spend all his mornings for many weeks in the library of the British Museum, reading and making notes, after which he would sit writing at home. I should have found it very dull during the former of these times, had he not discovered that I had some capacity for music, and provided instruction for me. I believe he could not have found me a better teacher in all Europe. Her character was lovely, and her music the natural outcome of its harmony. I went to her, then, almost every day for a time.

"What my father wrote I cannot tell. How gladly would I now read the shortest sentence I knew to be his! He never told me for what journals or publishers he wrote. I fancy it was work in which his brain was more interested than his heart, and which he was always hoping to exchange for something more to his mind. After his death I could discover scarcely a scrap of his writings, and not a hint to guide me to what he had written.

"My happiest times were when my father asked me to play to him while he wrote, and I sat down to my old cabinet Broadwood—the one you see there is as like it as I could find—and played anything and everything I liked, for I never forgot what I learned.

"Even though we went to church on Sunday mornings, my father rarely talked much to me about religion. When he did, it was with evident awe in his spirit, and reverence in his demeanor. Waking one night after I had been asleep for some time, I saw him on his knees by my bedside. I did not move or speak, for fear of disturbing him, and when he lifted his head I caught a glimpse of a pale, tearful face. It is no wonder that the virtue of the sight should never have passed away. He was in the habit of reading chapters of the New Testament to me, but the consolations of religion were not yet mine, for I had not yet begun to think of God in any relation to myself.

"We lived then near the Museum where I would linger about looking at things, sometimes for hours, before my father came to me. He always came at the very minute he had said, though, and always found me at the appointed spot.

"One afternoon I was waiting as usual, but my father did not come at the time appointed. I waited on and on till it grew dark, and the hour for closing arrived, and I was forced to go home without him. I found he had been seized with some kind of fit in the reading room and had been carried home. . . . and after that I was alone in the world.

"Our landlady was very kind to me, at least until she found that my father had left no money. All our little effects were sold for less than half their value, in consequence of that conspiracy of the brokers which they call *knocking out*. I was especially miserable at losing my father's books, which I greatly valued, more miserable even than at seeing my beloved piano carried off.

"When the sale was over, I sat down on the floor, amidst the dust and bits of paper and straw and cord, without a single idea in my head as to what was to become of me, or what I was to do next. I didn't cry, but I doubt if in all London there was a more wretched child than myself just then, in the twilight of a November afternoon. While I sat on the floor, the landlady and someone else came into the room. They, not seeing me, talked about me, reflecting severely on my father, and announcing the decree that I must go to the workhouse. The moment they left me alone, I got up, glided down the stairs, and ran from the house.

"Within a few yards I ran up against Mrs. Conan, an old Irishwoman who did all the little charing we wanted. I broke out in sobs, and told her I was running away because they were going to send me to the workhouse. She burst into a torrent of Irish indignation, and assured me that such should never be my fate while she lived. She led me away to a large house in a square—the largest house I had ever been in, though it was rather desolate. Except in one little room below, where she had scarcely more than a bed and a chair, a slip of carpet and a frying pan, there was not an article of furniture in the whole place. She had been put there when the last tenant left, to take care of the place until another tenant should appear to turn her out. She had her houseroom and a trifle a week besides for her services, beyond which she depended entirely on what she could make by charing. When she had no house to live in on the same terms, she took a room somewhere.

"Here I lived for several months, and was able to be of use. Mrs. Conan was bound to be there at certain times to show anyone over the house who brought an order from the agent, and this necessarily took up a good part of her working time. But as I could open the door and walk about the place as well as another, she willingly left me in charge as often as she had a job elsewhere.

"I found it very dreary indeed, for few people called, and she would not infrequently be absent the whole day. I had not my piano, and only a single book and what do you think that was? An odd volume of the *Newgate Calendar*. It moved me, indeed, to the profoundest sympathy, not with the crimes of the malefactors, but with the malefactors themselves, and their mental condition after the deed was actually done. But it made me feel almost as if I had committed every crime. It was not until long afterward that I was able to understand that a man's actions are not the man, but may be separated from him. His character may be changed while he yet holds the same individuality—the man was blind though he now sees. And though the deeds may continue to be his, all stain of them may yet be washed out of him.

"I cannot think that the study of the *Newgate Calendar* could do an innocent child harm. Even familiarity with vice is not necessarily pollution. There cannot be many women of my age as familiar with it in every shape as I am, and I do not regard it with one atom less of absolute abhorrence, although I neither shudder at the mention of it, nor turn with disgust from the person in whom it dwells. I believe that volume threw down the first deposit of soil, from which afterward sprung what grew to be almost a passion for getting the people about me clean—a passion which might have done as much harm as good, if its companion, patience, had not been sent me to guide and restrain it. In a word, I came at length to understand, in some measure, the last prayer of our Lord for those who crucified Him, and the ground on which He begged from His Father their forgiveness—that they knew not what they did.

"The house was in an old square, built in the reign of Queen Anne but fallen far from its first high estate. No one would believe, to look at it from the outside, what a great place it was. The whole of the space behind it, corresponding to the small gardens of the other houses, was occupied by a large music room, under which was a low-pitched room of equal extent, while all under that were cellars, connected with the sunken story in front by a long vaulted passage, corresponding to a wooden gallery above, which formed a communication between the drawing room floor and the music room. Most girls of my age, knowing these vast empty spaces about them, would have been terrified at being left alone there, even in midday. But I was, I suppose, too miserable to be frightened. Sometimes Mrs. Conan was later than usual, and the night came down, and I had to sit, perhaps for hours, in the dark—for she would not allow me to have a candle, for fear of fire. I used to cry a good deal, although I did my best to hide the traces of it, because I knew it would annoy my kind old friend. She showed me a great deal of rough tenderness, and you may be sure I learned to love her dearly.

"One rainy winter evening I have a particular cause to remember, both for itself, and because of something that followed many years after. I was in the drawing room on the first floor, a double room with folding doors and a small cabinet behind communicating with a back stair. The stairs were double all through the house, adding much to the eeriness of the place. I had been looking out of the window all the afternoon upon the silent square—there were no tradesmen there, and no children playing in the garden. A gray cloud of fog and soot hung from the whole sky. A score of yellow leaves yet quivered on the trees, and the statue of Queen Anne stood bleak and disconsolate among the bare branches.

"I gazed at it all drearily without interest. I brooded over the past, not dreaming of looking forward. I had no hope, and it never occurred to me that things might grow better. I was dull and wretched.

"I think this experience enabled me to understand the peculiar misery of the poor in our large towns—they have no hope, no impulse to look forward, nothing to expect. They live but in the present, and the dreariness of that soon shapes the whole atmosphere of their spirits to its own likeness. Perhaps the first thing one who would help them has to do is to aid the birth of some small vital hope in them, for that is better than a thousand gifts.

"But it began to grow dark. Tired of standing, I sat down upon the floor, until long after it was quite dark. All at once a surge of self-pity arose in my heart. I burst out wailing and sobbing, and cried aloud, 'God has forgotten me altogether!' I was really thinking that I could do nothing for anybody. My little ambition had always been to be useful. I knew I was of some use to my father, for I kept the rooms tidy for him, and dusted his pet books oh, so carefully, for they were like household gods to me. I had also played for him, and I knew he enjoyed that—he said so, many times. And I had begun to think, just before he left me, how I should be able to help him better by and by. For I saw that he worked very hard, so hard that it made him silent. I knew that my music mistress made her livelihood, partly at least, by giving lessons; and I thought that I might, by and by, be able to give lessons too, and then papa would not be required to work so hard, for I too should bring money home.

"But now I was of use to nobody. I could not help even poor Mrs. Conan. I did not earn a penny of our living. I only gave the poor old thing time to work harder, that I might eat up her earnings! I always thought of myself as a lady, for was not Papa a gentleman, let him be ever so poor? Shillings and sovereigns in his pocket could not determine whether a man was a gentleman or not! And if he was a gentleman, his daughter must be a lady. But how could I be a lady if I was content to be a burden to a poor charwoman, instead of earning my own living, and something besides with which to help her? For I had the notion that position depended on how much a person was able to help other people, and here I was, worse than useless to anybody! 'I am of no use,' I cried, 'and God has forgotten me altogether!' And I went on weeping until I fell fast asleep on the floor.

"I have no theory about dreams and visions, but surely if one falls fast asleep without an idea in one's head, and a whole dismal world of misery in one's heart, and wakes up quiet and refreshed, without the misery and with an idea, there can be no great fanaticism in thinking that God may have had something—or everything—to do with it. Certainly, if it had a physical source, it wasn't that I was more comfortable, for I was hungrier than ever, and cold enough, having slept on the bare floor without anything to cover me on Christmas Eve—for Christmas Eve it was.

"The way Mrs. Conan kept Christmas Day was to comfort her old bones in bed until the afternoon, and then to have a good tea with a chop. So, as soon as I had washed up the few breakfast things, I dressed myself as neatly as I could, and set out to look for work.

"In a nearby shop I had seen a piano standing, and a girl of about my own age watching. I found the shop, although it was shut up, and knocked at the door. A stout matron opened it, and asked me what I wanted. I told her I wanted work. She seemed amused at the idea, but asked what I could do. I told her I could teach her daughter music. She asked me what made me come to her, and I told her. But how was she to know, she asked, that I could teach her properly? I told her I would let her hear me play; whereupon she led me into the shop, took down a shutter, and managed to clear me a passage through a crowd of furniture to the instrument. With a struggle I squeezed through and reached it; but at the first chord I struck, I gave a cry of dismay. In some alarm she asked what was the matter, calling me Child very kindly. I told her it was so dreadfully out of tune that I couldn't play on it at all; but, if she would get it tuned, I should show her that I could do what I professed. She told me she could not afford to have it tuned, and if I could not teach Bertha on it as it was, she couldn't help it. This, I assured her, was utterly impossible; and then, with some show of offense, she reached over a chest of drawers, and shut down the cover. I believe she doubted whether I could play at all, and had not been merely amusing myself at her expense. Nothing was left but to thank her and walk out of the house, dreadfully disappointed.

"Unwilling to go home at once, I wandered about the neighborhood, through street after street, and found myself in front of a pianoforte firm, and a thought came into my head. The next morning I returned, and asked to see the master, Mr. Perkins, who was amused with my story. If I had asked him for money, he would probably have got rid of me quickly enough. But to my request that he would spare a man to tune Mrs. Lampeter's piano, he replied at once that he would, provided I could satisfy him as to my efficiency. Thereupon he took me to a grand piano in the shop and told me to play. I could not help trembling a good deal, but I tried my best. In a few moments, however, the tears were drop-ping on the keys, and when he asked me what was the matter, I told him it was months since I had touched a piano. He asked very kindly how that was, and I had to tell him my whole story. Then he not only promised to have the piano tuned for me at once, but told me I might come and practice in his shop as often as I pleased, so long as I was a good girl, and did not take up with bad company. Imagine my delight! Then he sent for a tuner, and I suppose told him a little about me, for the man spoke very kindly to me as we went to the broker's.

"Mr. Perkins has been a good friend to me ever since.

"For six months I continued to give Bertha Lampeter lessons. Her mother introduced me to several families, and I found five or six new pupils.

"When the house was let, Mrs. Conan took a room in the neigh-borhood, that I might keep up my connection. Then I was first introduced to the scenes and experiences with which I am now familiar. Mrs. Percivale might well recoil if I were to tell her half the wretchedness, wickedness, and vulgarity I have encountered. For two years or so we changed about, at one time in an empty house, at another in a hired room, sometimes better, sometimes worse off, as regarded our neighbors. When Mrs. Conan came to the conclusion that it would be better for her to confine herself to charing, we at last settled down here, where I have now lived for many years.

"I had never thought of going back to Miss Harper, my former music mistress, until Mr. Perkins asked me one day who had taught me. I resolved to go and see her. She welcomed me with more than kindness, with tenderness, and told me I had caused her much uneasiness by not letting her know what had become of me. She looked quite aghast when she learned in what sort of place and with whom I lived. But I told her Mrs. Conan had saved me from the workhouse, and was as much of a mother to me as possible. that we loved each other, and that it would be very wrong of me to leave her now, especially since she was not so well as she had been. I believe she then saw the thing as I saw it. She made me play to her, was pleased—indeed surprised—until I told her how I had been supporting myself, and she insisted on my resuming my studies with her, which I was only too glad to do. I now, of course, got on much faster.

"Then Mrs. Conan fell ill, and we indeed had hard work of it.

Had it not been for the kindness of the neighbors, we should sometimes have been in want of bread; and when I hear hard things said of the poor, I often think that surely improvidence is not so bad as selfishness.

"Miss Harper said I must raise my terms, but I told her that would be the loss of my pupils. Then she said she must see what could be done for me, only no one she knew was likely to employ a child. One morning, however, within a week, a note came from Lady Bernard asking me to go and see her.

"I went, and found—a mother. You do not know her, I think? But you must one day. Good people like you must come together. She awed me at first—I was not much more than thirteen then— but with the awe came a certain confidence which was far better then ease. The immediate result was that she engaged me to go and play for an hour, five days a week, at a hospital for sick children in the neighborhood, which she partly supported. For she had a strong belief that there was in music a great healing power, and I do think that good has been and is the result of my playing to those children. I go still, though not quite so often, and it is music to me to watch my music thrown back in light from some of those sweet, pale, suffering faces.

"Lady Bernard was too wise to pay me much at first. She inquired how much I was already earning, asked me on how much I could support Mrs. Conan and myself, and then made up that amount. At the same time, however, she sent many things to warm and feed the old woman, so that my mind was set at ease about her. Mrs. Conan continued to suffer so much from rheumatism that she was quite unfit to go out charing any more, and we removed ourselves to this place. It was a good while before the inmates of this house and I began to know each other. They regarded us from the first with disapproval. The little girls would make grimaces at me, and the bigger girls would pull my hair, slap my face, and even occasionally push me down stairs, while the boys made themselves far more terrible in my eyes. But with time and a few events, things began to grow better.

"And this is not by any means one of the worst parts of London. I could take Mr. Walton to houses in the East End, where the manners are indescribable. We are all earning our bread here. Some have an occasional attack of drunkenness, and idle about, but they are sick of it again after a while. I remember asking a woman once if her husband would be present at a little entertainment to which Lady Bernard had invited them. She answered that he would be there if he was drunk, but if he was sober he couldn't spare the time.

"My main stay and comfort was an old woman who then occupied the room opposite to this. She was such a good creature! She was nearly blind, yet I never saw a speck of dust on that chest of drawers, which was hers then. Her floor and her little muslin window curtains, her bed, and everything about her were as clean as a lady could desire. She was very pleased when I asked her to pay a visit to Mrs. Conan, and I think she did us both good. I wish you could picture her coming in at that door, with the broad borders of her white cap waving, and her hands stretched out before her. The most remarkable thing to me was the calmness with which she looked forward to her approaching death, although without the expectation which so many good people seem to have in connection with their departure. Her belief amounted to this— that she had never known beforehand what lay round the next corner, or what was going to happen to her, but under Providence things always turned out right and good for her, and she did not doubt she would find it so when she came to the last turn.

"I also kept my rooms as clean and tidy as I could—indeed, the sight of the blind woman's room was a constant reminder. I also was able to get a few more articles of furniture and a bit of carpet. I whitewashed the walls myself, and after a while began to whitewash the walls of the landing as well, and all down the stair. Before long some of the other tenants began to whitewash their rooms also, and contrive to keep things a little tidier. Soon this one and that began to apply to me for help in various difficulties that arose. But they didn't call me Grannie then—they called the blind woman Grannie, and the name got associated with the top of the house. After her death, the name settled down upon me, and I came to be called Grannie by everybody in the house.

"By and by I got a few music pupils amongst tradespeople of a more superior class, and I both asked and obtained double my former fee, so that our financial situation grew gradually better. Some of Lady Bernard's friends engaged me to teach their children as well.

"Having come once or twice to see Mrs. Conan, Lady Bernard discovered that we were gaining a little influence over the people in the house; and it occurred to her, as she told me afterward, that the virtue of music might be tried there with a moral end in view

Hence I was astonished and delighted one evening by the arrival of a piano—not that one, for I wore the other out. First I asked some of the children to come and listen while I played. Even the least educated children are made for music: whatever the street organs may be to poets and mathematicians, they are certainly a godsend to the children of our courts and alleys. The only condition I made was that they should come with clean hands and faces and tidy hair. Considerable indignation was at first manifested by some parents whose children I refused to admit, but the grumbling passed away while the condition gathered weight. After a while I began to invite the mothers to join us, and at length it came to be understood that every Saturday evening, whoever chose to be tidy would be welcome to an hour or two of my music. Some of the husbands even began to come.

"There was another point. Never since my father's death had I attended public worship, and I hardly know what induced me one evening to step into a chapel of which I knew nothing. There was not even Sunday to account for it. I believe, however, it had to do with my feeling tired. I only felt empty all through—I felt that something was not right with me, that something was required of me which I was not rendering. I entered the chapel, and found about a dozen people present and singing. Something in the air of the place, meagre and waste as it looked, yet induced me to remain. An address followed from a pale-faced, weak-looking man of middle age, who had no gift of person, voice, or utterance to recommend what he said. But there dwelt a powerful enforcement in him, that of earnestness. I went again and again, and slowly the sense of life and its majesty grew upon me.

"To one hungering for bread, it is of little consequence in what sort of platter it is handed him. This was a dissenting chapel—of what order, it was long before I knew—and my father had accustomed me to the Church services. And now, although a communicant of the Church of England, I do not prefer one over against the other.

"I gathered from this good man one practical thought which was the main fruit—the fruit by which I know that he was good. If all the labor of God was to bring sons into glory, lifting them out of the abyss of evil bondage up to the rock of His pure freedom, the only worthy end of life must be to work in the same direction— to be a fellow worker with God. Might I not, then, do such in my own small way? The urging, the hope, grew in me. Then my teacher taught me that the way for *me* to help others was not to tell them of their duty, but myself to learn of Him who bore our griefs and carried our sorrows. As I learned of Him, I should be able to help them. I have never had any theory since then but just to be their friend—to do for them the best I can. When I feel I may, I tell them what has done me good, but I never urge any belief of mine upon their acceptance.

"And so I remain where I am. I was sixteen when Mrs. Conan died. Then my friends, including Lady Bernard and Miss Harper, expected me to move. Indeed, Lady Bernard said she knew precisely the place for me. When I told her I should remain where I was, she was silent, and soon left me—offended, I thought. I wrote to her at once, explaining why I chose my part here, saying that I would not hastily alter anything that had been appointed me; that I loved the people; that they called me Grannie; that they came to me with their troubles; that there were few changes in the house now; that the sick looked to me for help, and the children for teaching; that they seemed to be steadily rising in the moral scale; and that I knew some of them were trying hard to be good. So I put it to her whether, if I were to leave them in order merely to better myself, I should not be forsaking my post, almost my family. If I was at all necessary to them, I knew they were yet more necessary to me.

"I have a burning desire to help in the making of the world clean, if it be only by sweeping one little room in it. I want to lead some poor stray sheep home—not home to the church, Mr. Walton. I would not be supposed to curry favor with you. I never think of what they call the church. I only care to lead them home to the bosom of God, where alone man is true man.

"I could talk to you all night about what Lady Bernard has been to me since, and what she has done for me and my grandchildren. But I have said enough to explain how it is that I am in such a questionable position."

FIFTEEN

A FEW MORE FACTS

A silence followed. My father had scarcely interrupted, and I had not spoken a word, for her story moved us deeply. My father sat perfectly composed, betraying his emotion in silence alone. I had a great lump in my throat, but in part from the shame which mingled with my admiration. The silence had not lasted more than a few seconds, when I yielded to a struggling impulse, rose, and kneeling before her, put my hands on her knees, and said, "Forgive me," and could say no more. She put her hand on my shoulder, whispered, "My dear Mrs. Percivale!" bent down her face, and kissed me on the forehead.

"How could you help being shy of me?" she said "Perhaps I ought to have come to you and explained it all, but I shrink from self-justification—at least before a fit opportunity makes it comparatively easy."

"That is the way to give it all its force," remarked my father.

"You see, Mr. Walton, it is not in the least as if, living in comfort, I had taken notice of the misery of the poor for the want of such sympathy and help as I could give them, and had therefore gone to live amongst them that I might so help them. It is quite different from that. If I had done so, I might be in danger of magnifying not merely my office but myself. On the contrary, I have been trained to it in such slow and continuous ways, that it would be a far greater trial to me to forsake my work than it has ever been to continue it."

My father said no more, but I knew he had his own thought. I remained kneeling, and understood for the first time what had led to saint worship.

"Won't you sit, Mrs. Percivale?" she said, as if merely expostulating with me for not making myself comfortable.

"Have you forgiven me?" I asked.

"How can I say I have, when I never had anything to forgive?"

"Well then, I must go unforgiven, for I cannot forgive myself," I said.

"O Mrs. Percivale! If you think how the world is flooded with forgiveness, you will just dip in your cup, and take what you want."

I rose, humbled, and took my seat.

The work to which Miss Clare had given herself seemed more like that of the Son of God than any other I knew. For she was not helping her friends from afar, but as one of themselves; nor with money, but with herself. She was not condescending to them, but finding her highest life in companionship with them. It seemed at least more like what His life must have been before He was thirty, than anything else I could think of. At length I ventured to remind her of something she seemed to have forgotten.

"When you were telling us, Miss Clare," I said, "of the help that came to you that dreary afternoon in the empty house, you mentioned that something which happened afterward made it still more remarkable."

"Oh, yes!" she answered. "I forgot about that. I did not carry my history far enough to be reminded of it again.

"About five years ago, Lady Bernard asked me to give an entertainment to my friends, and to as many of the neighbors as I pleased, to the number of about a hundred. She wanted to put the thing entirely in my hands, and it should be my entertainment, she claiming only the privilege of defraying expenses. I told her I should be delighted to convey *her* invitation, but that the entertainment must not pretend to be mine.

"She had bought a large house to be a home for young women out of employment, and she proposed the entertainment be given in it. There were a good many nice young women there who would help us to wait upon our guests. The idea was carried out, and the thing succeeded admirably. We had music and games, the latter such as the children were mostly acquainted with, only producing more merriment and conducted with more propriety than was usual in the court or the streets. Had these been children of the poorest sort, we should have had to teach them, for one of the saddest things is that they, in London at least, do not know how to play.

"In one of the games, I was seated on the floor with a handkerchief tied over my eyes, waiting, I believe, for some gentle trick to be played upon me, that I might guess who played it. There was a delay of only a few seconds, long enough, however, for a sudden return of that dreary December afternoon in which I sat on the floor too miserable even to think that I was cold and hungry. It was not the picture of it that came back to me first, but the sound of my voice calling aloud in the ringing echo of desolate rooms that I was of no use to anybody, and that God had forgotten me utterly.

"Then I jumped to my feet, and tore the bandage from my eyes. I stared about the room, convinced that it was the very room in which I had so sat in desolation and despair. I hurried into the back room—and there was the cabinet beyond! In a few moments more I was absolutely satisfied that this was indeed the house in which I had first found refuge. I sat down in the corner, and cried for joy. Someone went for Lady Bernard, whom I told that there was nothing the matter but a little too much happiness, and, that if she would come into the cabinet, I would tell her all about it. She did so, and a few words made her a hearty sharer in my pleasure. She insisted that I should tell the company all about it, 'for,' she said, 'you do not know how much it may help some poor creature to trust in God.' I promised I would. Then she left me alone for a little while, and after that I was able to join in the games again.

"At supper I stood up, and gave them all a little sketch of my history, and told what had happened that evening. Many of the simpler hearts about me received it without question, as a divine arrangement for my comfort and encouragement. But presently a man stood up—one who thought more than the rest of them, perhaps because he was blind—a man at once conceited, honest, and sceptical. Silence was made for him, and he began to speak, 'Ladies and gentlemen,' as if he had been addressing a public meeting, 'you've all heard what Grannie has said. It's very kind of her to give us so much of her history. It's a very remarkable one, *I* think, and she deserves to have it. As to what upset her this very night as is—and I must say for her, I've knowed her now for six years, and I never knowed her upset afore—and as to what upset her, all I can say is, it may or may not ha' been what phylosophers call a coincydence. But at the same time, if it wasn't a coincydence, and if the Almighty had a hand in it, it were no more than you might expect. He would look at it in this light, you see, that maybe she was wrong to fancy herself so down on her luck as all that, but she was a good soul, notwithstandin,' and He would let her know He hadn't forgotten her. And so He set her down in that room there for a minute, jest to put her in mind o' what had been, and what she had said there, an' how it was all so different now. In my opinion, it were no wonder as she broke down, God bless her. I beg leave to propose her health.'

"So they drank my health in lemonade and ginger beer. Then we had more music and singing; and a clergyman, who knew how to be neighbor to them that had fallen among thieves, read a short chapter and a collect or two, and said a few words to them. Then Grannie and her children went home together, all happy, but Grannie the happiest of them all."

"Strange and beautiful!" said my father. "But," he added, after a pause, "you must have met with many strange and beautiful things in such a life as yours, for such a life must open to the entrance of all simple wonders. Conventionality and routine and arbitrary law banish their very approach."

"I believe," said Miss Clare, "that every life has its own private experience of the strange and beautiful. But I have sometimes thought that perhaps God took pains to bar out such things of the sort as we should be no better for. The reason why Lazarus was not allowed to visit the brothers of Dives was, that the repentance he would have urged would not have followed, and they would have been only the worse in consequence."

"Admirably said," remarked my father.

Before we took our leave, I had engaged Miss Clare to dine with us while my father was in town.

SIXTEEN

LADY BERNARD

When Miss Clare came we had no other guests, and so had plenty of talk with her. Before dinner I showed her my husband's pictures, and she was especially pleased with that which hung in the little room off the study with a curtain before it. My father has described it in *The Seaboard Parish*: a pauper lies dead, and they are bringing in his coffin. She said it is no wonder it had not been sold, notwithstanding its excellence and force, and asked if I would allow her to bring Lady Bernard to see it.

Percivale succeeded in persuading her to sit for him— but not, however, before I had joined my entreaties with his, and my father had insisted that her face was not her own, but belonged to all her kind.

The very next morning she came with Lady Bernard. I wish I could give a photograph of that lady. She was slight and appeared taller than she was, being rather stately than graceful, with a commanding forehead and blue eyes. She gave at first the impression of coldness, with a touch of haughtiness. She said she knew my husband well by reputation and had, before our marriage, asked him to her house, but had not been fortunate enough to possess sufficient attraction. Percivale was much taken with her, for when her eyes lighted up, her seeming coldness vanished in the light that flashed into her eyes and the smile that illumined her face. She was much pleased with some of his pictures, criticising freely and with evident understanding. She bought both the pauper picture and that of the dying knight.

"But I am sorry to deprive your lovely room of such treasures, Mrs. Percivale," she said, with a kind smile.

"Of course I shall miss them," I returned, "but the thought that you have them will console me. Besides, it is good to have a change and there are only too many lying in the study, from which he will let me choose another."

"Will you let me come and see which you have chosen?" she asked.

"With the greatest pleasure."

"And will you come and see me? Do you think you could persuade your husband to bring you to dine with me?"

I told her I could promise the one with more than pleasure, and had little doubt of being able to do the other, now that my husband had seen her.

A reference to my husband's dislike to fashionable society followed, and I had occasion to mention his feeling about being asked without me. Of the latter, Lady Bernard expressed the warmest approval; and of the former, she said that it would have no force in respect of her parties, for they were not at all fashionable.

This was the commencement of a friendship for which we have much cause to thank God. (Nor did we forget that it came through Miss Clare.)

Lady Bernard interested me in many of her schemes of helping the poor. Some of the programs were for providing them with work in hard times, but more for giving them an interest in life itself, without which no one would begin to inquire into its relations and duties. She felt that one ought not, where avoidable, give them anything they *ought* to provide for themselves, such as food or clothing or shelter. But she heartily approved of making them an occasional present of something they could not be expected to procure for themselves—flowers, for instance. "You would not imagine," I have heard her say, "how they delight in flowers. I am sure they prize and enjoy them far more than most people with gardens and greenhouses do. A gift of that sort can only do them good. I would rather give a workman a gold watch than a leg of mutton. By a present you mean a compliment, and none feel more grateful for such an acknowledgment of your human relation to them than those who look up to you as their superior."

If ever there was a woman who lived this outer life for the sake of others, it was she. Her inner life was sufficient for herself, and found its natural outward expression in blessing others. I believe no one, not even Miss Clare, knew half the munificent things she did, or what an immense proportion of her large income she spent upon other people. But, as she said herself, no one understood the worth of money better, and no one liked better to have the worth of it. Therefore, she always administered her charity with some view to the value of the probable return, with some regard to the amount of good likely to result to others from the aid given to one. She always took into consideration whether the good was likely to be propagated, or to die with the receiver.

It was some time after our encounter with Lady Bernard that I judged I might give another little dinner party. I now knew Lady Bernard sufficiently well to know also that she would willingly accept an invitation from me, and would be pleased to bring Miss Clare with her.

I proposed the dinner and Percivale consented to it. My main object was the glorification of Miss Clare, who had more engagements of one kind or another than anybody I knew; so I first invited her, asking her to fix her own day. Next I invited Mr. and Mrs. Morley, and next Lady Bernard. Then I invited Mr. Blackstone, and Roger—for I was much interested in his meeting Miss Clare. He had been absent from London for some time, and had not seen her since he and I had quarreled.

On the evening, Roger arrived first, then Mr. Blackstone. Lady Bernard brought Miss Clare, and Mr. and Mrs. Morley came last. There were several introductions to be gone through, and I failed to observe how the presence of Miss Clare affected Mr. and Mrs. Morley. But my husband told me that Judy turned red, and that Mr. Morley bowed to her with studied politeness. I took care that Mr. Blackstone should take her down to dinner, which was served in the studio as before.

The conversation was broken and desultory at first, but eventually centered around Lady Bernard and my husband at the foot of the table.

"Then you do believe," my husband was saying, "in the importance of birth and descent—of *havage,* as some call it?"

"I believe that descent involves very important considerations," Lady Bernard returned.

"No one," interposed Mr. Morley, "can have a better right than your ladyship to believe that."

"One cannot have a better right than another to believe a fact,

Mr. Morley," she answered with a smile. "It is but a fact that you start better or worse according to the position of your starting point."

"Undeniably," said Mr. Morley. "And for all the growth of leveling notions in this country, it will be many generations before a profound respect for birth is eradicated from the feelings of the English people."

He drew in his chin with a jerk, and devoted himself again to his plate. He was not permitted to eat in peace, however.

"No growth of nations," said Mr. Blackstone, "will blot love, honesty, and kindness out of the human heart."

"Then," said Lady Bernard archly, "am I to understand, Mr. Blackstone, that you don't believe it of the least importance to come of decent people?"

"Your ladyship puts it well," said Mr. Morley, laughing mildly, "and with authority. The longer the descent—"

"The more doubtful," interrupted Lady Bernard, laughing. "One can hardly have come of decent people all through. Let us only hope, without inquiring too closely, that their number preponderates in our own individual cases."

Mr. Morley stared for a moment, and then tried to laugh, but unable to determine where he stood, returned to his glass of sherry.

"On the contrary," Mr. Blackstone rejoined, "it must be a serious fact to anyone like myself who believes that the sins of the fathers are visited on the children."

"I can't imagine you believing such a manifest injustice," objected Roger. "I must either disbelieve that, or disbelieve in a God."

"But don't you see it is a fact? Don't you see children born with the sins of their parents nestling in their very bodies?"

"Wouldn't you rather *not* believe in a God than in an unjust one?"

"An unjust god," said Mr. Blackstone, with the honest evasion of one who will not answer an awful question hastily, "must be a false god—that is, no god. But I will go further on my original statement. I will assert that it is an honor to us to have the sins of our fathers laid upon us. For thus it is given into our power to put a stop to them, so that they shall descend no further."

"I would differ from you in only one thing," said Lady Bernard. "The chain of descent is linked in such a complicated pattern that the choices of one link, or of many links, cannot break the transmission of qualities."

"If I understand you rightly, Lady Bernard," said Roger, "it is the personal character of your ancestors, and not their social position, that you regard as of importance."

"It was of their character alone I was thinking."

"Then we are all equally descended," I remarked, "for we have each had about the same number of ancestors, with characters of some sort or other, whose faults and virtues have to do with ours."

"Certainly," returned Lady Bernard. "And it is impossible to say in whose descent the good or the bad may predominate. I cannot tell, for instance, how much of the property I inherit has been honestly come by, or is the spoil of rapacity and injustice."

"You are doing the best you can to atone for such a possible fact, then, by its redistribution," said my husband.

"I have no right to throw up my stewardship, for that was none of my seeking, and I do not know anyone who has a better claim to it—but I count it only a stewardship. I am not at liberty to throw my orchard open, for that would result not only in its destruction, but in a renewal of the fight for its possession. However, I will try to distribute my apples properly to the poor and needy. I have not the same right to give away that I have to keep wisely."

"For my part," said Mr. Morley, "I don't see what is to be done. The poor go on increasing."

"It cannot be denied," said Lady Bernard, "whoever may be to blame for it, that the separation between rich and poor has greatly widened of late. Or perhaps we have become more aware of the breadth and depth of the gulf. Certainly the rich withdraw themselves from the poor. Instead of helping them to bear their burdens, they leave the still struggling poor of whole parishes to sink into hopeless want, under the weight of those who have already sunk beyond recovery. At all events, he that hates his brother is a murderer."

"But there is no question of hating here," objected Mr. Morley.

"I am not certain that absolute indifference to one's neighbor is not as bad. It came to pretty nearly the same thing in the case of the priest and the Levite, who passed by on the other side," said Mr. Blackstone.

"Still," said Mr. Morley, in all the self-importance of one who prided himself on the practical, "I do not see that anyone has proposed a remedy. What is to be *done?* What can *I* do?"

"I will not dare to answer what *you* can do. I can only speak of what principles I have discovered. But until a man begins to behave to those with whom he comes into personal contact as partakers of the same nature—to recognize, for instance, between himself and his tradespeople a bond superior to that of supply and demand—I cannot imagine how he is to do anything toward the drawing together of the edges of the gaping wound in the social body."

"But," persisted Mr. Morley who, I began to think, showed some real desire to come at a practical conclusion, "suppose a man finds himself incapable of that sort of thing—for it wants some rare qualification or other to be able to converse with an uneducated person—"

"Especially amongst those of the trades," interposed Mr. Blackstone, "there are many who think a great deal more than most of the so-called educated. There is a truer education to be got in the pursuit of a trade than in the life of a mere scholar. But I beg your pardon, Mr. Morley."

"Suppose," resumed Mr. Morley, accepting the apology without disclaimer, "suppose I find I can do nothing of that sort—is there nothing I can do?"

"Nothing of the best sort, I firmly believe," answered Miss Clare, "for the genuine recognition of the human relationship can alone give value to whatever else you may do, and indeed can alone guide you to what might serve toward the filling up of the gulf between the classes."

"Well, will not all kindness shown to the poor by persons in a superior station tend in that direction?"

"I maintain that you can do nothing for them in the way of kindness that shall not result in more harm than good, except you do it from and with genuine charity of soul—with some of that love, in short, which is the heart of religion. Except what is done for them is so done as to draw out their trust and affection, and so raise them consciously in the human scale, it can only tend either to hurt their feelings and generate indignation, or to encourage fawning and beggary. But—"

"I am entirely of your mind," said Mr. Blackstone. "But do go on."

"I was going to add," said Miss Clare, "that while no other charity than this can touch the sore, a good deal might yet be effected by bare justice. It seems to me high time that we dropped talking about charity and took up the cry of justice.

"Is it just in the nation," she continued, "to abandon those who can do nothing to help themselves, to be preyed upon by bad landlords, railway companies, and dishonest tradespeople with their false weights, balances, and measures, and adulterations to boot—from all of which their more wealthy brethren are completely safe? Does not a nation exist for the protection of its parts? Have these no claims on the nation? Would you call it just in a family to abandon its less gifted to any moral or physical spoiler who might be bred within it?

"To say a citizen must take care of himself *may* be just in those cases where he *can* take care of himself, but *cannot* be just wherever that is impossible. A thousand causes, originating mainly in the neglect of their neighbors, have combined to sink the poor into a state of moral paralysis. Are we to say the paralyzed may be run over in our streets with impunity? *Must* they take care of themselves? Have we not to awake them to the very sense that life is worth caring for? I cannot but feel that the bond between such a neglected class, and any nation in which it is to be found, is only or as strong as that between slaves and their masters. Who could preach to them their duty to the nation, except on grounds which such a nation acknowledges only with the lips?"

"You have to prove, Miss Clare," said Mr. Morley, in a tone that seemed intended to imply that he was not in the least affected by mistimed eloquence, "that the relation is that of a family."

"I believe," she returned, "that it is closer than the mere human relation of the parts of any family. But, at all events, until we *are* their friends, it is worse then useless to pretend to be such. And until they feel that we are their friends, it is worse than useless to talk to them about God and religion. They will have none of it from our lips."

"Will they from any lips? Are they not already too far sunk toward the brutish to be capable of receiving any such rousing influence?" suggested Mr. Blackstone with a smile, evidently wishing to draw Miss Clare yet further.

"You turn me aside, Mr. Blackstone. I wanted to urge Mr. Morley to go into Parliament as spiritual member for the poor of our large towns. Besides, I know you don't think as your question would imply. As far as my experience guides me, I am bound to believe that there is a spot of soil in every heart sufficient for the growth of a gospel seed. And I believe, moreover, that not only is he a fellow worker with God who sows that seed, but that he also is one who opens a way for that seed to enter the soil. If such preparation were not necessary, the Saviour would have come the moment Adam and Eve fell, and would have required no Baptist to precede Him."

A good deal followed which I would gladly record, but I fear I have already given too much conversation.

SEVENTEEN

THE END OF THE EVENING

A special delight during the evening was the marked attention, and the serious look in the eyes, with which Roger listened. It was not often that he did look serious. He preferred, if possible, to get a joke out of a thing; but when he did enter into an argument, he was always fair.

Mr. Morley, on the other hand, seemed an insoluble mass, inca·pable of receiving impressions from other minds. He regarded any suggestion of his own mind as reasonable and right, and was more than ordinarily prejudiced in his own favor. The day after they thus met at our house, Miss Clare had a letter from him, in which he took the high hand with her, rebuking her solemnly for her presumption in saying, as he represented it, that no good could be done except after the fashion she had laid down, and assuring her that she would thus alienate valuable assistance for any scheme to ameliorate the condition of the lower classes. It ended with the offer of a yearly subscription of five pounds to any project of the wisdom of which she would take the trouble to convince him. She replied, thanking him both for his advice and his offer, but saying that, as she had no scheme on foot requiring such assistance, she could not at present accept the offer. However, should anything show itself for which that sort of help was desirable, she would take the liberty of reminding him of it.

When the ladies rose, Judy took me aside, and said, "What does it all mean, Wynnie?"

"Just what you hear," I answered.

"You asked us, just to have a triumph over me, you naughty thing."

"Well, partly—if I am to be honest—but far more to make you do justice to Miss Clare. You being my cousin, she had a right to that at my hands."

"Does Lady Bernard know as much about her as she seems?"

"She knows everything about her, and visits her too, in her very questionable abode. You see, Judy, a report may be a fact and yet be untrue."

"I'm not going to be lectured by a chit like you. But I should like to have a little talk with Miss Clare."

"I will make you an opportunity."

I did so, and could not help overhearing a very pretty apology, to which Miss Clare replied that she feared she only was to blame, inasmuch as she ought to have explained the peculiarity of her circumstances before accepting the engagement. It had not appeared to her necessary, she said; but now she would make a point of explaining before she accepted any fresh duty of the kind, for she saw it would be fairer to both parties. It was no wonder such an answer should entirely disarm cousin Judy, who forthwith begged she would, if she had no objection, resume her lessons with the children at the commencement of the next quarter.

"But I understand from Mrs. Percivale," objected Miss Clare, "that the office is filled to your satisfaction."

"Yes, the lady I have is an excellent teacher, but the engagement was only for a quarter."

"If you have no other reason for parting with her, I could not think of stepping into her place. It would be a great disappointment to her, and my want of openness with you would be the cause of it. If you should part with her for any other reason, I should be very glad to serve you again."

Judy tried to argue with her, but Miss Clare was immovable.

"Will you let me come and see you, then?" said Judy.

"With all my heart," she answered. "You had better come with Mrs. Percivale, though, for it would not be easy for you to find the place."

We went up to the drawing room to tea, passing through the study, and taking the gentlemen with us. Miss Clare played to us, and sang several songs.

When my husband would have put her into Lady Bernard's carriage, as they were leaving, she said she should prefer walking home; and, as Lady Bernard did not press her to the contrary, Percivale could not remonstrate. "I am sorry I cannot walk with you, Miss Clare," he said. "I must not leave my duties, but—"

"There's not the slightest occasion," she interrupted. "I know every yard of the way. Good night."

The carriage drove off in one direction, and Miss Clare tripped lightly along in the other. Percivale darted into the house and told Roger, who snatched up his hat and bounded after her. Already she was out of sight; but he, following lightfooted, overtook her in the crescent. It was, however, only after persistent entreaty that he prevailed on her to allow him to accompany her.

"You do not know, Mr. Roger," she said pleasantly, "what you may be exposing yourself to, in going with me. I may have to do something you wouldn't like to have a share in."

"I shall be only too glad to have the humblest share in anything you draw me into," said Roger.

As it fell out, they had not gone far before they came upon a little crowd, chiefly of boys who ought to have been in bed long before, gathered about a man and woman. The man was forcing his company on a woman who was evidently annoyed that she could not get rid of him.

"Is he your husband?" asked Miss Clare, making her way through the crowd.

"No, Miss," the woman answered. "I never saw him afore. I'm only just come in from the country."

She looked more angry than frightened. Roger said her black eyes flashed dangerously, and she felt about the bosom of her dress—for a knife, he was certain.

"You leave her alone," he said to the man, getting between him and her.

"Mind your own business," returned the man, in a voice that showed he was drunk.

For a moment Roger was undecided what to do, for he feared involving Miss Clare in a row. But when the fellow pushed past him suddenly and laid his hand on Miss Clare and shoved her away, Roger gave him a blow that sent him staggering into the street. Whereupon, to his astonishment, Miss Clare left the woman, followed the man, and laid her hand on his arm and spoke to him, but in a voice so low and gentle that Roger could not hear a word. For a moment or two the man seemed to try to listen, but his condition was too much for him; and he rose and began to follow the woman again, who was now walking wearily away. Roger again interposed.

"Don't strike him, Mr. Roger," cried Miss Clare. "He's too drunk for that. But keep him back if you can, while I take the woman away. If I see a policeman, I will send him."

The man heard her last words, and they roused him to fury. He rushed at Roger, who only dodged and again confronted him, engaging his attention until help arrived. He was, however, by this time so fierce and violent, that Roger felt bound to assist the policeman.

As soon as the man was locked up, Roger went to Lime Court. The moon was shining and the narrow passage lay bright beneath her. Along the street people were going and coming, though it was past midnight, and the court was very still. He walked into it as far as the spot where we had together seen Miss Clare. The door at which she had entered was open, but he knew nothing of the house or its people, and feared to compromise her by making inquiries. He walked several times up and down, somewhat anxious, but gradually persuading himself that in all probability no further annoyance had befallen her, and at last he felt able to leave the place. He came back to our house, where, finding his brother at his final pipe in the study, he told him all about their adventure.

EIGHTEEN

MY FIRST TERROR

I will pass lightly over the next two years—not because nothing of importance happened, but because what came after was of greater importance and still looms large in my heart.

On the fourth anniversary of our marriage, Percivale took a holiday in order to give me one, and we went to spend it at Richmond. We wanted to enjoy it thoroughly, and so left our children at home. (As precious as children are, not *every* pleasure is enhanced by their company!) I say *children*, for Ethel's brother Roger (named after Percivale's father) was now nearly a year old.

It was a lovely day, with just a sufficient number of passing clouds to glorify the sunshine, and a gentle breeze, which itself seemed to be taking a holiday, for it blew just when you wanted it, and then only enough to make you think of that wind which, blowing where it lists, always blows where it is wanted. We took the train to Hammersmith, for my husband wished to row me from there to Richmond. How gay the riverside looked, with its fine broad landing stage and the numberless boats ready to push off on the swift water! Percivale hired his boat at a certain build-er's shed, that I might see the shed—such a picture of loveliest gloom—as if it had been the cave where the twilight abode its time! You could not tell whether to call it light or shade—that diffused presence of a soft elusive brown. But is what we call shade anything but subdued light?

Not having been used to boats, I felt nervous as we got into the long, sharp-nosed, hollow fish which Percivale made shoot out on

112

the rising tide. Then the slight fear vanished almost the moment we were afloat. Ignorant as I was of the art of rowing, I could not help seeing how perfectly Percivale was at home in it. The oars in his hands were like knitting needles in mine, so deftly, so swimmingly, so variously, did he wield them. Only once my fear returned, when he stood up in the swaying thing—a mere length without breadth—to pull off his coat and waistcoat. But he stood steady, sat down gently, took his oars quietly, and the same instant we were shooting so fast through the rising tide that it seemed as if *we* were pulling the water up to Richmond.

How merrily the water rippled in the sun and the wind! And so responsive were our feelings to the play of light and shade around us, that more than once when a cloud crossed us, I saw its shadow turn almost into sadness on the countenance of my companion, to vanish the next moment when the one sun above and the thousand mimic suns below shone out in universal laughter. Percivale suffered me to steer us, and so when a steamer came in sight, or announced its approach by the far-heard sound of its beating paddles, it brought with it a few moments of almost awful responsibility. But I found that the presence of danger and duty together enabled me to concentrate on getting the head of the boat as nearly possible at right angles with the waves from the paddles, for Percivale had told me that if one of any size struck us on the side, it would most probably capsize us.

I will say nothing more of the delights of that day. They were such a contrast to its close, and I could not rid myself of the foolish feeling that our enjoyment had been somehow to blame for what was happening at home while we were thus reveling in blessed carelessness.

When we returned to our little nest, rather late in the evening, I found to my annoyance that the front door was open. It had been a fault of which I thought I had cured the cook—to leave it thus when she ran out to fetch anything. Percivale went down to the study, and I walked into the drawing room, about to ring the bell in anger. There, to my surprise and further annoyance, I found Sarah seated on the sofa with her head in her hands, and little Roger wide awake on the floor.

"What *does* this mean?" I cried. "The front door open! Master Roger still up!"

"O Ma'am!" she almost shrieked as she rose. "Have you found her, Ma'am?"

"Found whom?" I returned in alarm. Her face was very pale, and her eyes were red with crying.

"Miss Ethel," she answered in a cry choked with a sob, and dropping again on the sofa, she hid her face once more between her hands.

I rushed to the study door, and called Percivale, then returned to question the girl. I wonder now that I did nothing outrageous, but fear kept down folly and made me unnaturally calm.

"Sarah," I said, as quietly as I could, while I trembled all over, "tell me what has happened. Where is the child?"

"Indeed it's not my fault, Ma'am. I was busy with Master Roger, and Miss Ethel was downstairs with Jemima."

"Where is she?" I repeated sternly.

"I don't know no more than the man in the moon, Ma'am."

"Where's Jemima? Run out to look for her? How long have you missed her?"

"An hour, or perhaps two hours. I don't know, my head's in such a whirl. I can't remember when I saw her last. O Ma'am! What *shall* I do?"

Percivale had come up and was standing beside me. When I looked round, he was as pale as death, and at the sight of his face, I nearly dropped on the floor. But he caught hold of me and said, in a voice so dreadfully still that it frightened me more than anything, "Come, my love—don't give way, for we must go to the police at once." Then, turning to Sarah, "Have you searched the house and garden?"

"Yes, Sir. Every hole and every corner. We've looked under every bed, and into every cupboard and chest—the coal cellar, the boxroom—everywhere."

"Have there been any tramps about the house since we left?" Percivale asked.

"Not that I know of, but the nursery window looks into the garden, you know, Sir. Jemima didn't mention it."

"Come, my dear," said my husband, and he led me away to the nearest cabstand. He glanced calmly along the line and chose the horse whose appearance promised the best speed. In a few minutes we were telling the inspector at the police station in Albany Street what had happened. He asked one question after another about her age, appearance, and dress, and wrote down our answers. He then gave the paper and some words of direction to another man.

"The men are now going on their beats for the night," he said, turning again to us. "They will all hear the description of the child."

"Thank you," said my husband. "Which station had we better go to next?"

"The news will be at the farthest before you can reach the nearest," he answered. "We shall telegraph to the suburbs first."

"Then what more can we do?" asked Percivale.

"Nothing," said the inspector, "except you find out whether any of the neighbors saw her, and when and where. It would be something to know in what direction she was going. Have you any ground for suspicion? Have you ever discharged a servant? Were any tramps seen about the place?"

"I know who it is!" I cried. "It's the woman that took Theodora! It's Theodora's mother! I know it is!"

Percivale explained what I meant.

"That's what people get, you see, when they take on themselves other people's business," returned the inspector. "That child ought to have been sent to the workhouse. But I have your address," he continued. "The child shall be brought back to you the moment she's found."

"Where are you going now?" I said to my husband, as we left the station to reenter the cab.

"I don't know," he answered, "except we go home and question all the shops in the neighborhood."

"Let us go to Miss Clare first," I said.

"By all means," he answered, and soon we were at the entrance of Lime Court.

When we turned the corner, we heard the sound of a piano. We entered the house and ascended the stairs in haste, hearing now the sounds of dancing as well as of music. In a moment, with our load of gnawing fear and helpless eagerness, we stood in the midst of a merry assembly of men, women and children, who filled Miss Clare's room to overflowing.

They made way for us, and Miss Clare left the piano, and came to meet us with a smile on her beautiful face. But when she saw our faces, hers fell.

"What *is* the matter, Mrs. Percivale?" she asked in alarm.

"We've lost Ethel," said my husband quietly.

"What do you mean? You don't—"

"No, no: she's gone—stolen. We don't know where she is," he answered with faltering voice. "We've just been to the police."

Miss Clare turned white. But, instead of making any remark, she called out to some of her friends whose good manners were making them leave the room.

"Don't go, please—we want you." Then turning to me, she asked, "May I do as I think best?"

"Yes, certainly," answered my husband.

"My friend, Mrs. Percivale," she said, addressing the whole assembly, "has lost her little girl."

A murmur of dismay and sympathy arose.

"What can we do to find her?" she went on.

They fell to talking among themselves. Then two men came up to us—one a keen-faced, elderly man, with iron-gray whiskers and clean-shaved chin, the other a young bricklayer. The elder addressed my husband, while the other listened without speaking.

"Tell us what she's like, Sir, and how she was dressed—though that ain't much use. She'll be different by this time."

The words shot a keen pang to my heart. My darling stripped of her nice clothes and covered with dirty, perhaps infected garments!

My husband repeated the description he had given the police, loud enouqh for the whole room to hear.

"Tell them also, please, Mr. Percivale, about the child Mrs. Percivale's father and mother found and brought up. That may have something to do with this."

My husband told them all the story, adding that the mother of the child might have found out who we were, and taken ours as a pledge for the recovery of her own.

Here one of the women spoke. "That dark woman you took in one night—two years ago, Miss Clare—she say something. I was astin' of her on the mornin' what her trouble was, for that trouble *she* had on *her* mind was plain to see, and she come over something, halfway like, about losin' of a child. But whether it were dead or strayed or stolen or what, I couldn't tell—and no more, I believe, she wanted me to."

Here another woman spoke. "I'm most sure I saw her—the same woman—two days ago, and no furrer off than Gower Street," she said. "You're too good by half, Miss," she went on, "to the likes of sich. They ain't none of them respectable."

"Perhaps you'll see some good come out of it before long," said Miss Clare in reply.

The words sounded like a rebuke, for all this time I had hardly sent a thought upward for help. The image of my child had so filled my heart, that there was no room left for the thought of duty, or even of God.

Miss Clare went on, still addressing the company, and her words had a tone of authority. "I will tell you what you must do, every one of you. Run and tell everybody you know, and tell everyone to tell everybody else. No time should be lost in making it as quickly and as widely known as possible. Go, please."

In a few moments the room was empty of all but ourselves. The rush on the stairs was tremendous for a single minute, and then all was still. Even the children had rushed out to tell what other children they could find.

"What must we do next?" said my husband.

"I would go and tell Mr. Blackstone," Miss Clare said. "It is a long way from here, but whoever has taken the child would not be likely to linger in the neighborhood. It is best to try everything."

"Right," said my husband. "Come, Wynnie."

We parted instantly, and drove to Mr. Blackstone's. What a long way it was! Down Oxford Street and Holborn we rattled and jolted, and then through many narrow ways, emerging at length in a broad road with many poor and a few fine old houses in it. We found the parsonage, and Mr. Blackstone in his study. The moment he heard our story he went to the door and called his servant. "Run, Jabez," he said, "and tell the sexton to ring the church bell. I will come to him directly I hear it."

About ten minutes passed, during which little was said. When the first boom of the big bell filled the little study in which we sat, I gave a cry and jumped up from my chair: it sounded in my ears like the knell of my lost baby, for at the moment I was thinking of her as once when a baby she lay for dead in my arms. Mr. Blackstone got up and left the room. It was a dreadful half hour before he returned; to sit doing nothing, not even being carried somewhere to do something, was frightful.

"I've told them all about it," he said. "I couldn't do better than follow Miss Clare's example. But my impression is that if the woman you suspect be the culprit, she would make her way out to the open as quickly as possible. Such people are most at home on the commons. They are of a less gregarious nature than the wild animals of the town. What shall you do next?"

"That is just what I want to know," answered my husband. He never asked advice except when he did not know what to do, and never except from one whose advice he meant to follow.

"Well," returned Mr. Blackstone, "I should put an advertisement into every one of the morning papers."

"But the offices will all be closed," said Percivale.

"Yes, the publishing, but not the printing offices. I know one or two of them, and the people there will tell us the rest."

"Then you mean to go with us?"

"Of course I do—that is, if you will have me. You don't think I would leave you to go alone?"

So we all left, and found a cab outside.

"Are you sure," said my husband, "that they will take an advertisement at the printing office?"

"I think they will. The circumstances are pressing. They will see that we are honest people, and will help us."

"We must pay, though," said Percivale, putting his hand in his pocket, and taking out his purse. "There! Just as I feared! No money—two—three shillings—and sixpence!"

Mr. Blackstone stopped the cab. "I've got as much," he said. "But it's of no consequence. I'll borrow five pounds at the Blue Posts."

"Let me do it, then," said Percivale. "You shouldn't be seen going into a public house."

"Pooh!" said Mr. Blackstone. "Do you think my character won't stand that much? Besides, they wouldn't do it for you."

We drove on to the Blue Posts. He got out, and returned in one minute with five sovereigns.

"What will people say to your borrowing five pounds at a public house?" said Percivale.

"If they say what is right, it won't hurt me."

"But if they say what is wrong?"

"That they can do any time, and that won't hurt me either."

"But what will the landlord think himself?"

"I have no doubt he feels grateful to me for being so friendly. You can't oblige a man more than by asking a *light* favor of him."

"Do you think it well in your position to be obliged to a man in his?" asked Percivale.

"I do. I am glad of the chance. It will bring me into friendly relations with him. I have done quite a stroke of business in borrowing that money of him."

Mr. Blackstone laughed, and the laugh sounded frightfully harsh in my ears.

"A man"—my husband went on, who was surprised that a

clergyman should be so liberal—"a man who sells drink! In whose house so many of your parishioners will tomorrow night get too drunk to be in church the next morning!"

"I wish having been drunk were what *would* keep them from being in church. Drunk or sober, it would be all the same. Few of them care to go. They are turning out better, however, than when I first came. As for the publican, who knows what chance of doing him a good turn it may put in my way?"

"You don't expect to persuade him to shut up shop?"

"No. He must persuade himself to do that. But you can't tell what good may or may not come out of it, any more than you can tell which of your efforts, or which of your helpers, may this night be the means of restoring your child."

"What, then, do you mean to tell him?" asked Percivale.

"The truth, the whole truth, and nothing but the truth," said Mr. Blackstone. "I shall go in tomorrow morning, just at the time when there will probably be far too many people in the bar—a little after noon. I shall return him his five sovereigns, ask for a glass of ale, and tell him the whole story—how my friend, the celebrated painter, came with his wife, and the rest of it, adding, I trust, that the child is all right, and at the moment probably going out for a walk with her mother, who won't let her out of her sight for a moment."

He laughed again, and again I thought him heartless, but I understood him better now. I wonder too that Percivale *could* go on talking, and yet I found that their talk did make the time go a little quicker. At length we reached the printing office of *The Times,* where an overseer agreed to find the best place in the morning paper for our advertisement.

We spent the greater part of the night in driving from one printing office to another. Mr. Blackstone declared he would not leave us until we had found her.

"You have to preach twice tomorrow," said Percivale. It was then three o'clock.

"I shall preach all the better," he returned. "I shall give them *one* good sermon tomorrow."

"The man talks as if the child were found already!" I thought, with indignation. "It's a pity he hasn't a child of his own. He would be more sympathetic." At the same time, if I had been honest, I should have confessed to myself that his confidence and hope helped to keep me up.

At last, having been to the printing office of every daily paper in London, we were on our dreary way home.

Oh, how dreary it was, and the more dreary that the cool, sweet light of a spring dawn was growing in every street, no smoke having yet begun to pour from the chimneys to sully its purity! From misery and want of sleep, my soul and body both felt like a gray foggy night. Every now and then the thought of my child came with a fresh pang. I pictured her little face—white with terror and misery and smeared with the dirt of the pitiful hands that rubbed the streaming eyes. They might have beaten her! She might have cried herself to sleep in some wretched hovel, or worse, in some fever-stricken and crowded lodging house, with horrible sights about her and horrible voices in her ears! Or she might at that moment be dragged wearily along a country road, farther and farther from her mother! I could have shrieked, and torn my hair. What if I should never see her again? She might be murdered, and I never know it!

At that thought a groan escaped my lips. My husband laid his hand on my arm, and Mr. Blackstone's voice was in my ear.

"Do you think God loves the child less than you do? Or do you think He is less able to take care of her than you are? When the disciples thought themselves sinking, Jesus rebuked them for being afraid. Be still, and you will see the hand of God in this. Good you cannot forsee will come out of it."

I could not answer him, but I felt both rebuked and grateful. Then all at once I thought of Roger. What would he say when he found that his pet was gone, and we had never told him?

"Roger!" I said to my husband. "We've never told him!"

"Let us go now," he returned.

When we arrived, Percivale rushed up the stairs and returned with Roger. They got into the cab, and a great talk followed. Roger was very indignant with his brother for having been out all night without him to help.

"I never thought of you, Roger," said Percivale.

"So much the worse!" said Roger.

" No," said Mr. Blackstone. "A thousand things make us forget. I dare say your brother all but forgot God in the first misery of his loss. To have thought of you—and not to have told you—would have been another thing."

A few minutes after, we stopped at our desolate house, where only a dim light was burning in the drawing room. Percivale took his passkey and opened the front door. I hurried in, and went straight to my own room, for I longed to be alone that I might weep, but not only weep. I fell on my knees by the bedside, buried my face and sobbed and tried to pray. But I could not collect my thoughts and, overwhelmed by a fresh access of despair, I started again to my feet.

Could I believe my eyes? What was that on the bed? Trembling in terror lest the vision vanish, I stooped toward it. It was my darling fast asleep, without one trace of suffering on her angelic loveliness! They tell me I gave a great cry and fell on the floor. When I came to, I was lying on the bed, my husband bending over me, and Roger and Mr. Blackstone both in the room. I could not speak, but my husband understood me.

"Yes, yes, my love," he said quietly, "she's all right—safe and sound, thank God!"

And I did thank God.

Mr. Blackstone came to the bedside, with a look and a smile that seemed to my conscience to say, "I told you so." I held out my hand to him, but could only weep.

Then I remembered how we had vexed Roger, and I called to him. "Dear Roger," I said, "forgive me, and go and tell Miss Clare."

I had some reason to think this the best amends I could make him.

"I will go at once," he said. "She will be anxious."

"And I will go to my sermon," said Mr. Blackstone, with the same quiet smile.

They shook hands with me, and went away. And my husband and I rejoiced over our firstborn.

NINETEEN

THE AFTERMATH

Later we found that my darling had been recovered by the police, and not through Miss Clare's injunctions or Mr. Blackstone's bell ringing. A woman had been walking steadily westward, carrying the child asleep in her arms, when a policeman stopped her at Turnham Green. She betrayed no fear, only annoyance, and offered no resistance, only begged he would not wake the child, or take her from her. He brought them in a cab to the station house, whence the child was sent home. As soon as Ethel arrived, Sarah gave her a warm bath and put her to bed, but she scarcely opened her eyes.

Jemima had run about the streets till midnight, and then fallen asleep on the doorstep, where the policeman found her when he brought the child. (For a week she went about like one dazed, and the blunders she made were marvelous. She ordered a brace of cod from the poulterer, and a pound of anchovies at the crockery shop. One day at dinner, we could not think how the chops were so pulpy, and why we got so many bits of bone in our mouth: she had powerfully beaten them, as if they had been steaks. She sent up melted butter for bread sauce, and stuffed a hare with sausages.)

After breakfast, Percivale walked to the police station to thank the inspector, pay what expenses had been incurred, and see the woman. I was not well enough to go with him and I suggested that he should take Miss Clare. She accompanied him willingly, and recognized the woman as the one she had befriended.

Percivale told the magistrate he did not wish to punish her, but that there were certain circumstances which made him desirous of detaining her until a gentleman who could identify her should arrive. The magistrate therefore remanded her.

The next day but one my father came. When he saw the woman, he had little doubt she was the same who had carried off Theo. He told the magistrate the whole story, saying that if she should prove the mother of the child, he was most anxious to do what he could for her. The magistrate expressed grave doubts whether he would find it possible to befriend her to any effectual degree.

Now came the benefit of the kindness Miss Clare had shown the woman. I doubt if anyone else could have got the truth from her. Even she found it difficult, for to tell her that if she was Theo's mother she should not be punished, might be only to tempt her to lie. All Miss Clare could do was to assure her of the kindness of everyone concerned, and to urge her to disclose her reasons for doing such a grievous wrong as to steal another woman's child.

"*They* stole *my* child," she blurted out at last, when the cruelty of the action was pressed upon her.

"Oh, no!" said Miss Clare. "You left her to die in the cold."

"No, no!" she cried. "I wanted somebody to hear her and take her in. I wasn't far off, and was just going to take her again, when I saw a light, and heard them searching for her. Oh, dear! Oh, dear!"

"Then how can you say they stole her? You would have had no child at all, but for them. She was nearly dead when they found her. And in return you go and steal their grandchild!"

"They took her from me afterward. They wouldn't let me have my own flesh and blood. I wanted to let them know what it was like to have *their* child taken from them."

"How could they tell she was your child, when you stole her away like that? It might, for anything they knew, be some other woman stealing her, as you stole theirs the other day. What would have become of you if it had been so?"

To this reasoning she made no answer, but only moaned, "I want my child—I want my child. I shall kill myself if I don't get my child! O Lady, you don't know what it is to have a child and not have her! I shall kill myself if they don't let me have her back. They can't say I did their child any harm. I was as good to her as if she had been my own."

"They know that quite well, and don't want to punish you. Would you like to see your child?"

She clasped her hands above her head, fell on her knees at Miss Clare's feet, and looked up in her face without uttering a word.

"I will speak to Mr. Walton," said Miss Clare, and left her.

The next morning the woman was discharged with the warning that, if ever she came to the attention of the law again, this would be brought up against her, and she would have the severest punishment the law could inflict. It may be right to pass a first offense, and wrong to pass a second.

My husband brought her home with him. Sympathy with the mother-passion in her bosom had melted away my resentment. She was a fine young woman, about twenty-five, though her weather-browned complexion made her look much older. With the help of the servants, I persuaded her to have a bath, during which they removed her clothes and substituted others. She objected to putting them on—seemed half-frightened at them, as if they might involve some shape of bondage, and begged to have her own again. At last Jemima (who, although so sparingly provided with brains, is not without genius) prevailed upon her, insisting that her little girl would turn away from her if she wasn't well dressed, for she had been used to seeing ladies about her. With a deep sigh, she yielded, begging, however, to have her old garments restored to her.

She had brought with her a small bundle tied up in a cotton handkerchief, and from it she now took a scarf of red silk, and twisted it up with her black hair in a fashion I had never seen before. In this headdress she had almost a brilliant look, while her carriage had a certain dignity. My husband admired her even more than I did, and made a very good sketch of her. Her eyes were large and dark—unquestionably fine—and if there was not much of the light of thought in them, they had a certain wildness which in a measure made up for want. She had a Spanish rather than an Eastern look, I thought, with an air of defiance that prevented me from feeling at ease with her. In the presence of Miss Clare she seemed humbler, and answered her questions more readily than ours. If Ethel was in the room, her eyes would be constantly wandering after her, with a wistful, troubled, eager look. Surely, the mother-passion must have infinite relations and destinies.

As I was unable to leave home, my father persuaded Miss Clare to accompany him and help him to take charge of her. I confess it was a relief to me when she left the house; for though I wanted to be as kind to her as I could, I felt considerable discomfort in her presence.

When Miss Clare returned, the next day but one, I found she had learned the main points of the woman's history, fully justifying my father's previous conjectures.

She belonged to one of the principal gypsy families in this country. The fact that they had no settled habitation but lived in tents, like Abraham and Isaac, had nothing to do with poverty. The silver buttons on her father's coat were, she had said, worth nearly twenty pounds. When friends of any distinction came to tea with them, they spread a tablecloth of fine linen on the grass, and set out upon it the best of china, and a tea service of hallmarked silver. She said her friends scorned stealing, and affirmed that no real gypsy would "risk his neck for his belly," except he were driven by hunger. All her family could read, she said, and they carried a big Bible with them.

One summer they were encamped (as was their custom) for several months in the neighborhood of Edinburgh, making horn spoons and baskets, and some of them working in tin. There they were visited by a clergyman, who talked and read the Bible to them and prayed with them. But all their visitors were not of the same sort. One young fellow of loose character, a clerk in the city, was attracted by her appearance and prevailed upon her to meet him often. She was not then eighteen. Any aberration from the paths of modesty is exceedingly rare among the gypsies, and regarded with severity. Therefore, her father gave her a terrible punishment with the whip he used in driving his horses. In terror of what would follow when the worst came to be known, she ran away. She was soon forsaken by her so-called lover, and wandered about, a common vagrant, until her baby was born—under the stars on a summer night, in a field of long grass.

For some time she wandered up and down, longing to join a tribe of her own people, but dreading unspeakably the disgrace of her motherhood. At length, having found a home with our family for her child, she associated herself with a gang of gypsies of inferior character, amongst whom she had many hardships to endure. Although she had no intention of carrying off her child to share her present lot, the urgings of mere mother-hunger that drove her to the Hall for a sight of her child. When she had succeeded in enticing her out of sight of the house, however, the longing to possess her grew fierce and—braving all consequences, or unable to weigh them—she did carry her away. Foiled in this attempt, and seeing that her chances of future success in any similar one were diminished by it, she sought some other plan. Learning that one of the family had married and moved to London, she succeeded, through gypsy acquaintances who lodged occasionally near Tottenham Court Road, in finding out where we lived. Then she carried off Ethel with the vague intent, as we had conjectured, of using her to recover her own child.

Theodora was now about seven years of age and almost as wild as ever. Miss Clare was present with my father and the rest of the family when the mother and daughter met. They were all more than curious to see how the child would behave, and whether there would be any instinct to draw her to her parent. In this, however, they were disappointed.

It was a fine warm forenoon when she came running onto the lawn where they were assembled, the gypsy mother with them.

"There she is!" said my father to the woman. "Make the best of yourself you can."

Miss Clare said the poor creature turned very pale, but her eyes glowed with such a fire!

With the cunning of her race, she knew better than to bound forward and catch up the child in her arms. She walked away from the rest and stood watching the little damsel romp merrily with Mr. Wagtail. They thought she recognized the dog and was afraid of him. She had put on a few silver ornaments which she had either kept or managed to procure, notwithstanding her poverty. The glittering of these in the sun, and the glow of her red satin scarf in her dark hair, along with the strangeness of her whole appearance, attracted the child who approached to look at her. Then the mother took from her pocket a large gilded ball and rolled it gleaming along the grass. Theo and Mr. Wagtail bounded after it with a shriek and a bark. The child examined it for a moment and threw it again along the lawn, and this time the mother, lithe as a leopard and fleet as a savage, joined in the chase, caught it first, and again sent it spinning away, farther from the assembled group. Once more all three followed in swift pursuit, but this time the mother allowed the child to seize the treasure. After the sport had continued a little while, a general consultation of mother, child, and dog took place over the bauble, and presently the watchers saw that Theo was eating something.

"I trust," said my mother, "she won't hurt the child with any nasty stuff."

"She will not do so wittingly," said my father, "you may be sure. Anyhow, we must not interfere."

In a few minutes more the mother approached them with a subdued look of triumph, and her eyes overflowing with light, carrying the child in her arms. Theo was playing with some foreign coins which adorned her hair, and with a string of coral and silver beads round her neck.

For the rest of the day they were left to do much as they pleased—only everyone kept watch.

In the joy of recovering her child, the mother seemed herself to have gained a new and childlike spirit. She hastened to do what was requested of her, as if she fully acknowledged the right of authority in those now around her. Whether this would last when the novelty of the new experience had worn off, whether jealousy would not then come in for its share in the ordering of her conduct, remained to be shown; but in the meantime the good in her was uppermost.

She was allowed to spend a whole fortnight in making friends with her daughter, before a word was spoken about the future, for the design of my father was to win the mother through the child. (Certain people considered him not eager enough to convert the wicked. Whatever apparent indifference he showed in that direction arose from his utter belief in their guiding of God, and his dread of outrunning His designs. He would *follow* the operations of the Spirit. "Your forced hothouse fruits," he would say, "are often finer to look at than those which have waited for God's wind and weather, but what are they worth in respect of all for the sake of which fruit exists?")

Until an opportunity, then, was thrown his way, he would hold back. But when it was clear to him that he had to minister, then he was thoughtful, watchful, instant, and unswerving. You might have seen him during this time, as the letters cf Connie informed me, often standing for a time watching the mother and daughter, and pondering in his heart concerning them. The fortnight had not passed before, to all appearance, the unknown mother had become the greatest favorite of the child.

One twilight, he overheard the following talk between them. When they came near where he sat, Theodora, carried by her mother, and pulling at her neck with her arms, was saying, "Tell me! Tell me! Tell me!" in the tone of one who would compel an answer to a question repeatedly asked in vain.

"What do you want me to tell you?" said the mother.

"You know well enough. Tell me your name."

In reply, she uttered a few words my father did not comprehend. The child shook her petulantly and with violence crying, "That's nonsense. I don't know what you say, and I don't know what to call you."

My father had desired the household, if possible, to give no name to the woman in the child's hearing.

"Call me Ma'am, if you like."

"But you're not a lady, and I won't say Ma'am to you," said Theo, rude as a child will sometimes be when she least intends offense.

Her mother set her down and gave a deep sigh. Was it only that the child's restlessness and roughness tired her? My father thought otherwise.

"Tell me! Tell me!" the child persisted, beating her with her little clenched fist. "Take me up again, and tell me, or I will make you."

My father thought it time to interfere. As he stepped forward, the mother started with a little cry and caught up the child.

"Theo," said my father, "I cannot allow you to be rude, especially to one who loves you more than anyone else loves you."

The woman set her down again, dropped on her knees, and caught and kissed his hand. The child stared, but she stood in awe of my father, and perhaps the more that she had none for anyone else. When her mother lifted her once more she was carried away in silence.

The difficulty was solved by telling the child to call the woman *Nurse*.

My father was now sufficiently satisfied with immediate results to carry out the remainder of his contingent plan, of which my mother heartily approved. The gardener and his wife were elderly and without family, and therefore did not require the whole of their cottage, which was within a short distance of the house. My mother arranged their spare room for the gypsy, and there she was housed, with free access to her child, and the understanding that when Theo liked to sleep with her, she was at liberty to do so.

But before long her old habits were working in her and making her restless. She was pining after the liberty of her old wandering life, with sun and wind, space and change, all about her. It was spring, and the reviving life of nature was rousing in her the longing for motion and room and variety. My father had foreseen the probability, and had already thought over what could be done for her if the wandering passion should revive too powerfully. He reasoned that there was nothing bad in such an impulse—one doubtless felt by Abraham himself—however much its indulgence might place her at a disadvantage in the midst of a settled social order. He saw too that the love of her child could, like an elastic but infrangible cord, gradually tame her down to a more settled life.

He proposed, therefore, that she go and visit her parents and let them know of her welfare. She looked alarmed.

"Your father will show you no unkindness, I am certain, after the lapse of so many years," he added. "Think it over, and tell me tomorrow how you feel about it. You shall go by train to Edinburgh, and once there you may find them. The child will be safe with us till you come back."

So she went, found her people, spent a fortnight with them, and returned. The rest of that year she remained quietly at home, stilling her desires by frequent and long rambles with her child. Mr. Wagtail alone accompanied them, for my father thought it better to run the risk of her escaping than to force the thought on her by appearing not to trust her. She no doubt suspected that the dog was there to prevent, or at least expose, any such imprudence. The following spring she went on a second visit to her friends, but was back within a week, and the next year did not go at all.

My father continued to do what he could to teach her, presenting every truth as something it was necessary she should teach her child. With this duty, he said, he always baited the hook with which he fished for her.

What will be the final result, who dares to prophesy? At my old home she still resides—grateful, and in some measure useful, idolizing, but not altogether spoiling her child, who understands the relation between them and now calls her Mother.

Dora teaches Theo, and the mother comes in for what share she inclines to appropriate. She does not take much to reading, but she is fond of listening, and is a regular and devout attendant at public worship. Above all, they have sufficing proof that her conscience is awake, and that she gives some heed to what it says.

Mr. Blackstone was right when he told me that good would result from the loss which then drowned me in despair.

TWENTY

TROUBLES

In the beginning of the following year, the lady who filled Miss Clare's music-teaching position with the Morleys was married, and Miss Clare resumed the teaching of Judy's children.

In the spring, great trouble fell upon the Morleys. One of the children was taken with scarlet fever, and then another and another in such rapid succession—until five of them were lying ill together. Cousin Judy would accept no assistance in nursing them, beyond that of her own maids. But then her strength gave way, and she contracted the infection herself in the form of diphtheria, and was compelled to take to her bed.

There she lay moaning, with her eyes shut, when a hand was laid in hers and Miss Clare's voice came in her ear. She had come to give her usual lesson to one of the girls who had as yet escaped the infection, and when she heard that Mrs. Morley had been taken ill, she walked straight to her room.

"Go away!" said Judy. "Do you want to die too?"

"Dear Mrs. Morley," said Miss Clare, "I will just run home and make a few arrangements, and then come back and nurse you."

"Never mind me," said Judy. "The children! The children! What shall I do?"

"I am quite able to look after you all, if you will allow me to bring a young woman to help me."

"You are an angel!" said poor Judy. "But there is no occasion to bring anyone with you. My servants are quite competent."

"I must have everything in my own hands," said Miss Clare, "and therefore must have someone who will do exactly as I tell her. This girl has been with me now for some time, and I can depend upon her."

"Do whatever you like, you blessed creature," said Judy. "If any one of my servants behaves improperly to you, or neglects your orders, she shall go as soon as I am up again."

"I would rather give them as little opportunity as I can of running the risk. If I may bring this friend of my own, I shall soon have the house under hospital regulations."

She had hardly left the room before Judy fell asleep. Ere she awoke, Miss Clare was in a cab on her way back to the Morley residence on Bolivar Square, with her friend and two carpetbags. Within an hour, she had entrenched herself in a spare bedroom, lighted a fire, arranged all the medicines on a chest of drawers, made the round of the patients (who were all in adjoining rooms) and the round of the house to see that the disinfectants were fresh and active, added to their number, and then gone to await the arrival of the medical attendant in Mrs. Morley's room.

"Dr. Brand might have been a little more gracious," said Judy, "but I thought it better not to interrupt him by explaining that you were not the professional nurse he took you for."

"Indeed, there was no occasion," answered Miss Clare. "I should have told him so myself, had it not been that I have done a nurse's regular work in St. George's Hospital. Anyhow, I understood every word he said."

Meeting Mr. Morley in the hall, the doctor advised him not to go near his wife, diptheria being so infectious, but comforted him with the assurance that the nurse appeared an intelligent young person who would attend to all his directions. He added, "I could have wished that she had been older, but there is a great deal of illness about, and experienced nurses are scarce."

Miss Clare was a week in the house before Mr. Morley saw her, or knew she was there. One evening, needing brandy for medicine, she ran down to the dining room where he sat over his lonely glass of Madiera, and went straight to the sideboard. As she turned to leave the room, he recognized her and said, in some astonishment, "You need not trouble yourself, Miss Clare. The nurse can get what she wants from Hawkins. Indeed, I don't see—"

"Excuse me, Mr. Morley. If you wish to speak to me, I will return in a few minutes, but I have a good deal to attend to now."

She left the room and, as he had said nothing in reply, she did not return.

Two days after, about the same hour, whether suspecting the fact, or for some other reason, he requested the butler to send the nurse to him.

"The nurse from the nursery, Sir, or the young person as teaches the young ladies the piano?" asked Hawkins.

"I mean the sick-nurse," said his master.

In a few minutes Miss Clare entered the dining room and approached Mr. Morley.

"How do you do, Miss Clare?" he said stiffly, for to anyone in his employment he was gracious only now and then. "Allow me to say that I doubt the propriety of your being here so much. You cannot fail to carry the infection. I think your lessons had better be postponed until *all* your pupils are able to benefit by them. I have just sent for the nurse, and, if you please—"

"Yes. Hawkins told me you wanted me," said Miss Clare.

"I did not want you. He must have been mistaken."

"I *am* the nurse, Mr. Morley."

"Then I *must* say it is not with my approval!" he returned, rising from his chair in anger. "I was given to understand that a properly qualified person was in charge of my wife and family. This is no ordinary case, where a little coddling is all that is wanted."

"I am perfectly qualified, Mr. Morley."

He walked up and down the room several times, and said, "I must speak to Mrs. Morley about this."

"I entreat you will not disturb her. She is not well this afternoon."

"How *is* this, Miss Clare? Pray explain to me how you have come to take a part in the affairs of this family so very different from that arranged between Mrs. Morley and yourself."

"It is but an illustration of the law of supply and demand," answered Miss Clare. "A nurse was wanted, Mrs. Morley had strong objections to a hired nurse, and I was very glad to be able to set her mind at rest."

"It was very obliging of you, no doubt," he returned, "but—but—"

"Let us leave it thus for the present, if you please, for while I am nurse, I must mind my business. Dr. Brand expresses himself quite satisfied with me, and it is better for the children, not to mention Mrs. Morley, to have someone they are used to."

She left the room without waiting for further parley.

When a terrible time of anxiety was at length over, during which one after another, and especially Judy herself, had been in great danger, Dr. Brand assured Mr. Morley that, but for the vigilance and intelligence of Miss Clare, he did not believe he could have brought Mrs. Morley through.

Judy and the little Morleys had recovered so far that they were to set out the next morning for Hastings, when Mr. Morley sent for Miss Clare once more.

"I hope you will accompany them, Miss Clare," he said. "By this time you must be in no small need of a change yourself."

"The best change for me will be Lime Court," she answered, laughing. "I am anxious about my friends there. I fear they have not been getting on quite so well without me. A Bible woman and a Roman Catholic have been quarreling dreadfully, I hear."

Mr. Morley compressed his lips. It *was* annoying to be so indebted to one who, from whatever motives, called such people her friends.

"Oblige me, then," he said loftily, taking an envelope from the mantle piece, and handing it to her, "by opening that at your leisure."

"I will open it now, if you please," she returned.

It contained a bank note for a hundred pounds. Mr. Morley, though a hard man, was not by any means stingy. She replaced it in the envelope, and laid it again upon the chimneypiece.

"You owe me nothing, Mr. Morley," she said.

"Owe you nothing! I owe you more than I can ever repay."

"Then don't try it, please. You are *very* generous—but indeed I could not accept it."

"You must oblige me. You *might* take it from *me*," he added, almost pathetically, as if the bond was so close that money was nothing between them.

"You are the last—one of the last—I *could* take money from, Mr. Morley."

"Why?"

"Because you think so much of it, and yet would look down on me all the more if I accepted it."

He bit his lip, rubbed his forehead with his hand, threw back his head, and turned away from her.

"I should be very sorry to offend you," she said, "and, believe me, there is hardly anything I value less than money. I have enough, and could have plenty more if I liked. I would rather have your friendship than all the money you possess. But that cannot be, so long as—"

"So long as what?"

"So long as you are a worshiper of mammon," she answered, and left the room.

This she told me later, saying, "I am afraid it was very wrong, and very rude as well. But just think—there was a generous heart, clogged up with self-importance and wealth! As he stood there on the hearthrug, he was a most pitiable object, with an impervious wall betwixt him and the kingdom of heaven! He seemed like a man in a terrible dream, from which I *must* awake him by calling aloud in his ear! Alas! The dream was not terrible to him, only to me! If he had been one of my poor friends, guilty of some plain fault, I should have told him so without compunction—and why not, being what he was? There he stood, a man of estimable qualities, of benevolence, if not bounty, no miser, nor consciously unjust, yet a man whose heart the moth and rust were eating into a sponge. A man who went to church every Sunday, and who had many friends, not one of whom, not even his own wife, would tell him that he was a mammon-worshiper and losing his life. It may have been useless, and it may have been wrong, but I felt driven to it by bare human pity."

Strange tableau—a young and poor woman prophetlike rebuking a wealthy London merchant on his own hearthrug, as a worshiper of mammon!

And no one can tell what effects the words may have had upon him. I do not believe he ever mentioned the circumstance to his wife. At all events, there was no change in her manner to Miss Clare. Indeed, I could not help fancying that a little halo of quiet reverence now encircled the love in every look Judy cast upon her.

She firmly believed that Miss Marion Clare had saved her life, and that of more than one of her children. Nothing, she said, could equal the quietness and tenderness and tirelessness of her nursing. She was never flurried, never impatient, and never frightened. Even when the tears would be flowing down her face, the light never left her eyes nor the music her voice. And when she had the nursery piano brought out on the landing in the middle of the sickrooms, and there played and sang to them, it was, she said, like the voice of an angel, come fresh to the earth with the same old news of peace and goodwill.

But even so, Miss Clare came out of it very pale and a good deal worn. The day the Morleys set off for Hastings, she returned to Lime Court. The next day she resumed her lessons, and soon recovered her usual appearance. A change of work, she always said, was the best restorative. But before a month was over, I succeeded in persuading her to accept my mother's invitation to spend a week at the Hall, and from this visit she returned quite invigorated.

TWENTY-ONE

MR. MORLEY

As soon as my cousin Judy returned from Hastings, I called to see her, and found them all well restored except Amy, a child between eight and nine. There was nothing very definite the matter with her, but she was white and thin, and looked wistful; the blue of her eyes had grown pale, and her fair locks had nearly lost the curl which had so well suited her rosy cheeks. She had been her father's pride for her looks, and her mother's for her sayings—at once odd and simple.

Judy that morning reminded me of how, one night, when Amy was about three years old, she had gone to bed, and some time after had called out for her mother. There had been jam-making that day, and Judy feared Amy had been having more than the portion which on such an occasion fell to her share. But Amy only begged to be taken up that she might say her prayers over again. Amy accordingly kneeled by the bedside in her nightgown and, having gone over all her petitions from beginning to end, paused a moment before the final word, and inserted the following special and peculiar request: "And please, God, give me some more jam tomorrow-day, forever and ever. Amen."

(I remember my father being quite troubled when he heard that the child had been rebuked for offering what was probably her very first genuine prayer. The rebuke, however, had little effect on the petitioner, for she was fast asleep a moment after it.)

"There is one thing that puzzles and annoys me," said Judy. "I can't think what it means. My husband tells me that Miss Clare was so rude to him the day before we left for Hastings, that he would rather not be aware of it any time she was in the house. Those were his very words. 'I will not interfere with your doing as you think proper,' he said, 'seeing you consider yourself under such obligation to her. And I should be very sorry to deprive her of the advantage of giving lessons in a house like this, but I wish you to be careful that the girls do not copy her manners. She has not by any means escaped the influence of the company she keeps.' I was utterly astonished, you may well think, but I could get no further explanation from him. He only said that when I wished to have her society of an evening, I must let him know, because he would then dine at his club.

"I said that he must have misunderstood her. 'Not in the least,' he said. 'I have no doubt she is to you everything amiable, but she has taken some unaccountable aversion to me, and loses no opportunity of showing it. And I *don't* think I deserve it.' I told him I was so sure he did not deserve it, that I must believe there was some mistake. But he only shook his head and raised his newspaper. You must help me, little coz."

"How am I to help you, Judy dear?" I returned. "I can't interfere between husband and wife, you know. If I dared such a thing, he would quarrel with me too—and rightly."

"No, no," she said, laughing. "I don't want your intercession. I only want you to find out from Miss Clare whether she knows how she has so mortally offended my husband. I believe she knows nothing about it. Help me, now, there's a dear!"

I promised I would, and hence came the story I have already given. But Miss Clare was so distressed at the result of her words, and so anxious that Judy should not be hurt, that she begged me to avoid disclosing the matter, especially seeing Mr. Morley himself judged it too heinous to impart to his wife.

How to manage it I could not think, but at length we arranged it between us. I told Judy that Miss Clare confessed to having said something which had offended Mr. Morley, that she was very sorry, and hoped she need not say that such had not been her intention; and that, as Mr. Morley evidently preferred what had passed between them to remain unmentioned, to disclose it would be merely to swell the mischief. It would be better for them all, she requested me to say, that she should give up her lessons for the present, and therefore she hoped Mrs. Morley would excuse her. When I gave the message, Judy cried and said nothing. When the children heard that Miss Clare was not coming for a while, Amy cried, the other girls looked very grave, and the boys protested. Judy insisted that I should let Mr. Morley hear Miss Clare's message.

"But the message is not to Mr. Morley," I said. "Miss Clare would never have thought of sending one to him."

"But if I ask you to repeat it in his hearing, you will not refuse?"

To this I consented, but I fear she was disappointed in the result. Her husband only smiled sarcastically, drew in his chin, and showed himself a little more cheerful than usual.

One morning, about two months after that, as I was sitting in the drawing room with my baby on the floor beside me, I was surprised to see Judy's brougham pull up at the little gate. When she got out, I saw that something was amiss, and I ran to open the door. Her eyes were red, her cheeks were ashy, and the moment we reached the drawing room, she sunk on the couch and burst into tears.

"Judy!" I cried, "what *is* the matter? Is Amy worse?"

"No, no, Cozzy dear, but we are ruined. We haven't a penny in the world. The children will be beggars."

And there were the gay little horses champing their bits at the door, and the coachman sitting in all his glory, erect and impassive!

I did my best to quiet her. With difficulty she managed to let me understand that her husband had been speculating, and had failed. I could hardly believe myself awake. Mr. Morley was the last man I should have thought capable either of speculating or of failing in it if he did.

Judy said he had not been like himself for months; but it was only on the previous night he had told her they must give up their house in Bolivar Square, and take a small one in the suburbs. For anything he could see, he said, he must look out for a situation.

"Still you may be happier than ever, Judy. I can tell you that happiness does not depend on riches," I said, though I could not help crying with her.

"It's a different thing though, after you've been used to them," she answered. "But the question is of bread for my children, not of putting down my carriage."

She rose hurriedly.

"Where are you going? Is there anything I can do for you?" I asked.

"Nothing," she answered. "I left my husband at Mr. Baddeley's. He is as rich as Croesus, and could write him a check that would float him."

When she reached Mr. Baddeley's her husband was gone. Having driven to his countinghouse, and been shown into his private room, she found him there with his head between his hands. The great man had declined doing anything for him, and had even rebuked him for his imprudence, without wasting a thought on the fact that every penny he himself possessed was the result of the boldest speculation on the part of his father.

And now only a very few days would elapse before the falling due of certain bills would disclose the state of his affairs.

As soon as she left me, I put on my bonnet, and went to find Miss Clare. I must tell *her* everything that caused me either joy or sorrow; and besides, she had all the right that love could give to know of Judy's distress.

I told her my sad news and after a pause, she asked, "Is there anything to be done?"

"I know of nothing," I answered.

Again she sat silent for a few minutes. "One can't move without knowing all the circumstances and particulars," she said at length. "And how to get at them? He wouldn't make a confidante of *me*," she said, smiling sadly. "It will be best," she continued, "to go to Mr. Blackstone. He has a wonderful acquaintance with business for a clergyman, and knows many of the city people."

"What could any clergyman do?" I returned. "Mr. Morley would not accept even consolation at his hands."

"The time for that is not come yet," said Miss Clare. "We must try to help him some other way first. We will, if we can, make friends with him by means of the very Mammon that has all but ruined him. Mr. Blackstone can find out for me what Mr. Morley's liabilities are, and how much would serve to tide him over the bar of his present difficulties. I suspect he has few friends who would risk anything for him. You believe him an honorable man, do you not?" she asked abruptly.

"It never entered my head to doubt it," I replied.

"Then let us go see Mr. Blackstone now!" she said, and we descended and found a cab to drive us to Mile End.

"I fear I can't go with you so far, Marion," I said. "I must go home. I don't know what you intend, but *please* don't let anything come out. I can trust *you*, but—"

"If you can trust me, I can trust Mr. Blackstone. He is the most cautious man in the world. Shall I get out, and take another cab?"

"No. You can drop me at Tottenham Court Road, and I will go home by omnibus. But you must let me pay the cab."

"No, no—I am richer than you: I have no children. What fun it is to spend money for Mr. Morley, and lay him under an obligation he will never know!" she said, laughing.

As a result of her endeavors, Mr. Blackstone, by a circuitous succession of introductions, reached Mr. Morley's confidential clerk who, satisfied concerning the object in desiring the information, made a full disclosure of the condition of affairs, and stated what sum would be sufficient to carry them over their difficulties. The clerk added, though, that the greatest care, and every possible reduction of expenditure for some years, would be indispensible to their complete restoration.

Mr. Blackstone carried his discoveries to Miss Clare and she to Lady Bernard.

"My dear Marion," said Lady Bernard, "this is a serious matter you suggest. The man may be honest, and yet it may be of no use trying to help him. I don't want to bolster him up for a few months in order to see my money go after his. That's not what I have to do with my money. No doubt I could lose as much as you mention, without being crippled by it. I hope it's no disgrace in me to be rich, as it's none in you to be poor. But I hate waste, and I will *not* be guilty of it. If Mr. Morley will convince me that there is good probability of his recovering himself by means of it, then, and not till then, I shall feel justified in risking the amount. For, as you say, it would prevent much misery to many besides that good-hearted creature, Mrs. Morley, and her children. It is worth doing if it can be done, but not worth trying if it can't."

The same evening Lady Bernard's shabby one-horse brougham stopped at Mr. Morley's door. Without circumlocution, she told him that if he would lay his affairs before her and a certain accountant she named, to use their judgment in the hope of finding it possible to serve him, they would wait upon him for that purpose at any time and place he pleased. Mr. Morley expressed his obligation—not very warmly, she said—repudiating, however, the slightest objection to her ladyship's knowing now what all the world must know the next day but one.

Early the following morning Lady Bernard and the accountant met Mr. Morley at his place in the city, and by three o'clock in the afternoon fifteen thousand pounds were handed in to his account at his bank.

At Miss Clare's earnest entreaty, no one told either Mr. or Mrs. Morley of the share she had had in saving his credit and social position.

Immediately after that, the carriage was put down; the butler, one of the footmen, and the lady's maid were dismissed; and household arrangements fitted to a different scale. The whole family drew yet more closely and lovingly together, and I must say for Judy that, after a few weeks of what she called poverty, her spirits seemed in no degree the worse for the trial.

But that it was not all the trial needful for Mr. Morley was soon apparent. His favorite Amy began to pine more rapidly, and Judy saw that except some change speedily took place, they could not have her with them for long. The father, however, refused to admit the idea that she was in danger. I suppose he felt that if, he were once to allow the possibility of losing her, from that moment there would be no stay between her and the grave—it would be a giving of her over to death. When the chills of autumn drew near, her mother took her to Ventnor, but little change followed, and before the new year she was gone. It was the first death, beyond that of an infant, they had had in their family, and took place at a time when business obligations rendered it impossible for her father to be out of London. He could only go to lay her in the earth, and bring back his wife.

Judy had never seen him weep before. Certainly I never saw such a change in a man. He was literally bowed with grief, as if he bore a material burden on his back. The best feelings of his nature, unimpeded by any jar to his self-importance or his prejudices, had been able to spend themselves on the lovely little creature, and I do not believe any other suffering than the loss of such a child could have brought into play that in him which was purely human.

He was at home one morning, ill for the first time in his life, when Miss Clare called on Judy. While she waited in the drawing-room, he entered. He turned the moment he saw her, but had not taken two steps toward the door when he turned again and approached her. She went to meet him, and he held out his hand.

"She was very fond of you, Miss Clare," he said. "She was

talking about you the very last time I saw her. Let bygones be bygones between us."

"I was rough and rude to you, Mr. Morley, and I am very sorry," said Miss Clare.

"But you spoke the truth," he rejoined. "I thought I was above being spoken to like a sinner, but now I don't know why."

He sat down on a couch, and leaned his head on his hand. Miss Clare took a chair near him, but could not speak.

"It is very hard," he murmured at length.

"Whom the Lord loveth He chasteneth," said Miss Clare.

"That may be true in some cases, but I have no right to believe it applies to me. He loved the child, I believe—for I dare not think of her either as having ceased to be, or as alone in the world to which she has gone. You do think, Miss Clare, do you not, that we shall know our friends in another world?"

"I believe," answered Miss Clare, "that God sent you that child for the express purpose of enticing you back to Himself. And if I believe anything at all, I believe that the gifts of God are without repentance."

At this point Judy came in. Seeing them together she would have withdrawn again, but her husband called her with more tenderness in his voice than Miss Clare could have imagined belonging to it.

"Come, my dear. Miss Clare and I were talking about our little angel. I didn't think ever to speak of her again, but I fear I am growing foolish. All the strength is out of me, and I feel so tired, so weary of everything!"

She sat down beside him and took his hand, and Miss Clare crept away to the children. An hour after, Judy found her in the nursery, with the youngest on her knee and the rest all about her. She was telling them that we were sent into this world to learn to be good, and then to go back to God from whom we came, like little Amy.

"When I go out tomowwow," said one little fellow, about four years old, "I'll look up in the sky vewy hard, wight up, and then I shall see Amy, and God saying to her, 'Hushaby, poo' Amy! You bette' now, Amy?' Shan't I, Mawion?"

She had taught them to call her Marion.

"No, my pet. You might look and look, all day long and every day, and never see God or Amy."

"Then they *ain't* there!" he exclaimed indignantly.

"God is there, anyhow," she answered, "only you can't see Him that way."

"I don't care about seeing God," said the next elder. "It's Amy I want to see. Do tell me, Marion, how we are to see Amy?"

"I will tell you the only way I know. When Jesus was in the world, He told us that all who had clean hearts should see God. That's how Jesus Himself saw God. And how can you see Amy if you can't even see God? If Amy be in God's arms, the first thing, in order to find her, is to find God. To be good is the only way to get near to anybody. When you're naughty, Willie, you can't get near your mamma, can you?"

"Yes, I can. I can get close up to her."

"Is that near enough? Would you be quite content with that? Even when she turns away her face and won't look at you?"

The little boy was silent.

"Did you ever see God, Marion?" asked one of the girls.

She thought for a moment before giving her answer. "No," she said. "I've seen things just after He has done them, and I think I've heard Him speak to me, but I've never seen Him yet."

"Then you're not good, Marion," said the free-thinker of the group.

"No—that's just it. But I hope to be good someday, and then I *shall* see Him."

"How do you grow good, Marion?" asked the girl.

"God is always trying to make me good," she answered, "and I try not to interfere with Him."

"But sometimes you forget, don't you?"

"Yes, I do."

"And what do you do then?"

"Then I'm sorry and unhappy, and begin to try again."

"And God don't mind much, does He?"

"He minds very much until I mind, but after that He forgets it all, takes all my naughtiness and throws it behind His back, and won't look at it."

"That's very good of God," said the reasoner, but with such a self-satisfied air in his approval, that Miss Clare thought it time to stop.

She came straight to see me and told me, with a perfectly radiant face, of the alteration of Mr. Morley's behavior to her, and, what was of much more consequence, the evident change that had begun to be wrought in him.

He has not, as yet, shown a very shining light, but some change is evident. The eternal wind must now be able to get in through the chink which the loss of his child has left behind. And if the changes were not going on, surely he would by now have returned to his wallowing in the mire of Mammon, for his former fortune is all but restored to him.

I fancy his growth in goodness is measured by his progress in appreciating Marion. He still regards her as extreme in her notions, but it is curious to see how, as they gradually sink into his understanding, he comes to adopt them as, and even to mistake them for, his own.

TWENTY-TWO

PERCIVALE

I should say a few words concerning my husband, if possible, because women differ much in the degree and manner in which their feelings will permit them to talk about their husbands. I have known women who set a whole community against their husbands by the way in which they trumpet their praises; and I have known one woman who set everybody against herself by the way in which she published her husband's faults. I find it difficult to believe either sort. To praise one's husband is so much like praising one's self that it seems immodest and subject to suspicion; while to blame one's husband, even justly and openly, seems to border upon treachery.

My father had long been concerned about Percivale's opinions. Now my father is large-minded, but I am not certain that he has done Percivale justice—although Percivale is partly to blame himself, for he never took pains to show my father what he was. Had he done so, my father of all men would have understood him.

My husband left the impression on my father's mind that he had some definite repugnance to Christianity itself. I, however, had soon been satisfied (perhaps from Percivale being more open with me) that certain representations of Christianity, coming to him with authority, had cast discredit on the whole idea. We had had many talks, and I was astonished at the things he imagined to be acknowledged essentials of Christianity, but which have no place whatever in the New Testament. There was little or no outward difference to be perceived in him as he came to see his misconceptions, but I could clearly distinguish an undercurrent of thought and feeling setting toward the faith which Christianity preaches. He said little or nothing, for he was almost morbidly careful not to seem to know anything he did not know or to appear to be what he was not.

I remember one occasion, some time before we began to go to Marion's on Sunday evenings, when I had asked him to go with me to a certain little chapel in the neighborhood—the very chapel, in fact, into which Marion had stepped on that evening so miserable to her.

"What!" he said merrily, "the daughter of a clergyman being seen going to a conventicle?"

"If I went, I would be seen doing it," I answered.

"Don't you know that the man is no conciliator, or even mild dissenter, but a decided enemy to church and state and all that?" pursued Percivale.

"I don't care," I replied. "He's a poet and a prophet both in one, and he stirs up my heart within me and makes me long to be good. He is no studied orator, as you profess such a great aversion to, yet he often breaks into eloquence."

"I don't mind going if you wish. I suppose he believes what he says, at least."

"Not a doubt of it, else he could not speak as he does."

"Do you mean he is *sure* of everything—is he *sure* that the story of the New Testament is, in the main, actual fact? I should be very sorry to trouble your faith, but—"

"My father says," I interrupted, "that a true faith is like the pool of Bethesda—it is when it is troubled that it shows its healing power."

"That may depend on where the trouble comes from," said Percivale.

"It is only that which cannot be shaken that shall remain."

"Well, here is a common sense difficulty: how is anyone to be *sure* of the things recorded? I cannot imagine a man of our time absolutely certain of them. If you tell me I have testimony, I answer that the testimony itself requires testimony. I never even saw the people who bear it, so I have just as good reason to doubt their existence as I do His. I have no means of verifying their testimony, and have so little confidence in what is called 'evidence,' knowing how it can be twisted, that I distrust any conclusion I should come to on one side or the other. If the thing were of God, He would have made it possible for an honest man to place a hearty confidence in its record."

He had never talked to me so openly, and I felt it a serious matter to answer him, for how could I have any better assurance of that external kind than Percivale himself? For a short time I was silent, while he regarded me with a look of concern, fearful, I fancied, lest he should have involved me in his own perplexity.

"Isn't it possible, Percivale," I said "that God may not care so much for beginning at that end? A man might believe every fact concerning our Lord, and yet not have the faith that God wishes him to have."

"Yes, certainly. But is the converse true? Will you say a man may have the faith God cares for without the faith you say He does not care for?"

"I didn't say that God does not care about our assurance of the facts. I only expressed a doubt whether He cares that we should have that assurance first. Perhaps He means it to be the result of that higher kind of faith which rests in the will."

"How can the higher faith precede the lower?"

"What is the test of discipleship the Lord laid down? Is it not obedience? 'If you love Me, keep My commandments.' Suppose a man feels in himself that he must have some Saviour or perish— suppose he feels drawn by conscience, admiration, or early memories to Jesus, dimly seen through the mists of ages. Suppose he cannot be sure there ever was such a Man, but reads about Him, and ponders over the words attributed to Him, until he feels they are the right thing, whether He said them or not, and that if he could be sure there were such a Being, he would believe in Him with heart and soul. Suppose also that he comes upon the words, 'If any man is willing to do the will of My Father, he shall know whether I speak of Myself or He sent Me.' Suppose the man then says to himself, 'I cannot tell whether all this is true, but I know nothing else that seems half so good, and I will try to do the will of the Father in the hope of the promised knowledge.' Do you think God would, or would not, count that to the man for faith?"

I had no more to say. After a pause of some duration, Percivale said, "I will go with you, my dear," and that was all his answer.

When we came out of the little chapel, we walked homeward in silence and reached our own door ere a word was spoken.

But Percivale followed me into our room and said, "Whether that man is *certain* of the fact or not, I cannot tell, but I am perfectly satisfied he believes in the manner of which you were speaking—that of obedience, Wynnie. He must believe with his heart and will and life."

"If so, he can well afford to wait for what light God will give him on things that belong to the intellect and judgment."

"I would rather think," he returned, "that purity of life must react on the judgment, so as to make it likewise clear, and enable it to recognize the true force of the evidence."

"That is how my father came to believe," I said.

"But your father seems to me to rest his conviction more upon external proof."

"Only because it is easier to talk about. He told me once that he was never able to estimate the force and weight of the external arguments until after he had believed for the very love of the eternal truth he saw in the story. His heart, he said, had been the guide of his intellect."

"That is just what I would fain believe. But O Wynnie! The pity of it if that story should not be true after all!"

"That very word makes me surer than ever that it cannot but be true! Let us go on putting it to the hardest test. Let us try it until it crumbles in our hands. Let us try it by the touchstone of action founded on its requirements."

"There may be no other way," said Percivale, "of becoming capable of recognizing the truth. It may be beyond the grasp of all but the mind that has thus yielded to it. Such a conviction, then, could neither be forestalled nor communicated. Its very existence must remain doubtful until it asserts itself."

And so we went on to other things.

TWENTY-THREE

A STRANGE TEXT

For some time after the events last related, things went on pretty smoothly with us for several years. What with my children and the increase of social duty resulting from the growth of acquaintance—occasioned in part by my success in persuading Percivale to mingle a little more with his fellow painters—my heart and mind and hands were all pretty fully occupied. But I still managed to see Miss Clare two or three times a week, sometimes alone, sometimes with her friends as well. Her society did much to keep my heart open, and to prevent it from becoming selfishly absorbed in its cares for husband and children. For love which is *only* concentrating its force—that is, not widening its circle—is itself doomed, and for its objects is ruinous, be those objects ever so sacred. God Himself could never be content that His children should love Him only, nor has He allowed the few to succeed who have tried after it; perhaps their divinest success has been their most mortifying failure. Indeed, for exclusive love, sharp suffering is often sent as the needful cure.

For some time I had seen a considerable change in Roger, reaching even to his dress. Hitherto, when got up for dinner, he was what I was astonished to hear my boy call "a howling swell"; but at other times he did not even escape remark, not for the oddity merely, but for the slovenliness of his attire. He had worn (for more years than I dare guess) a brown coat of some rich-looking stuff, whose long pile was stuck together in so many places with spots and dabs of paint that he looked like our long-haired

Bedlington terrier toward the end of a muddy week. This coat was now discarded—so far at least as to be hung up in his brother's study, to be at hand when he did anything for him there. It was replaced by a more civilized garment of tweed, of which he actually showed himself a little careful. While his necktie *was* red, it was of a very deep and rich red, and he had seldom worn one at all before. His brigand-looking felt hat was exchanged for one of half the altitude, which he did not crush on his head with quite as many indentations as its surface could hold. He also began to go to church with us sometimes.

But there was a greater and more significant change than any of these. We found that he was sticking more steadily to work. I can hardly say *his* work, for he was jack-of-all-trades. His forte was engraving on wood, and my husband said that if he could do so well with so little practice as he had had, he must be capable of becoming an admirable engraver. To our delight, then, we discovered, all at once, that he had been working steadily for three months for the Messrs. Danby, whose place was not far from our house. He had said nothing about it to his brother, probably from having good reason to fear that he would regard it only as a *spurt*. Having now, however, executed a block which greatly pleased himself, he had brought a proof impression to show Percivale. He, more pleased with it than even Roger himself, gave him a hearty congratulation, and told him it would be a shame if he did not bring his execution in that art to perfection, from which, judging by the present specimen, he said it could not be far off. The words brought into Roger's face an expression of modest gratification which it rejoiced me to behold. He accepted Percivale's approbation more like a son than a brother, with a humid glow in his eyes and hardly a word on his lips. It seemed to me that the child in his heart had begun to throw off the swaddling clothes which foolish manhood had wrapped around it, and the germ of his being was about to assert itself. Indeed, I have seldom seen Percivale look so pleased.

"Do me a dozen as good as that," he said, "and I'll have the proofs framed in silver gilt."

(It *has* been done, but the proofs had to wait longer for the frames than Percivale for the proofs.)

But he need have held out no such bribe of brotherly love, for there was another love already at work in himself more than sufficing to the affair. Roger always took a half-holiday on Saturdays, and now generally came to us. On one of these occasions I said to him, "Wouldn't you like to come and hear Marion play to her friends this evening, Roger?"

"Nothing would give me greater pleasure," he answered, and we went.

It was delightful, for Marion is a real artist. While she uttered from herself, she heard with her audience, and while she played and sang with her own fingers and mouth, she at the same time listened with their ears, knowing what they must feel, as well as what she meant to utter. And hence it was, I think, that she came into such vital contact with them, even through her piano.

As we returned home, Roger said, after some remark of mine, "Does she never try to teach them anything, Wynnie?"

"She is constantly teaching them, whether she tries or not," I answered. "If you can make anyone believe that there is something somewhere to be trusted, is not that the best lesson you can give them? That can be taught only by being such that people can but trust you."

"I don't need to be told that," he answered. "I want to know whether or not she ever teaches them by word of mouth, by an ordinary and inferior mode, if you will."

"If you had ever heard her, you would not call hers an ordinary or inferior mode," I returned. "Her teaching is the outcome of her life, the blossom of her being, and therefore has the whole force of her living truth to back it. She teaches them every Sunday evening, and I never heard anything like it."

"Could you take me with you sometime?" he asked, in an assumed tone of ordinary interest, out of which, however, he could not keep a slight tremble.

"I don't know. I don't quite see why I shouldn't. And yet—"

"Men do go," urged Roger, as if it were a mere half-indifferent suggestion.

"Oh, yes! You would have plenty to keep you in countenance! Men enough—and worth teaching too—some of them, at least!"

"Then, I don't see why she should object to me for another."

"I don't know that she would. You are not exactly of the sort, you know, that—"

"I see no essential difference. I am in want of teaching as much as any of them. And, if she stands on circumstances, I am a workingman as much as any of them, perhaps more than most of them. Few of them work after midnight, as I do not unfrequently."

151

"Still, all admitted, I should hardly like—"

"I didn't mean you were to take me without asking her," he said. "I should never have dreamed of that."

"And if I were to ask her, I am certain she would refuse. But," I added, thinking over the matter a little, "I will take you without asking her. Come with me tomorrow night. I don't think she will have the heart to send you away."

"I will," he answered, with more gladness in his voice than he intended.

We arranged that he should call for me at a certain hour. I told Percivale, and he pretended to grumble that I was taking Roger instead of him.

"It was Roger, and not you, that made the request," I returned. "If you really want to go, I don't see why you shouldn't. It's ever so much better than going to any church I know of—except one. But we must be prudent. I can't take more than one the first time. We must get the thin edge of the wedge in first."

"And you count Roger the thin edge?"

"Yes."

"I'll tell him so."

"Do. The thin edge, mind, without which the thicker rest is useless! But, seriously, I quite expect to take you there too, the Sunday after."

Roger and I went. Intending to be a little late, we found that the class had already begun. When we reached the last stair we could hear her saying, "I will now read to you the chapter of which I spoke."

The door was open, and we could hear well enough, although she was sitting where we could not see her. We would not show ourselves until the reading was ended—so much, at least, we might overhear without offense.

Before she had read many words, Roger and I began to cast strange looks to each other. For this was the chapter she read:

"And Joseph, wheresoever he went in the city, took the Lord Jesus with him, where he was sent for to work, to make gates or milk pails, or sieves, or boxes. And as often as Joseph had anything in his work to make longer or shorter, or wider or narrower, the Lord Jesus would stretch His hand toward it. And presently it became as Joseph would have it. And he had no need to finish anything with his own hands, for he was not very skillful at his carpenter's trade.

"On a certain time the king of Jerusalem sent for him, and said, 'I would have thee make me a throne of the same dimensions with that place in which I commonly sit.' Joseph obeyed, and forthwith began with the work, and continued two years in the king's palace before he finished. And when he came to fix it in its place, he found it wanted two spans on each side of the appointed measure. Which, when the king saw, he was very angry with Joseph, and Joseph, afraid of the king's anger, went to bed without his supper, taking not anything to eat. Then the Lord Jesus asked him what he was afraid of. Joseph replied, 'Because I have lost my labor in the work which I have been about these two years.' Jesus said to him, 'Fear not, neither be cast down. Do thou lay hold on one side of the throne, and I will the other, and we will bring it to its just dimensions.' And when Joseph had done as the Lord Jesus said, and each of them had with strength drawn his side, the throne obeyed, and was brought to the proper dimensions of the place. They who stood by saw this miracle, and were astonished, and praised God. The throne was made of the same wood which was in being in Solomon's time, namely, wood adorned with various shapes and figures."

Her voice ceased, and a pause followed.

"We must go in now," I whispered.

"Now, what do you think of it?" asked Marion in a meditative tone.

We crept within the scope of her vision, and stood. A voice (which I knew) was at that moment replying to her question.

"I don't think it's much of a chapter, that, Grannie."

The speaker was the keen-faced, elderly man with iron-gray whiskers, who had helped us search for little Ethel. He sat near the door, between two respectable looking women who had been listening to the chapter as devoutly as if it had been of the true Gospel.

"Sure, Grannie, that ain't out o' the Bible?" said another voice, from somewhere farther off.

"We'll talk about that presently," answered Marion. "I want to hear what Mr. Jarvis has to say. He's a carpenter himself, you see."

All the faces in the room were now turned toward Jarvis.

"Tell me why you don't think much of it, Mr. Jarvis," said Marion.

"Tain't a bit likely," he answered.

"What isn't likely?"

"First and foremost, 'tain't a bit likely the old man 'ud ha' been sich a duffer."

"Why not? There must have been stupid people then as well as now."

"Well, it ain't likely sich a workman 'ud ha' stood so high i' the trade that the king of Jerusalem would ha' sent for *him* of all the tradesmen in the town to make his new throne for him. No more it ain't likely—and let him be as big a duffer as ever was, to be a jiner at all—that he'd ha' been two years at work on that there throne—an' a carvin' of it in figures too—and never found out it was four spans too narrer for the place it had to stand in. Do ye 'appen to know now, Grannie, how much is a span?"

"I don't know. Do you know, Mrs. Percivale?"

The sudden reference took me very much by surprise, but I had not forgotten, happily, the answer I received to the same question, when anxious to realize the monstrous height of Goliath.

"I remember my father telling me," I replied, "that it was as much as you could stretch between your thumb and little finger."

"There!" cried Jarvis triumphantly, parting the extreme members of his right hand against the back of the woman in front of him. "That would be seven or eight inches! Four times that? Two foot and a half at least! Think of that!"

"I admit the force of both your objections," said Marion. "And what do you think of the way He got His father out of his evil plight?"

Before Jarvis had time to make any reply, the blind man struck in.

"*I* make more o' that pint than the t' other," he said. "A man as is a duffer may well make a mull of a thing, but a man as knows what he's up to can't. I don't make much o' them miracles, you know, Grannie—but what I'm sure of is this here one thing—that man or boy as *could* work a miracle, you know, Grannie, wouldn't work no miracle as there wasn't no good working of."

"It was to help His father," suggested Marion.

Here Jarvis broke in almost with scorn. "To help him to pass for a clever fellow, when he was as great a duffer as ever broke bread!"

"I'm quite o' your opinion, Mr. Jarvis," said the blind man. "It'ud ha' been more like Him to tell His father what a duffer he was, and send him home to learn his trade."

"He couldn't do that, you know," said Marion gently. "He *couldn't* use such words to His father, if he were ever so stupid."

"I think, though," said Jarvis, "for as hard as He'd ha' found it, it would ha' been more like Him to set up to work and teach His father, than to scamp up his mulls."

"Certainly," acquiesced Marion. "To hide any man's faults, and leave him not only stupid but, in all probability, obstinate and self-satisfied, would not be like *Him*. What do you think our Lord would have done?"

"He'd ha' done all He could to make a man of him," answered Jarvis.

"Wouldn't He have set about making him comfortable then, in spite of his blunders?" said Marion.

A significant silence followed this question.

"Well, no, not first thing, I don't think," returned Jarvis at length. "He'd ha' got him some good first, and gone in to make him comfortable after."

"Then I suppose you would rather be of some good and uncomfortable, than of no good and comfortable?" said Marion.

"I hope so, Grannie," answered Jarvis, and "I would," "Yes," and "That I would" came from several voices in the little crowd.

"Then," she said—and I saw by the light which rose in her eyes that she was now coming to the point—"then, surely it must be worth our while to bear discomfort in order to grow of some good! Mr. Jarvis has truly said that if Jesus had had such a father, He would have made him of some good before He made him comfortable. That is just the way your Father in heaven is acting with you. Not many of you would say you are of much good yet, but you would like to be better. And yet, put it to yourselves: do you not grumble at everything that comes to you that you don't like, and call it bad luck, and worse—yes, even when you know it comes of your own fault? You think if you only had this or that to make you comfortable, you would be content. You forget that to make you comfortable as you are would be the same as to pull out Joseph's misfitted thrones and doors, and make his misshapen buckets over again for him. And that you think so absurd that you can't believe the story a bit. Yet you would wish to be helped out of all *your* troubles, even those you bring on yourselves, not thinking what the certain consequence would be, namely, that you would grow of less and less value, until you were of no good, either to God or man.

"When, for instance, are you most willing to do right? When are you most ready to hear about good things? When are you most inclined to pray to God? When you have plenty of money in your pockets, or when you are in want? When you have had a good dinner, or when you have not had enough to get one? When you are in jolly health, or when the life seems ebbing out of you in misery and pain? If suffering drives you to God, that is its end and there will be an end of it.

"Now, however, that we have got a lesson from a false gospel, we may as well get one from the true."

As she spoke, she turned to her New Testament which lay beside her. But Jarvis interrupted her.

"Where did you get that stuff you was a readin' of to us, Grannie?" he asked.

"The chapter I read to you," she answered, "is part of a pretended gospel called *The First Gospel of the Infancy of Jesus Christ.* Very early in the history of the church, there were some people who indulged themselves in inventing things about Jesus, who had no idea of the importance of keeping to facts—of speaking and writing only the truth. It is long before some people learn to speak the truth, even after they know it is wicked to lie. Perhaps, however, they did not expect their stories to be received as facts, intending them only as a sort of recognized fiction about Him—an amazing presumption at the best."

"Did anybody, then, believe the likes of that, Grannie?" asked Jarvis.

"Yes. What I read to you seems to have been believed within a hundred years after the death of the apostles. There are several such writings, with a great deal of nonsense in them, which were generally accepted by Christian people for many hundreds of years.

"One comfort is, that such a story is sure not to be consistent with itself. It is sure to show its own falsehood to anyone who is good enough to doubt it, and who will look into it and examine it well. You don't, for instance, want any other proof than the things themselves to show you that what I have just read to you can't be true."

"Then don't you think it likely this much is true, Grannie," said Jarvis, "that He worked with His father, and helped him in his trade?"

"I do indeed," answered Marion. "I believe that to be the one germ of truth in the whole story. Is it likely that He, who came down for the express purpose of being a true man, would see His father toiling to feed Him and His mother and His brothers and sisters, and go idling about, instead of putting in His hand to help him? Would that have been like Him?"

"Certainly not," said Mr. Jarvis.

"Mr. Jarvis, will you tell me whether you think the work of the carpenter's Son would have been in any way distinguishable from that of another man?"

"Well, I don't know, Grannie. He wouldn't want to be putting of a private mark upon it. He wouldn't want to be showing of it off, would He? He'd use His tools like another man, anyhow."

"We may be certain of that. But do you suppose you would have been able to distinguish His work from that of any other carpenter?"

A silence followed. Jarvis was thinking, and at last his face brightened.

"Well, Grannie," he said, "I think it would be very difficult in anything easy, but very easy in anything difficult." Then he laughed, for he had not perceived the paradox before uttering it.

"Explain yourself, if you please, Mr. Jarvis. I am not sure that I understand you," said Marion.

"I mean that in an easy job, which any fair workman could do well enough, it would not be easy to tell His work. But, where the job was difficult, His would be so much better done that it would not be difficult to see the better hand in it."

"Then the chief distinction would lie in the quality of the work—that whatever He did, he would do in such a thorough manner that, over the whole of what He turned out, the perfection of the work would be a striking characteristic. Is that it?"

"That is what I do mean, Grannie."

"And that is just the conclusion I had come to myself."

"I should like to say just one word to it, Grannie," said the blind man. "Mr. Jarvis, he say as how the jiner-work done by Jesus Christ would be better done than e'er another man's—tip-top fashion—and there would lie the difference. Now, it do seem to me as I've got no call to come to that 'ere conclusion. For the works o' God—there ain't one on' em as I can see downright well managed—tip-top jiner's work, as I may say. We ha' got most uncommon bad weather more'n at times, and the walnuts they turns out, every now an' then, full o' mere dirt, an' the oranges

157

awful. There ain't been a good crop o' hay, they tells me, for many's the year. An' i' furren parts, what wi' earthquakes an' wolcanies an' lions an' tigers, an' savages as eats their wisiters, an' chimley-pots blowin' about, an' ships goin' down, an' fathers o' families choked an' drownded an' burnt i' coal pits by the hundreds—it do seem to me that if His jinerin' hadn't been tip-top, it would ha' been but like the rest on it. There, Grannie! Mind, I mean no offense, an' I don't doubt you ha' got somethink i' your weskit pocket as'll turn it all topsy-turvy in a moment. Anyhow, I won't purtend to nothink, and that's how it looks to me."

"I admit," said Marion, "that the objection is a reasonable one. Allow me just to put a question or two to Mr. Jarvis, because he's a joiner himself, and that's a great comfort to me tonight. What would you say, Mr. Jarvis, of a master who planed the timber he used for scaffolding, and tied the crosspieces with ropes of silk?"

"I should say he was a fool, Grannie, not only for losin' his money and his labor, but for weakenin' of his scaffoldin'."

"What's the object of a scaffold, Mr. Jarvis?"

"To get at something else by means of—say, to build a house."

"Then, so long as the house was going up all right, the probability is there wouldn't be much amiss with the scaffold?"

"Certainly, provided it stood till it was taken down."

"If you saw a scaffold," said Marion, "would you mistake it for a permanent erection?"

"Nobody wouldn't be such a fool," he answered. "The look of it would tell you that."

"You wouldn't complain, then, if it should be a little out of the square, and if there should be no windows in it?"

Jarvis only laughed.

"Mr. Evans," Marion went on, turning to the blind man, "do you think the design of this world was to make men comfortable?"

"If it was, it don't seem to ha' succeeded," answered Evans.

"And you complain of that, don't you?"

"Well, yes, rather," said the blind man.

"You think, perhaps, that God, having gone so far to make this world a pleasant and comfortable place to live in, might have gone farther and made it quite pleasant and comfortable for everybody?"

"Whoever could make it at all could na' done that, Grannie."

"Then, as He hasn't done it, the probability is He didn't mean to do it?"

"Of course. That's what I complain of."

"Then He meant to do something else?"

"It looks like it."

"The whole affair has an unfinished look, you think?"

"I just do."

"What if it were not meant to stand, then? What if it were meant only for a temporary assistance in carrying out something finished and lasting, and of unspeakably more importance? Suppose God were building a palace for you, and had set up a scaffold, upon which He wanted you to help Him. Would it be reasonable for you to complain that you didn't find the scaffold at all a comfortable place to live in? Or that it was draughty and cold? This world is that scaffold, and if you were busy carrying stones and mortar for the palace, you would be glad of all the cold to cool the glow of your labor.

"But what will all the labor of a workman who does not fall in with the design of the builder come to? Instead of working away at the palace, like men, will you go on tacking bits of matting and old carpet about the corners of the scaffold to keep the wind off, while that same wind keeps tearing them away and scattering them? You keep trying to live in a scaffold, which not all eternity would make a house of. God wants to build you a house whereof the walls shall be *goodness*. You want a house with walls of *comfort*. But God knows that such walls cannot be built—that that kind of stone crumbles away in the foolish workman's hands. He would make you comfortable, but neither is that His first object, nor can it be gained without the first, which is to make you good. He loves you so much that He would infinitely rather have you good and uncomfortable—for then He could take you to His heart as His own children—than comfortable and not good, for then He could not come near you, or give you anything He counted worth having."

"So," said Jarvis, "you've just brought us round, Grannie, to the same thing as before."

"I believe so," returned Marion. "It comes to this, that when God would build a palace for Himself to dwell in with His children, He does not want His scaffold so constructed that they shall be able to make a house of it for themselves, and live like apes instead of angels.

"You see, then, it is not inconsistent with the apparent imperfections of the creation around us, that Jesus should have done the best possible carpenter's work, for those very imperfections are actually through their imperfections the means of carrying out the higher creation God has in view, and at which He is working all the time.

"Now let me read you what King David thought upon this question."

She read Psalm 107. Then they had some singing, and Roger and I slipped out. We had agreed it would be best to make no apology, but just vanish, and come again with Percivale the following Sunday.

The greater part of the way home we walked in silence.

"What do you think of that, Roger?" I asked at length.

"Quite Socratic as to method," he answered, and said no more.

I sent a full report of the evening to my father, who was delighted with it, although, of course, much was lost in the reporting of the mere words, not to mention the absence of her sweet face and shining eyes, and of her quiet, earnest, musical voice.

TWENTY-FOUR

MY SECOND TERROR

"Please, Ma'am, is Master Fido to carry Master Zohrab about?" said Jemima, in indignant appeal one afternoon late in November, bursting into the study where I sat with my husband.

Fido was our Bedlington terrier which, having been reared by Newcastle colliers and taught to draw a badger, had a passion for burrowing after anything buried. Swept away by the current of the said passion, he had unearthed poor Zohrab the tortoise, who had ensconced himself (he thought) for the winter in the earth at the foot of a lilac tree. Now, much to his jeopardy, he was being triumphantly borne about the garden in Fido's jaws.

Alarmed at the danger to the poor powerless animal, Percivale threw down his palette and brushes and ran out the door.

"Do put on your coat and hat, Percivale!" I cried, but he was gone.

Cold as it was, he had been sitting in the light blouse he had worn at his work all summer. The stove was red-hot, and the room like an oven, while outside a dank fog filled the air. I hurried after him with his coat, and found him pursuing Fido about the garden. The brute declined to obey his call or to drop the tortoise. Percivale was equally deaf to my call, and not until he had chastised the dog did he return with the rescued tortoise in his hands. The consequences were serious—first the death of Zohrab, and next a terrible illness to my husband. A cold settled into his lungs and passed into bronchitis.

It was a terrible time for me, for I had no doubt that he was dying. The measures taken seemed thoroughly futile.

It is an awful moment when first Death looks in at the door. The positive recognition of his presence is so different from any vividest imagination of it! For the moment I believed nothing—felt only the coming blackness of absolute loss. I cared neither for my children, nor for my father or mother. Nothing appeared of any worth anymore. I had conscience enough left to try to pray, but no prayer would rise from the frozen depths of my spirit. I could only move about in mechanical and hopeless ministration to one whom it seemed of no use to go on loving any more. For what was nature but a soulless machine, the constant clank of whose motion sounded only, "Dust to dust, dust to dust," forevermore?

But my husband caught a glimpse of my despair, motioned me to him with a smile as of sunshine upon snow, and whispered in my ear, "I am afraid you haven't much more faith than myself, after all, Wynnie."

It stung me into life, not for the sake of my professions, not even for the honor of our Heavenly Father, but by waking in me the awful thought of my beloved passing through the shadow of death with no one beside him to help or comfort him, in absolute loneliness and uncertainty. For a moment I wished he might die suddenly, and so escape the vacuous despair of a conscious lingering betwixt life and the something or the nothing beyond it.

"But I cannot go with you!" I cried, and forgetting all my duty as a nurse, I wept in agony.

"Perhaps another will, my Wynnie—One who knows the way," he whispered, for he could not speak aloud, and closed his eyes.

It was as if an arrow of light had slain the python coiled about my heart. If *he* believed, *I* could believe also. If *he* could encounter the vague dark, *I* could endure the cheerless light. I was myself again and, with one word of endearment, left the bedside to do what had to be done.

At length a faint hope began to glimmer in the depths of my cavernous fear, though it was long ere it swelled into confidence. For a whole week I did not once undress, and for weeks I was half-awake all the time I slept. The softest whisper would rouse me thoroughly, and it was only when Marion took my place that I could sleep at all.

I am afraid I neglected my poor children dreadfully, but then I knew that they were well attended to. Friends were very kind— especially Judy—in taking them out, and Marion's daily visits were like those of a mother. (Indeed, she was able to mother anything human except a baby, to whom she felt no attraction, anymore than to animals, for which she had little regard. She would hurt no creature that was not hurtful, but she had scarcely an atom of kindness for dog or cat, or anything that is petted of woman. It is the only defect I am aware of in her character.)

My husband slowly recovered, but it was months before he was able to do anything he would call work. But, even in labor, success is not only to the strong. Working a little at the short best time of the day, he managed, long before his full recovery, to paint a small picture which better critics than I have thought worthy of Fra Angelico. I will attempt to describe it.

Through the lighted windows of a great hall, the spectator catches broken glimpses of a festive company. At the head of the table, pouring red wine, he sees One like unto the Son of man, upon whom all eyes are turned. At the other end of the hall, seated high in a gallery, with rapt looks and quaint yet homely angelic instruments, he sees the orchestra pouring out their souls through their strings and trumpets. The hall is filled with a jewelly glow, the radiating center is the red wine on the table. Mingled wings of all gorgeous splendors hovering in the dim height are suffused and harmonized by the molten ruby tint that pervades the whole.

Outside, in the drizzly darkness, stands a lonely man. He stoops, listening with one ear laid almost against the door. His half-upturned face catches a ray of the light reflected from a muddy pool in the road. It discloses features wan and wasted with sorrow and sickness, but glorified with the joy of the music. He is like one who has been four days dead, to whose body the music has recalled the soul. Down by his knee he holds a violin, fashioned like those of the orchestra within and, as he listens, he is tuning to their pitch.

The origin of all this was a poem of Dr. Donne's—"Hymn to God, my God in my sickness." I had read some verses of it to him in his convalescence, and having heard them once, he requested them often again. The first stanza runs thus:

> Since I am coming to that holy room
> Where with the choir of saints forevermore
> I shall be made Thy musique, as I come,
> I tune the instrument here at the door;
> And what I must do then, think here before.

The painting is almost the only one he has yet refused to let me see before it was finished, but when it was, he hung it up in my own little room off the study, and I became thoroughly acquainted with it. I think I love it more than anything else he has done. I got him, without telling him why, to put a touch or two to the listening figure, which made it really like himself.

During this period of recovery, I often came upon him reading his Greek New Testament, which he would shove aside when I entered. At length, one morning, I said to him, "Are you ashamed of reading the New Testament, Percivale? One would think it was a bad book from the way you try to hide it."

"No, my love," he said. "It is only that I am jealous of appearing to do that from suffering and weakness only, which I did not do when I was strong and well. But sickness has opened my eyes a good deal, I think, and I am sure of this much, that, whatever truth there is here, I want it all the same whether I am feeling the want or not. I had no idea what there was in this Book."

"Would you mind telling me," I said, "what made you take to reading it?"

"I will try. When I thought I was dying, a black cloud seemed to fall over everything. It was not so much that I was afraid to die—although I did dread the final conflict—as that I felt so forsaken and lonely. It was of little use saying to myself that I mustn't be a coward, and that it was the part of a man to meet his fate, whatever it might be, with composure; for I saw nothing worth being brave about. The heart had melted out of me. There was nothing to give me joy, nothing for my life to rest upon, no sense of love at the heart of things. Didn't you feel something the same that terrible day?"

"I did," I answered. "For one fearful moment the skeleton of Death seemed to swell and grow till he blotted out the sun and the stars, and the life beyond was too shadowy to show behind him. And so Death was victorious, until the thought of your loneliness in the dark valley broke the spell, and for your sake I hoped in God again."

Percivale then continued, "And I asked myself if God would set His children down in the dark, and leave them to cry aloud in anguish at the terrors of the night? Would He not make the very darkness light about them? Or, if they must pass through such tortures, would He not at least let them know that He was with them? Then arose in my mind all at once the old story how, in the person of His Son, God Himself had passed through the darkness now gathering about me, had gone down to the grave, and had conquered death by dying. If this was true, this was to be a God indeed. Well might He call us to endure, who had Himself borne the far heavier share. If there were an Eternal Life who would perfect my life, I could be brave, I could endure what He chose to lay upon me, I could go whither He led."

"And were you able to think all that when you were so ill, my love?" I said.

"Something like it," he answered. "It kept growing in my mind, coming and going, and gathering clearer in shape. If there was a God, He certainly knew that I would give myself to Him if I could—that if I knew Jesus to be verily and really His Son, however it might seem strange to believe in Him and hard to obey Him—I would try to do so. Then the verse about the smoking flax and the bruised reed came into my head, and a great hope arose in me. I do not know if it was what the good people would call faith, but I had no time and no heart to think about words. I wanted God and His Christ. A fresh spring of life seemed to burst up in my heart. All the world grew bright again, and I seemed to love you and the children twice as much as before. A calmness came down upon my spirit which seemed to me like nothing but the presence of God; and, although I dare say you did not then perceive a change, I am certain that the same moment I began to recover."

The little money we had in hand rapidly vanished during Percivale's illness. While he was making nothing, the expenses of the family went on as usual, and the doctor was yet to pay. Even up to the time when he had been taken ill, we had been doing little better than living from hand to mouth, for as often as we thought income was about to get a few yards ahead in the race with expense, something invariably happened to disappoint us.

While Percivale was ill, not a picture had been disposed of, and even after he was able to work a little, I could not encourage visitors. He was fatigued, and he shrunk with irritability from seeing anyone. I watched my little stock—which was bodily in my hand, for we had no banking account—rapidly approach its final evanishment.

Some may think that, with parents in the position of mine, a temporary difficulty need have caused me no anxiety.

In the first place, my husband could not feel toward my father as I felt. Percivale had married me as a poor man who yet could keep a wife, and I knew it would be a bitter humiliation to him to ask my father for money, on the ground that he had given his daughter.

In the second place, even I, in my fullest freedom, could not have asked help from my father just at this time. He had taken upon himself to pay some two thousand pounds of injudicious debts incurred by my eldest brother—incurred through no other vice beyond that of thoughtlessness and folly. Indeed, he had to borrow part of the money on a fresh mortgage in order to clear him. Some lawyer told him that he was not bound to pay, but my father said that although such creditors deserved no protection of the law, he was not bound to give them a lesson in honesty at the expense of weakening the bond between himself and his son, for whose misdeeds he acknowledged a large share of responsibility. On the other hand, he was bound to give his son the lesson of the suffering he brought on his family by his selfishness, and therefore would pay the money—if not gladly, yet willingly. How the poor boy got through the shame and misery of it, I can hardly imagine. But this I can say for him, that it was purely of himself that he accepted a situation in Ceylon, with the intention of repaying my father. If he succeeds in doing so, he will doubtless make a fairer start the second time—because of the discipline—than if he had gone out with money in his pocket.

It was natural, then, that in such circumstances a daughter should shrink from adding her troubles to those caused by a son. My father had also of late been laying out a good deal in building cottages for the laborers on his farms, and the land itself was not entirely freed from the mortgages my mother had inherited with it.

Percivale continued so weak that for some time I could not bring myself to say a word to him about money. But to keep the household debts as low as possible did not prevent them from accumulating, and the servants' wages were on the point of coming due. I had been careful to keep the milkman paid and, if the worse came to the worst, there was plenty of furniture in the house to pay the rest of the tradesmen. Still, of all burdens, next to sin, that of debt must be heaviest.

"What *is* the matter, my darling?" asked Percivale.

I took a half crown out of my pocket, and held it out on the palm of my hand.

"That's all I've got, Percivale," I said.

166

"Oh! That's all, is it?" he returned lightly.

"Yes, isn't that enough?" I said with some indignation.

"Certainly, for tonight," he answered, "seeing the shops are shut. But is that all that's troubling you?"

"It seems to me quite enough," I said again, "and if you had the housekeeping to do, and the bills to pay, you would think a solitary half crown quite enough to make you miserable."

"Never mind, so long as it's a good one," he said. "I'll get you more tomorrow."

"How can you do that?" I asked.

"Easily," he answered. "You'll see. Don't you trouble your dear heart about it for a moment."

I felt relieved, and asked him no more questions.

The next morning, when I went into the study to speak to him, he was not there. I guessed that he had gone to town to get the money, for he had not been out before since his illness, at least not without me. But I hoped of all things he was not going to borrow it of a moneylender, of which I had a great and justifiable horror. I would have sold three-fourths of the things in the house rather. But as I turned to leave the study, anxious both about himself and his proceedings, I thought something was different, and soon discovered that a certain favorite picture was missing from the wall. It was clear he had gone either to sell it or raise money upon it.

He soon returned and put two five-pound notes into my hands, although with a look of forced cheerfulness.

"Is that all you got for that picture?" I said.

"That is all Mr. Spencer would advance me," he answered. "I thought he had made enough by me to have risked a little more than that, but the picture dealers—well, never mind. That is enough to give time for twenty things to happen."

And no doubt twenty things did happen, but none of them of the sort he meant. The ten pounds sank through my purse like water through gravel. I paid a number of small bills at once, for they pressed the more heavily upon me that I knew the money was wanted, and by the end of another fortnight we were as badly off as before, with an additional trouble.

Jemima gave warning, for it was out of my power to pay her wages, and there was no sign of her yielding.

I tried to pray to God to deliver us, but a whole day would sometimes pass under a weight of care that amounted often to misery, and not until its close would I see that I had been all the weary hours without God. Even when more hopeful, I would keep looking and looking for the impossibility of something to happen of itself, instead of looking for some good and perfect gift to come down from the Father of lights.

It was, indeed, a miserable time. There was, besides, one definite thought that always choked my prayers: I could not say in my conscience that I had been sufficiently careful either in my management or my expenditures. "If," I thought, "I could be certain that I had done my best, I should be able to trust in God for all that lies beyond my power. But now He may mean to punish me for my carelessness." Then why should I not endure it calmly and without complaint? Alas! It was not I alone that thus would be punished, but my children and my husband as well.

Sometimes, however, in more faithful moods, I would reason with myself that God would not be hard upon me, even if I had not been so saving as I ought. My father had taken his son's debts on himself, and would not allow him to be disgraced more than could be helped. And, if an earthly parent would act thus for his child, would our Father in heaven be less tender with us?

Things went on, and grew no better.

Percivale at length asked Roger if he had any money by him to lend him a little. Roger gave him all he had, amounting to six pounds, a wonderful amount for Roger to have accumulated. The next step I had in view was to take my little valuables to the pawnbroker's—amongst them a watch, whose face was encircled with a row of good-sized diamonds. It had belonged to my great-grandmother, and my mother had given it to me when I was married.

Percivale had gone out, and I was sitting in the drawing room, lost in anything but a blessed reverie, with the children chattering amongst themselves beside me, when Jemima entered, looking subdued.

"If you please, ma'am, this is my day," she said.

"Have you got a place, then, Jemima?" I asked, for I had been so much occupied with my own affairs that I had thought little of the future of the poor girl to whom I could have given but a lukewarm recommendation for anything prized amongst housekeepers.

"No, Ma'am. Please, Ma'am, mayn't I stop?"

"No, Jemima. I am very sorry, but I can't afford to keep you. I shall have to do all the work myself when you are gone."

Jemima burst into an Irish wail, mingled with sobs and tears, crying between the convulsions of all three, "I thought there was something wrong, Mis'ess. You and master looked so scared-like. Please, Mis'ess, don't send me away."

"I never wanted to send you away, Jemima. You wanted to go yourself."

"No, Ma'am, *that* I didn't. I only wanted you to ask me to stop. Wirra! Wirra! It's myself is sorry I was so rude. It's not me—it's my temper, Mis'ess. I do believe I was born with a devil inside me."

I could not help laughing, partly from amusement, partly from relief.

"But you see I can't ask you to stop," I said. "I've no money, not even enough to pay you today."

"I don't want no money, Ma'am. Let me stop, and I'll cook for yez, and wash and scrub for yez, to the end o' my days. An' I'll eat no more than'll keep the life in me. Please 'm, I ha' got fifteen pounds in the savings bank. I'll give ye all of that, if ye'll let me stop wid ye."

"Thank you very much, Jemima," I said, as soon as I could speak. "I won't take your money, for then you would be as poor as I am. But if you would like to stop with us, you shall, and I won't pay you till I'm able."

The poor girl was profuse in her thanks, and left the room sobbing in her apron.

It was a gloomy, drizzly, dreary afternoon. The children were hard to amuse, and I was glad when their bedtime arrived. It was getting late before Percivale returned. He looked pale, and I found afterward that he had walked home. He had got wet, and had to change some of his clothes. When I related to him what had passed with Jemima, he laughed merrily and was evidently a good deal relieved. Then I asked him where he had been.

"To the city," he answered.

"Have you sold another picture?" I asked. As much as we wanted the money, I could ill bear the thought of his pictures going for the price of mere pot-boilers.

"No," he replied. "The last picture is blocking the way. Mr. Tait has been advertising it as a bargain for a hundred and fifty. But he hasn't sold it yet, and can't—he says—risk ten pounds more on another. What's to come of it, I don't know. But meantime it's a comfort that Jemima can wait for *her* money."

Later I thought I saw a look on Percivale's face which I had never seen there before. After a long pause, during which we had been both looking into the fire, he said, "Wynnie, I'm going to paint a better picture than I've ever painted yet. I can, and I will."

"But how are we to live in the meantime?" I said.

His face fell, and I saw with shame what a Job's comforter I was. Instead of sympathizing with his ardor, I had quenched it. What if my foolish remark had ruined a great picture! Anyhow, it had wounded a great heart, which had turned to labor as its plainest duty, and would thereby have been strengthened to endure and to hope. It was too cruel of me. I knelt by his knee, and told him I was both ashamed and sorry I had been so faithless and unkind. He made little of it, and even tried to be merry over it. But I could see well enough that I had let a gust of the foggy night into his soul, and I was thoroughly vexed with myself. We went to bed gloomy, but slept well and awoke more cheerful in the morning.

TWENTY-FIVE

THE RAYS OF SUNSHINE

As we were dressing, it came into my mind that I had forgotten to give Percivale a black-bordered letter which had arrived the night before. It looked like a business letter, and I feared it might be a demand for the overdue rent of the house. By this time I dreaded opening any letter if I did not recognize the writing.

"Here is a letter, Percivale," I said. "I'm sorry I forgot to give it to you last night."

"Who is it from?" he asked, talking through his towel from his dressing room.

"I don't know. I didn't open it. It looks like something disagreeable."

He came in, opened it, and read it. Then suddenly his arms were around me and his cheek on mine.

"Read that," he said, putting the letter into my hand.

It was from a lawyer in Shrewsbury, informing him that his godmother, with whom he had been a great favorite when a boy, had died, and had left him three hundred pounds.

Death itself may sometimes be a release, but the gift out of this woman's death was a reprieve to us. I could only weep and thank God, once more believing in my Father in heaven. But it was a humbling thought that, if He had not thus helped me, I might have ceased to believe in Him. I saw plainly that my own faith was but a wretched thing. It is all very well to have noble theories about God; but where is the good of them except we actually trust in Him as a real, present, living, loving Being, who counts us of

171

more value than many sparrows, and will not let one of them fall to the ground without Him?

"I thought, Wynnie, if there was such a God as you believed in, and with you to pray to Him, we shouldn't be long without a hearing," said my husband.

But our troubles weren't nearly over yet. Percivale wrote, acknowledging the letter, and requesting the money as he was in immediate want of it. The reply was that the trustees were not bound to pay the legacies for a year, but that possibly they might stretch a point in his favor if he applied to them. Percivale did so, but received a very curt answer, with little encouragement to expect anything but the extreme of legal delay. He received the money, however, about four months after, lightened, to the great disappointment of my ignorance, of thirty pounds legacy-duty.

In the meantime, although our minds were much relieved, and Percivale was working away at his new picture with great energy and courage, the immediate pressure of circumstances was nearly as painful as ever. It was a comfort, however, to know that we might borrow on the security of the legacy, but, greatly grudging the loss of the interest which that would involve, I would have persuaded Percivale to ask a loan of Lady Bernard. He objected, on the ground that it would be disagreeable to Lady Bernard to be repaid the sum she had lent us! He would have finally consented, however, I have little doubt, had the absolute necessity for borrowing arrived.

About a week or ten days after the blessed news, he had a note from Mr. Tait, whom he had authorized to part with the picture for thirty guineas. (How much this was under its value, it is not easy to say, but, if the fairy godmother's executors had paid her legacy at once, that picture would not have been sold for less than five times the amount. The last time it changed hands, it fetched five hundred and seventy pounds.)

Mr. Tait wrote that he had an offer of five and twenty for it, desiring to know whether he might sell it for that sum. Percivale at once gave his consent, and the next day received a check for eleven pounds and some odd shillings, the difference being the borrowed amount upon it, its interest, the commission charged on the sale, and the price of a small picture frame.

The next day, Percivale had a visitor at the studio—no less a person than Mr. Baddeley, with his shirtfront in full blossom, and his diamond wallowing in light on his fifth finger. His hands were as huge as they were soft and white—hands descended of generations of laborious ones, but which had never themselves done any work beyond paddling in money.

He greeted Percivale with a jolly condescension and told him that, having seen and rather liked a picture of his the other day, he had come to inquire whether he had one that would do for a pendant to it, as he should like to have it, provided he did not want a fancy price for it.

Percivale felt as if he were setting out his children for sale, as he invited him to look about the room, and turned round a few from against the wall. The great man flitted hither and thither, spying at one after another through the cylinder of his curved hand, Percivale going on with his painting as if no one were there.

"How much do you want for this sketch?" asked Mr. Baddeley, at length, pointing to one of the most highly finished paintings in the room.

"I put three hundred on it at the Academy Exhibition," answered Percivale. "My friends thought it too little, but as it has been on my hands a long time now, and pictures don't rise in price in the keeping of the painter, I shouldn't mind taking two for it."

"Two tens, I suppose you mean," said Mr. Baddeley.

Percivale gave him a look, and I know what kind of phenomenon that look must have been.

"Come, now," Mr. Baddeley went on, perhaps misinterpreting the look, for it was such as a man of his property was not in the habit of receiving. "You mustn't think I'm made of money, or that I'm a green hand in the market. I know what your pictures fetch, and I'm a pretty sharp man of business, I believe. What do you really mean to say and stick to? Ready money, you know."

"Three hundred," said Percivale coolly.

"Why, Mr. Percivale!" cried Mr. Baddeley, drawing himself up with the air of one who knew a trick worth two of that, "I paid Mr. Tait fifty pounds, neither more nor less, for a picture of yours yesterday—a picture, allow me to say, worth—"

He turned again to the one in question with a critical air, as if about to estimate to a fraction its value as compared with the other.

"Worth three of that, some people think," said Percivale.

"The price of this, then, joking aside, is—?"

"Three hundred pounds," answered Percivale quietly.

"I understood you wished to sell it," said Mr. Baddeley, begin-

ning, for all his good nature, to look offended, as well he might.
"I do wish to sell it. I happen to be in want of money."

"Then I'll be liberal, and offer you the same I paid for the other. I'll send you a check this afternoon for fifty—with pleasure."

"You cannot have that picture under three hundred."

"Why!" said the rich man, puzzled. "You offered it for two hundred, not five minutes ago."

"Yes, and you pretended to think I meant two tens."

"Offended you, I fear."

"At all events, betrayed so much ignorance of painting, that I would rather not have a picture of mine in your house."

"You're the first man who ever presumed to tell me I was ignorant of painting," said Mr. Baddeley, now thoroughly indignant.

"You have heard the truth, then, for the first time," said Percivale, and resumed his work.

Mr. Baddeley walked out of the study.

I am not sure that he was so very ignorant. He had been buying popular pictures for some time, paying thousands for certain of them. I suspect he had eye enough to see that my husband's would probably rise in value, and, with the true huckster spirit, was ambitious of boasting how little he had given compared with what they were really worth.

Percivale in this case was doubtless rude. He had an insuperable aversion to men of Mr. Baddeley's class—men who could have no position but for their money, and who yet presumed upon it, as if it were their gifts and graces, genius and learning, judgment and art, all in one.

Before long, through Lady Bernard, he sold a picture at a fair price, and soon after, seeing in a shop window the one Mr. Tait had sold to Mr. Baddeley, marked ten pounds now, went in and bought it. Within the year he sold it for a hundred and fifty.

By working day and night almost, he finished his new picture in time for the Academy—and, as he had himself predicted, it proved the best that he had ever painted. It was bought at once for three hundred pounds, and never since then have we been in want of money.

TWENTY-SIX

LADY BERNARD AGAIN

I have not mentioned Marion in these troubles. I could not bring myself to tell her of them, partly because she was in some trouble herself, from strangers who had taken rooms in the house and made mischief between her and her grandchildren, and partly because I knew she would insist on going to Lady Bernard. Although I should not have minded it myself, I knew that nothing but seeing the children hungry would have driven my husband to consent to it.

One evening, after it was all over, I told Lady Bernard the story. She allowed me to finish it without saying a word. When I had ended, she still sat silent for a few moments. Then laying her hand on my arm, she said, "My dear child, you were very wrong, as well as very unkind. Why did you not let me know?"

"Because my husband would never have allowed me," I answered.

"Then I must have a talk with your husband," she said.

"I wish you would," I replied, "for I can't help thinking Percivale too severe about such things."

The very next day she called, and did have a talk with him in the study.

"I have come to quarrel with you, Mr. Percivale," said Lady Bernard.

"I'm sorry to hear it," he returned. "You're the last person I should like to quarrel with, for it would imply some unpardonable fault in me."

"It does imply a fault—and a great one," she rejoined, "though I trust not an unpardonable one. That depends on whether you can repent of it."

She spoke with such a serious air that Percivale grew uneasy, and began to wonder what he could possibly have done to offend her.

When she saw him troubled, she smiled.

"Is it not a fault, Mr. Percivale, to prevent one from obeying the divine law of bearing another's burden?"

"But," said Percivale, "I read as well, that every man shall bear his own burden."

"Ah!" returned Lady Bernard, "but I learn that two different Greek words are used there, which we translate only by the English *burden*. I cannot tell you what they are. I can only tell you the practical result. We are to bear one another's burdens of pain or grief or misfortune or doubt—whatever weighs one down is to be borne by another. But the man who is tempted to exalt himself over his neighbors is taught to remember that he has his own load of grace to bear and answer for. It is just a weaker form of the lesson of the mote and the beam. You cannot get out at that door, Mr. Percivale. I beg you will read the passage in your Greek Testament, and see if you have not misapplied it. You *ought* to have let me bear your burden."

"Well, you see, my dear Lady Bernard," returned Percivale, at a loss to reply to such a vigorous assault, "I knew how it would be. You would have come here and bought pictures you didn't want, and I, knowing all the time you did it only to give me the money, should have had to talk to you as if I were taken by it, and I really could *not* stand it."

"There you are altogether wrong. Besides depriving me of the opportunity of fulfilling a duty, and of the pleasure and the honor of helping you to bear your burden, you have deprived me of the opportunity of indulging a positive passion for pictures. I am constantly compelled to restrain it lest I should spend too much of the money given me for the common good on my own private tastes. But here was a chance for me! I might have had some of your lovely pictures in my drawing room now, with a good conscience and a happy heart, if you had only been friendly. It was too bad of you, Mr. Percivale! I am not pretending in the least when I assert that I am really and thoroughly disappointed."

"I haven't a word to say for myself," returned Percivale.

"You couldn't have said a better word, then," rejoined Lady Bernard. "I hope you will never have to say it again."

"That I shall not. If ever I find myself in any difficulty worth speaking of, I will let you know at once."

"Thank you. Then we are friends again. And now I do think I am entitled to a picture—at least, I think it will be pardonable if I yield to the *very* strong temptation I am under at this moment to buy one. Let me see, what have you in the slave market, as your wife calls it?"

She bought *The Street Musician*, as Percivale had named that first picture he painted after his illness. I was more miserable than I ought to have been when I found he had parted with it, but it was a great consolation to think it had gone to Lady Bernard's. She was the only one, except my mother or Miss Clare, I could bear to think of as its possessor.

Percivale had asked her what I thought a very low price for it, and I judge that Lady Bernard thought the same. But after what had passed between them, she would not have ventured to expostulate. With such a man as my husband, I fancy, she thought it best to let well enough alone. Anyhow, one day soon after this, her servant brought him a little box, containing a fine brilliant.

"The good lady's kindness is longsighted," said my husband, as he placed it on his finger. "I shall be hard up, though, before I part with this. Wynnie, I've actually got a finer diamond than Mr. Baddeley! It *is* a beauty, if ever there was one!"

My husband, with all his carelessness of dress and adornment, has almost a passion for stones. It is delightful to hear him talk about them, but he had never possessed a single gem before Lady Bernard made him this present. I believe he is child enough to be happier for all his life.

TWENTY-SEVEN

MRS. CROMWELL COMES

The moment the legacy was paid and all our liabilities discharged, my husband took us all to Hastings. I had never before been to any other seacoast town where the land was worthy of the sea, except Kilkhaven. Assuredly, there is no place within easy reach of London to compare with Hastings. The immediate shore with its earthy cliffs is vastly inferior to the magnificent rock about Tintagel, but there is no outlook on the sea that I know more satisfying than that from the heights of Hastings, especially East Hill. From the west side you may, when weary of the ocean, look straight down on the ancient port, with its old houses and fine, multiform red roofs, through the gauze of blue smoke which a eve of a summer day fills the narrow valley, softening the rough goings-on of life with the gentleness of sea and shore, field and sky.

On the brow of East Hill, just where it begins to sink towards Ecclesbourne Glen, stands a small, old, rickety house in the midst of the sweet grass of the downs. This house my husband was fortunate in finding to let, and took for three months. It was there I made the acquaintance of Mrs. Cromwell.

One bright day, about noon, a rather fashionable maid ran up to our little garden, begging for some water for her mistress. Sending her on with water, I followed myself with a glass of sherry.

The door in our garden house opened immediately on a green hollow in the hill, sloping toward the glen. As I stepped from the little gate onto the grass, I saw, to my surprise, that a white fog was blowing in from the sea. The heights on the opposite side of the glen, partially obscured thereby, looked more majestic than was their wont, and were mottled with patches of duller and brighter color as the drifts of the fog were heaped or parted here or there. Far down, at the foot of the cliffs, the waves of the rising tide caught and threw back what sunlight reached them, and thinned with their shine the fog between. It was all so strange and fine, and had come on so suddenly, that I stood for a moment or two and gazed, almost forgetting why I was there.

Then I saw, in the sheltered hollow before me, a lady seated in a curiously shaped chair, a kind of litter. It was plain she was an invalid, from her paleness, and the tension of the skin on her face which revealed the outline of the bones beneath. Her features were finely formed, but rather small, and her forehead low—a Greek-like face with large, pale blue eyes that reminded me of little Amy Morley. She smiled very sweetly when she saw me, and shook her head at the wine.

"I only wanted a little water," she said. "This fog stifles me."

"It has come on very suddenly," I said. "Perhaps it is the cold of it that affects your breathing. You don't seem very strong, and any sudden change of temperature—"

"I am not the most vigorous of mortals," she answered with a sad smile. "But the day seemed of such indubitable character that, after my husband had brought me here in the carriage, he sent it home, and left me with my maid, while he went for a long walk across the downs. When he sees the change in the weather, though, he will turn directly."

"It won't do to wait him here," I said. "We must get you in at once! Would it be wrong to press you to take a little of this wine, just to counteract a chill?"

"I daren't touch anything but water," she replied. "It would make me feverish at once."

"Run and tell the cook," I said to the maid, "that I want her here. You and she could carry your mistress in, could you not?"

"There's no occasion for that, Ma'am. She's as light as a feather," was the whispered answer.

"I am quite ashamed of giving you so much trouble," said the lady, either hearing or guessing at our words. "My husband will be very grateful to you."

"It is only an act of common humanity," I said.

But, as I spoke, her fair brow clouded a little, as if she was not accustomed to common humanity, and the word sounded harsh in her ear. The cloud, however, passed so quickly that I doubted whether it had really been there.

Jemima and her own maid lifted her with the utmost ease and bore her gently towards the house. The garden gate was just wide enough to let the chair through, and in a minute more she was on the sofa. Then a fit of coughing came on which shook her dreadfully. When it had passed she lay quiet, with closed eyes, and a smile hovering about her sweet, thin-lipped mouth. By and by she opened her eyes and looked at me with a pitiful expression.

"I fear you are far from well," I said.

"I'm dying," she returned quietly.

"I hope not," was all I could answer.

"Why should you hope not?" she returned. "I desire to depart. For me to die will be all gain."

"But your friends?" I ventured to suggest, feeling my way, and not quite relishing either the form or tone of her utterance.

"I have none but my husband."

"Then your husband?" I persisted.

"Ah!" she said mournfully, "He will miss me, no doubt, for a while. But it *must* be a weight off him, for I have been a sufferer so long!"

At this moment I heard a heavy, hasty step in the passage. Then the door opened, and in rushed a burly man, clumsy and active, wiping his face with his hand. He carried an umbrella, and was followed by a great, lumbering Newfoundland dog.

"Down, Polyphemus!" he said to the dog, which crept under a chair. He, taking no notice of my presence, hurried up to his wife.

"My love! My little dove!" he said eagerly. "Did you think I had forsaken you to the cruel elements?"

"No, Alcibiades," she answered with a sweet little drawl. "But you do not observe that I am not the only lady in the room." Then, turning to me, "This is my husband, Mr. Cromwell," she said. "I cannot tell him *your* name."

"I am Mrs. Percivale," I returned, almost mechanically.

"I beg your pardon, Ma'am," said Mr. Cromwell, bowing. "Permit my anxiety about my poor wife to cover my rudeness. I had climbed the other side of the glen before I saw the fog, and it is no such easy matter to get up and down these hills of yours. I am greatly obliged to you for your hospitality. You have doubtless saved her life, for she is a frail flower, shrinking from the least breath of cold."

The lady closed her eyes again, and the gentleman took her hand and felt her pulse. He seemed about twice her age—she not thirty, he well past fifty, the top of his head bald, and his gray hair sticking out fiercely over his good-natured red cheeks. He laid her hand gently down, put his hat on the table and his umbrella in a corner, wiped his face again, drew a chair near the sofa, and took his place by her side. I thought it better to leave them.

When I reentered after a while, I saw from the seaward window that the wind had risen, and was driving great, thick, white masses of seafog landwards. It was the storm wind of that southwest coast which dashes the pebbles over the Parade, and the heavy spray against the houses. Mr. Alcibiades Cromwell was sitting as I had left him, silent, by the side of his wife, whose blue-veined eyelids had apparently never been lifted from her large eyes.

"Is there anything I could offer Mrs. Cromwell?" I said. "Could she not eat something?"

"It is very little she can take," he answered, "but you are very kind. If you could let her have a little beef tea? She generally has a spoonful or two about this time of day."

"I am sorry we have none," I said, "and it would be far too long for her to wait. I have a nice chicken, though, ready for cooking. If she could take a little chicken-broth, that would be ready in a very little while."

"Thank you a thousand times, Ma'am," he said heartily. "Nothing could be better. She might even be induced to eat a mouthful of the chicken. But I am afraid your extreme kindness prevents me from being so thoroughly ashamed as I ought to be at putting you to so much trouble for perfect strangers."

"It is a pleasure to be of service to anyone in want of it," I said. Mrs. Cromwell opened her eyes and smiled gratefully.

I left the room to give orders about the chicken. When I returned, Mr. Cromwell had open in his hand a little hymnbook of mine, and his wife was saying to him, "That is lovely! Thank you, Husband. How can it be I never saw it before? I am quite astonished."

"She little knows what multitudes of hymns there are!" I thought. My father's collection had given me some idea of the extent of that department of religious literature.

"This is a hymnbook we are not acquainted with," said Mr. Cromwell, addressing me.

"It is not much known," I answered. "It was compiled by a

friend of my father's for his own schools."

"And this," he went on, "is a very beautiful hymn. You may trust my wife's judgment, Mrs. Percivale. She lives on hymns."

In telling them a few of the facts connected with the hymn, I presume I had manifested my admiration with some degree of fervor.

"Ah!" said Mrs. Cromwell, opening her eyes very wide, and letting the rising tears fill them, "Ah! Mrs. Percivale! You are— you must be one of us!"

"You must tell me first who you are," I said.

She held out her hand, and I gave her mine. She drew me toward her, and whispered almost in my ear—though why the secrecy I can only imagine—the name of a certain small and exclusive sect.

"No," I answered, speaking with the calmness of self-compulsion, for I confess I felt repelled. "I am not one of you, except as we all belong to the Church of Christ."

She gave a little sigh of disappointment, closed her eyes for a moment, opened them again with a smile and said, with a pleading tone, "But you do believe in personal religion?"

"I don't see," I returned, "how religion can be anything but personal."

Again she closed her eyes in a way that made me think how convenient bad health must be—conferring not only the privilege of passing into retirement at any desirable moment, but of doing so in such a ready and easy manner as the mere dropping of the eyelids.

I rose to leave the room once more. Mr. Cromwell, who had made way for me to sit beside his wife, stood looking out the window, against which came sweeping the great volumes of mist. Not only was the sea invisible, but even the brow of the cliffs.

When he turned toward me, I saw that his face had lost much of its rubicund hue, and looked troubled and anxious.

"There is nothing for it," I said to myself, "but to keep them all night." I did not much like it, I confess, for I was not much interested in either of them, while the sect to which she belonged was the narrowest and most sectarian in Christendom. It was a pity she had sought to claim me by a would-be closer bond than that of the Body of Christ. At the same time I did feel some curiosity concerning the oddly yoked couple, and wondered whether the lady was really so ill as she would appear. She might be using her illness both as an excuse for self-indulgence, and as a means of keeping her husband's interest. I did not like the wearing of her religion on her sleeve, nor the mellifluous drawl in which she spoke.

When the chicken broth was ready, she partook daintily, but before she ended had made a very good meal, including a wing and a bit of the breast, after which she fell asleep.

"There seems little chance of the weather clearing," said Mr. Cromwell in a whisper, as I approached the window where he once more stood.

"You must remain here for the night," I said.

"My dear Madam, I couldn't think of it," he returned. "She requires so many little comforts and peculiar contrivances to entice repose, that I must get her home."

"Where do you live?" I asked, not sorry to find his intention of going so fixed.

"We have a house in Warrior Square," he answered. "We live in London, but have been here all the past winter. I doubt if she improves, though."

He said the last words in a yet lower and more mournful whisper. Then, with a shake of his head, he turned and gazed again through the window.

A peculiar little cough from the sofa made us both look round. Mrs. Cromwell was awake and searching for her handkerchief. Her husband understood her movements and hurried to her assistance. When she took the handkerchief from her mouth, there was a red spot against the white. Mr. Cromwell's face turned the color of lead, but his wife looked up at him and smiled a sweet, consciously pathetic smile.

"He has sent for me," she said. "The messenger has come."

Her husband made no answer. His eyes seemed starting from his head.

"Who is your medical man?" I asked.

He told me, and I sent off my housemaid to fetch him. It was a long hour before he arrived. As often as I peeped in, I saw Mr. Cromwell sitting silent, and holding her head, until the last time, when I found him reading a hymn to her. She was apparently once more asleep.

When the doctor came, he proceeded to examine her with much care, and averred in her hearing that he found nothing serious. But he told her husband apart that there was considerable mischief, and assured me afterward that her lungs were all but gone, and that she could not live beyond a month or two. She had better be removed to her own house, he said, as speedily as possible.

"But it would be cruelty to send her out in a day like this," I returned.

"Yes, yes. I did not mean that," he said. "But tomorrow, perhaps. You'll see what the weather is like. Is Mrs. Cromwell an old friend?"

"I have never seen her until today," I replied.

"Ah!" he remarked, and said no more.

It was a week before she got up again, and a month before she was carried down the hill, during which time her husband sat up with her, or slept on a sofa in the room beside her, every night. During the day I took a share in the nursing, which was by no means oppressive, for she did not suffer much, and required little. Her chief demand was for hymns, and the only annoyance was that she often wished me to admire with her such as I could only half like, and occasionally such as were thoroughly distasteful to me. Her husband had brought her own collection from Warrior Square—volumes of hymns in manuscript, copied by her own hand, many of them strange to me. None of those I read were altogether devoid of literary merit, and some of them were lovely both in feeling and form. But all, even the best, belonged to one class—a class breathing a certain tone difficult to describe. What pleased me in them was their full utterance of personal devotion to the Saviour, and what displeased me was a sort of sentimental regard of self in the matter—an implied special, and thus partially exclusive, preference of the Saviour for the individual making use of them. It was a certain fundamental want of humility, therefore, although the forms of speech in which they were cast might be laboriously humble. They also not unfrequently manifested a great leaning to the forms of earthly show as representative of the glories of that kingdom which the Lord says is *within us*.

One morning, the fine weather returned in all its summer glory, and Mrs. Cromwell was lying on a couch in her own room near the window, where she could gaze on the expanse of sea below. This morning it was streaked with the most delicate gradations of distance, sweep beyond sweep, line and band and ribbon of softly varying hue, leading the eyes on and on into the infinite. There may have been some atmospheric illusion ending off the show, for the last reaches so mingled with the air that you saw no horizon line, only a great breadth of border—no spot you could assign with certainty either to sea or sky, while here and there was a vessel appearing to pursue its path in the sky, and not upon the sea. It was a still, gray forenoon, with a film of cloud over all the heavens, and many horizontal strata of deeper but varying density near the horizon.

Mrs. Cromwell had lain for some time with her large eyes fixed on the farthest confusion of sea and sky.

"I have been sending out my soul," she said at length, "to travel all across those distances, step by step, on to the gates of pearl. Who knows but that may be the path I must travel to meet the Bridegroom?"

"The way is wide," I said. "What if you should miss Him?"

I spoke almost involuntarily. The style of her talk was very distasteful to me, and I had just been thinking of what I had once heard my father say, that at no time were people in more danger of being theatrical than when upon their deathbeds.

"No," she returned, with a smile of gentle superiority. "No, that cannot be. Is He not waiting for me? Has He not chosen me, and called me for His own? Is not my Jesus mine? I shall *not* miss Him. He waits to give me my new name and clothe me in the garments of righteousness."

As she spoke, she clasped her thin hands and looked upward with a radiant expression. Far as it was from me to hint, even in my own soul, that the Saviour was not hers, yet tenfold more hers than she was able to think, I doubted whether her heart and soul and mind were as close to Him as she thought. She could not be wrong in trusting Him, but could she be right in her notion of the measure to which her union with Him had been perfected? A little fear, soon to pass into reverence, might be to her a salutary thing. The fear would heighten and deepen the love, and purify it from that self which haunted her whole consciousness, and of which she had not yet sickened, as one day she certainly must.

"My lamp is burning," she said. "I feel it burning. I love my Lord. It would be false to say otherwise."

"Are you sure you have oil enough in your vessel as well as in your lamp?" I said.

"Ah, you are one of the doubting!" she returned kindly. "Don't you know that sweet hymn about feeding our lamps from the olive trees of Gethsemane? The idea is taken from the lamp the Prophet Zechariah saw in his vision, into which two olive branches, through two golden pipes, emptied the golden oil out of them-selves. If we are thus one with the olive tree, the oil cannot fail us. It is not as if we had to fill our lamps from a cruse of our own. This is the cruse that cannot fail."

"True, true," I said, "but ought we not to examine our own selves whether we are in the faith?"

"Let those examine who doubt," she replied, and I could not but yield in my heart that she had had the best of the argument.

For I knew that the confidence in Christ which prevents us from thinking of ourselves, and makes us eager to obey His Word, leav-ing all the care of our feelings to Him, is a true and healthy faith. Hence I could not answer her, although I doubted for several reasons whether her peace came from such confidence. One, that she seemed full of herself. Another, that she seemed to find no difficulty with herself in any way, and surely, she was too young for all struggle to be over! I perceived no reference to the will of God in regard of anything she had to do, only in regard of what she had to suffer, and especially in regard of that smallest of matters, when she was to go. Here I checked myself, for what could she *do* in such a state of health? But then she never spoke as if she had any anxiety about the welfare of other people. That, however, might be from her absolute contentment in the will of God.

But why did she always look to the Saviour through a mist of hymns, and never go straight back to the genuine old Good News, or to the mighty thoughts and exhortations with which the first preachers of that news followed them up and unfolded the gran-deur of their goodness?

But I had no right to say anything, and to be uneasy about her was to distrust Him whose it was to teach her, and who would perfect that which He had certainly begun in her. For her heart, however poor and faulty and flimsy its faith might be, was yet certainly drawn toward the object of faith. I, therefore, said noth-ing. My plain duty was to serve her as one of those least whom the Saviour set forth as representing Himself. I would do it to her as unto Him.

My children were out the greater part of the day, and Dora was with me, so that I had more leisure than I had had for a long time. I therefore set myself to wait upon her as a kind of lady's maid in things spiritual. Her own maid, understanding her ways, was suffi-cient for things temporal. I resolved to try to help her after her own fashion, and not after mine, for however strange the nourishment she preferred, it must at length be of the kind she could best assimilate. My care should be to give her her gruel as good as I might, and her beef tea strong, with chicken broth instead of barley water and delusive jelly.

I could set myself to find fitting pabulum for her, and that of her chosen sort. This was possible for me in virtue of my father's collection of hymns, and the aid he could give me. I therefore sent him a detailed description of what seemed to me her condition, and what I thought I might do for her. His answer arrived in the shape of a box of books, each bristling with paper marks, many of them inscribed with some fact concerning, or criticism upon, the hymn indicated. And he wrote that he quite agreed with my notion of the right mode of serving her.

I judged that in all of my father's hymns there was something she must appreciate, although the main drift of several would be entirely beyond her apprehension. Accordingly, the next time she asked me to read from her collection, I made the request that she would listen to some of which I believed she did not know, but would, I thought, like. She consented with eagerness, was astonished to find she knew none of them, expressed much approbation of some, and showed herself delighted with others.

That she must have had some literary faculty seems evident from the genuine pleasure she took in simple, quaint, sometimes odd hymns of her own peculiar kind. But the very best of another sort she could not appreciate.

However, my endeavors were crowned with success in so far that she accepted better specimens of the sort she liked than any she had, and I think they must have had a good influence upon her.

She seemed to have no fear of death, contemplating the change she believed at hand, not with equanimity merely, but with expectation. She even wrote hymns about it—sweet, pretty, and weak, always with herself and the love of her Saviour for *her* in the foreground.

One of my conversations with her took place the evening before her departure for her own house. Her husband had gone to make some final preparations. For one who expected to be unclothed that she might be clothed upon, she certainly made a tolerable to-do about the garment she was so soon to lay aside, especially seeing she often spoke of it as an ill-fitting garment—never with peevishness or complaint, only, as it seemed to me, with far more interest than it was worth. Perhaps I should have been considerably less bewildered with her conduct had I suspected that she was not half so near death as she chose to think, and that she had as yet suffered little.

That evening, the stars just beginning to glimmer through the warm flush that lingered from the sunset, we sat together in the drawing room looking out on the sea. My patient appearing, from the light in her eyes, about to go off into one of her ecstatic moods, I hastened to forestall it.

"It seems like turning you out to let you go tomorrow, Mrs. Cromwell," I said, "but, you see, our three months are up two days after that, and I cannot help it."

"You have been very kind," she said, half abstractedly.

"And you are really much better. Who would have thought three weeks ago to see you so well today?"

"Ah, you congratulate me, do you?" she rejoined, turning her big full eyes upon me. "Congratulate me that I am doomed to be still a captive in the prison of this vile body? Is it kind? Is it well?"

"At least, you must remember, if you are doomed, who dooms you."

"Oh, that I had the wings of a dove!" she cried, avoiding my remark, of which I doubt she saw the drift. "Think, dear Mrs. Percivale, the society of saints and angels—all brightness and harmony and peace! Is it not worth forsaking this world to inherit a kingdom like that? Wouldn't *you* like to go? Don't you wish to fly away and be at rest?"

She spoke as if expostulating and reasoning with one she would persuade to some kind of holy emigration.

"Not until I am sent for," I answered.

"*I* am sent for," she returned, and then recited,

Here all my labor is so poor!
Here all my love so faint!
But when I reach the heavenly door,
I cease the weary plaint.

I couldn't help wishing she would cease her plaint a little sooner.

"But suppose," I ventured to say, "it were the will of God that you should live many years yet."

"That cannot be. And why should you wish it for me? Is it not better to depart and be with Him? What pleasure could it be to a weak, worn creature like me to go on living in this isle of banishment?"

"But suppose you were to recover your health? Would it not be delightful to *do* something for His sake? If you would think of how much there is to be done in the world, perhaps you would wish less to die and leave it."

"Do not tempt me," she returned reproachfully. And then she quoted a passage of application, which to her own case appeared to me so irreverent that I felt I could bear with her no longer.

She did leave the next day and I breathed more freely than since she had come

I concluded that Mrs. Cromwell was but a spoiled child, who would, somehow or other, be brought to her senses before all was over. I was ashamed of my impatience with her, and believed if I could have learned her history, it would have explained the rare phenomenon of one apparently able to look death in the face with so little of the really spiritual to support her; for she seemed to me to know Christ only after the flesh. But had she indeed ever looked death in the face?

TWENTY-EIGHT

MRS. CROMWELL GOES

I heard nothing more of Mrs. Cromwell for about a year. A note or two passed between us, and then all communication ceased. This, I am happy to think, was not immediately my fault; not that it mattered much, for we were not then fitted for much communion—we had too little in common.

We could not commune, that is, with any heartiness. The Saviour of whom she spoke so often, and evidently thought so much, was in a great measure a being of her own fancy. She manifested no desire to find out who the Christ was who had spent thirty-three years making a revelation of Himself to the world. The knowledge she had about Him was not even secondhand, but at many removes. She did not study His words or His actions to learn His thought or His meanings, but lived in a kind of dreamland of her own, which could be interesting only to the dreamer. She did not take the trouble to "know Him and the power of His resurrection." Therefore we had scarcely enough common ground to meet upon. I could not help contrasting her religion with that of Marion Clare.

At length I had a note from her, begging me to go and see her at her house in Richmond, and apologizing for not coming to me, on the score of her health. I felt it my duty to go, but sadly grudged the loss of time, for I expected neither pleasure nor profit from the visit. Percivale went with me, and left me at the door to have a row on the river, and to call for me at a certain hour.

The house and grounds were both luxurious and lovely—two

qualities often dissociated. She could have nothing to desire of this world's gifts, I thought. But the moment I saw her, I was shocked at the change. She was in a widow's cap, and disease and coming death were plain on every feature. The face I had held in my memory was healthy in contrast.

"My dear Mrs. Cromwell!" I gasped.

"You see," she said, and sitting down on a straight-backed chair, looked at me with lustreless eyes.

Death had been hovering about her windows before, but had entered at last—not to take the sickly young woman longing to die, but the hale man who would have clung to the last edge of life.

"He is taken and I am left," she said abruptly.

Her drawl had vanished. Pain and grief had made her simple. "Then," I thought with myself, "she did love him!" But I could say nothing. She took my silence for the sympathy it was, and smiled a heartrending smile, so different from that little sad smile she used to have—really pathetic now, and with hardly a glimmer in it of the old self-pity. I rose, put my arms about her, and kissed her on the forehead. She laid her head on my shoulder and wept.

"Whom the Lord loveth He chasteneth," I faltered out, for her sorrow filled me with new respect.

"Yes," she returned, as gently as hopelessly. "And whom He does not love, as well."

"You have no grounds for saying so," I answered. "The Apostle does not."

"My lamp is gone out," she said, "gone out in darkness, utter darkness. You warned me, and I did not heed the warning. I thought I knew better, but I was full of self-conceit. And now I am wandering where there is no way and no light. My iniquities have found me out."

I did not say what I saw plain enough—that her lamp was just beginning to burn. Neither did I try to persuade her that her iniquities were small.

"But the Bridegroom," I said, "is not yet come. There is time to go and get some oil."

"Where am I to get it?" she returned, in a tone of despair.

"From the Bridegroom Himself," I said.

"No," she answered. "I have talked and talked and talked, and you know He says He abhors talkers. I am one of those to whom He will say, 'I know you not.'

"And you will answer Him that you have eaten and drunk in

191

His presence, and cast out devils, and—?"

"No, no. I will say that He is right—that it was all my own fault, and that I thought I was something when I was nothing, but that I know better now."

A dreadful fit of coughing interrupted her. As soon as it was over, I said, "And what will the Lord say to you, do you think, when you have said so to Him?"

"Depart from Me," she answered in a hollow, forced voice.

"No," I returned. "He will say, 'I know you well. You have told Me the truth. Come in.' "

"*Do* you think so?" she cried. "You never used to think well of me."

"Those who were turned away," I said, avoiding her last words, "were trying to make themselves out better than they were. They trusted not in the love of Christ but in what they thought their worth and social standing. Perhaps, if their deeds had been as good as they thought them, they would have known better than to trust in them. If they had told Him the truth, if they had said, 'Lord, we are workers of iniquity. Lord, we used to be hypocrites, but we speak the truth now—forgive us,' do you think He would have them turned away? No, surely. If your lamp is gone out, make haste and tell Him how careless you have been. Tell Him all, and pray Him for oil and light, and see whether your lamp will not straightway glimmer—glimmer first, then glow."

"Ah, Mrs. Percivale!" she cried. "I would *do* something for His sake now if I might, but I cannot. If I had but resisted the disease in me for the sake of serving Him, I might have been able now. But my chance is over: I cannot now—I have too much pain. And death looks such a different thing now! I used to think of it only as a kind of going to sleep, easy though sad—sad, I mean, in the eyes of mourning friends. But I have no friends, now that my husband is gone! I never dreamed of him going first. He loved me—indeed he did, though I always took it as a matter of course. I never saw how beautiful and unselfish he was till he was gone. I have been selfish and stupid and dull, and my sins have found me out. A great darkness has fallen upon me, and although weary of life, instead of longing for death, I shrink from it with horror. My cough will not let me sleep, and there is nothing but weariness in my body, and despair in my heart. Oh, how black and dreary the nights are! I think of the time in your house as an earthly paradise. But where is the heavenly paradise I used to dream of then?"

"Would it content you," I asked, "to be able to dream of it again?"

"No, no. I want something very different now. Those fancies look so uninteresting and stupid now! All I want now is to hear God say, 'I forgive you.' And my husband—I must have troubled him sorely. You don't know how good he was, Mrs. Percivale. *He* made no pretenses like silly me. Do you know," she went on, lowering her voice, and speaking with something like horror in its tone, "do you know, I cannot *bear* hymns?"

As she said it, she looked up in my face, half-terrified with the anticipation of the horror she expected to see manifested there. I could not help smiling. The case was not one for argument of any kind. I thought for a moment, then merely repeated a verse:

When the law threatens endless death,
Upon the awful hill,
Straightway, from her consuming breath,
My soul goeth higher still—
Goeth to Jesus, wounded, slain,
And maketh Him her home again,
And where Death cannot come.

"Ah! That is good," she said. "If only I could get to Him. But I cannot. He is so far off! He seems to be—nowhere."

I think she was going to say *nobody*, but changed the word.

"If you felt for a moment how helpless and wretched I feel, especially in the early morning," she went on, "how there seems nothing to look for, and no help to be had—you would pity rather than blame me, though I know I deserve blame. I feel as if all the heart and soul and strength and mind, with which we are told to love God, has gone out of me, or rather, as if I had never had any. I doubt if I ever had. I tried very hard for a long time to get a sight of Jesus, to feel myself in His presence, but it was of no use, and I have quite given it up now."

I made her lie on the sofa, and I sat down beside her.

"Do you think," I said, "that anyone, before He came, could have imagined such a visitor to the world as Jesus Christ?"

"I suppose not," she answered listlessly.

"Then, no more can you come near Him now by trying to imagine Him. You cannot represent to yourself the reality, the Being who can comfort you. You cannot take Him into your heart.

Only He knows Himself, and only He can reveal Himself to you. And not until He does can you find any certainty or any peace."

"But He doesn't—He won't reveal Himself to me."

"Suppose you had forgotten what some friend of your childhood was like—say, if it were possible, your own mother. Suppose you could not recall a feature of her face or the color of her eyes. And suppose that while you were very miserable about it, you remembered all at once that you had a portrait of her in an old desk you had not opened for years. What would you do?"

"Go and get it," she answered like a child at the Sunday School.

"Then why shouldn't you do so now? You have such a portrait of Jesus, far truer and more complete than any other kind of portrait can be—the portrait His own deeds and words give us of Him."

"I see what you mean, but that is all about long ago, and I want Him now. That is in a book, and I want Him in my heart."

"How are you to get Him into your heart? How could you have Him there, except by knowing Him? But perhaps you think you do know Him?"

"I am certain I do not know Him—at least, as I want to know Him," she said.

"No doubt," I went on, "He can speak to your heart without the record and, I think, is speaking to you now in this very want of Him you feel. But how could He show Himself to you otherwise than by helping you to understand the revelation of Himself which cost Him such labor? If the story were millions of years old, so long as it were true, it would be all the same as if it had been only yesterday; for, being what He represented Himself, He can never change. To know what He was then is to know what He is now."

"But, if I knew Him so, that wouldn't be to have Him with me."

"No, but in that knowledge He might come to you. It is by the door of that knowledge that His Spirit, which is Himself, comes into the soul. You would at least be more able to pray to Him. You would know what kind of a being you had to cry to. *You* would thus come nearer to Him, and no one ever drew nigh to Him whom He did not also draw nigh. If you would but read the story as if you had never read it before, as if you were reading the history of a man you heard of for the first time—"

I ceased, and for some moments she sat silent. Then she said feebly, "There's a Bible somewhere in the room."

I found it and read the story of the woman who came from behind Him in terror, and touched the hem of His garment. I could hardly read it for the emotion it caused in myself, and when I ceased I saw her weeping silently.

A servant entered with the message that Mr. Percivale had called for me.

"I cannot see him today," she sobbed.

"Of course not," I replied. "I must leave you now, but I will come again—come as often as you like."

"You are as kind as ever!" she returned, with a fresh burst of tears. "Will you come and be with me when—when—?"

She could not finish for sobs.

"I will," I said, knowing well what she meant.

And I know her story now. When her husband died suddenly, of apoplexy, she was stunned for a time, gradually awaking to a miserable sense of unprotected loneliness, so much the more painful for her weakly condition and the overcare to which she had been accustomed. Left thus without shelter, like a delicate plant whose house of glass has been shattered, she speedily recognized her true condition. With no one to heed her whims, and no one capable of sympathizing with the genuine misery which supervened, her disease gathered strength rapidly, her lamp went out, and she saw no light beyond—for the smoke of that lamp had dimmed the windows at which the stars would have looked in. She saw that she was poor and miserable and blind and naked, that she had never had faith fit to support her.

But out of this darkness dawned at least a twilight, gradual, slow. She became aware of a deeper and simpler need than hitherto she had known—the need of life in herself, the life of the Son of God.

I went to see her often, going every other day and sometimes oftener, for her end seemed to be drawing nigh. Her weakness had greatly increased: she could but just walk across the room, and was constantly restless. She had no great continuous pain, but oft-returning sharp fits of it. She looked genuinely sad, and her spirits never recovered themselves. She seldom looked out of the window, for the daylight seemed to distress her. Flowers were the only links between her and the outer world—wild ones, for the scent of greenhouse flowers, and even that of most garden ones, she could not bear. She had been very fond of music, but could no longer endure her piano—every note seemed to strike on a nerve. But she was generally quiet in her mind and often peaceful. The more her body decayed, the more her spirit seemed to come alive. It was the calm of a gray evening, not so lovely as a golden sunset or a silvery moonlight, but more sweet than either. She talked little of her feelings, but evidently longed after the words of our Lord. As she listened to some of them, I could see the eyes, which had now grown dim with suffering, gleam with the light of holy longing and humble adoration.

She often referred to her coming departure, and confessed that she feared death—not so much what might be on the other side, as the dark way itself, the struggle, the torture, the fainting. But by degrees her allusions to it became rarer, and at length ceased almost entirely.

Once I said to her, "Are you afraid of death still, Eleanor?"

"No, not much," she replied, after a brief pause. "He may do with me whatever He likes."

Knowing so well what Marion could do to comfort and support, and therefore desirous of bringing them together, I took her one day with me. Before we left, it was plain that Marion had a far more soothing influence upon her than I had myself. She looked eagerly to her next visit, and my mind was now more at peace concerning her.

One evening, after listening to some stories from Marion about her friends, Mrs. Cromwell said, "Ah, Miss Clare! To think I might have done something for *Him* by doing it for *them!* Alas! I have led a useless life, and am dying out of this world without having borne any fruit! Ah, me, me!"

"You are doing a good deal for Him now," said Marion, "and hard work too! Harder far than mine."

"I am only dying," she returned, so sadly.

"You are enduring chastisement," said Marion. "The Lord gives one person one thing to do, and another person another. We have no right to wish for other work than He gives us. It is rebellious and unchildlike, whatever it may seem. Neither have we any right to wish to be better in *our* way; we must wish to be better in *His*.

"And what is the will of God? Is it not your sanctification? And why did He make the Captain of our salvation perfect through suffering? Was it not that He might in like manner bring many sons into glory? Then, if you are enduring, you are working with God for the perfection through suffering of one more. You are working for God in yourself, that the will of God may be done in you, that He may have His very own way with you. It is the only work He requires of you now; do it not only willingly, then, but contentedly. To make people good is all His labor. Be good, and you are a fellow worker with God in the highest region of labor. He does not want you for other people—yet."

One evening, when we were both with her, it had grown very sultry and breathless.

"Isn't it very close, dear Mrs. Percivale?" she said.

I rose to get a fan, and Marion, leaving the window as if moved by a sudden resolve, went and opened the piano. Mrs. Cromwell made a hasty motion, as if she must prevent her. But, such was my faith in my friend's soul as well as her heart, in her divine taste as well as her human faculty, that I laid my hand on Mrs. Cromwell's. It was enough for sweetness like hers; she yielded instantly and lay still, evidently nerving herself to suffer. But the first movement stole so "soft and soullike" on her ear, trembling as it were on the borderland between sound and silence, that she missed the pain she expected and found only the pleasure she looked not for. Marion's hands made the instrument sigh and sing, not merely as with a human voice, but as with a human soul. Marion's voice next stole its way into her heart, to set first one chord then another vibrating, until the whole soul was filled with responses.

Where she got the song she then sang, she always avoids telling me. I had told her all I knew and understood concerning Mrs. Cromwell, and have my suspicions. This was her song:

I fancy I hear a whisper
As of leaves in a gentle air:
Is it wrong, I wonder, to fancy
It may be the tree up there?
The tree that heals the nations,
Growing amidst the street,
And dropping, for who will gather,
Its apples at their feet?

I fancy I hear a rushing
As of waters down a slope:
Is it wrong, I wonder, to fancy
It may be the river of hope?
The river of crystal waters
That flows from the very throne,

And runs through the street of the city
With a softly jubilant sound?

I fancy a twilight around me,
And a wandering of the breeze,
With a hush in that high city,
And a going in the trees.
But I know there will be no night there—
No coming and going day;
For the holy face of the Father
Will be perfect light alway.

I could do without the darkness,
And better without the sun;
But, oh, I should like a twilight
After the day was done!
Would He lay His hand on my forehead,
On His hair as white as wool,
And shine one hour through His fingers,
Till the shadow had made me cool?

But the thought is very foolish:
If that face I did but see,
All else would be forgotten—
River and twilight and tree;
I should seek, I should care, for nothing,
Beholding His countenance;
And fear only to lose one glimmer
By one single sideway glance.

'Tis but again a foolish fancy
To picture the countenance so,
Which is shining in all our spirits,
Making them white as snow.
Come to me, shine in me, Master,
And I care not for river or tree—
Care for no sorrow or crying,
If only Thou shine in me.

I would lie on my bed for ages,
Looking out on the dusty street,

Where whisper nor leaves nor waters,
Nor anything cool and sweet;
At my heart this ghastly fainting,
And this burning in my blood—
If only I knew Thou wast with me—
Wast with me and making me good.

When Marion rose from the piano, Mrs. Cromwell stretched out her hand for hers, and held it for some time, unable to speak. Then she said, "That has done me good, I hope. I will try to be more patient, for I think *He* is teaching me."

She died, at length, in my arms. I cannot linger over the last time. She suffered a good deal, but went without a struggle. The last words I heard her utter were, "Yes, Lord," after which she breathed but once. A half-smile came over her face, which froze upon it and remained as the coffin lid covered it. But I shall see it, I trust, a whole smile some day.

TWENTY-NINE

DOUBLE, DOUBLE, TOIL
AND TROUBLE

I had for a day or two fancied that Marion was looking less bright than usual, as if some little shadow had fallen upon the morning of her life. She must now have been twenty-seven or twenty-eight. Unwilling at once to assert the ultimate privilege of friendship, I asked her if anything was amiss with her friends. She answered that all was going on well, at least so far that she had no special anxiety about any of them. Encouraged by a half-conscious and more than half-sad smile, I ventured a little further.

"I am afraid there is something troubling you," I said.

"There is," she replied, "Something is troubling me a good deal, but I hope it will pass away soon."

The sigh which followed, however, seemed to indicate a fear that the trouble might not pass away so very soon.

"I am not to ask you any questions, I suppose," I returned.

"Better not at present," she answered. "I am not quite sure that—"

She paused several moments before finishing her sentence, then added, "—that I am at liberty to tell you about it."

"Then don't say another word," I rejoined. "Only when I can be of service to you, you *will* let me know, won't you?"

The tears rose to her eyes. "I'm afraid it may be some fault of mine," she said. "I can't tell. I don't understand such things."

She sighed again, and held her peace.

It was enigmatic enough, but I held my peace, and in a few

minutes Marion went, with a more affectionate leave-taking than usual.

I pondered, but it was not of much use. Of course, the first thing that suggested itself was, Could my angel be in love? And with some mere mortal? Being a woman, she *might* be in love, but the two ideas, *Marion* and *love*, refused to coalesce. And again, was it likely that she, her mind occupied with so many other absorbing interests, would fall in love unprovoked, unsolicited? That was not likely. Then if solicited, she but returned love for love, why was she sad? The new experience might trouble her greatly. She would not know what to do with it, nor where to accommodate her new inmate so as to keep him from meddling with affairs he had no right to meddle with. It was easy enough to fancy him troublesome in a house like hers. But surely of all women *she* might be able to meet her own liabilities. And if this were all, why should she have said she hoped it would soon pass? That might, however, mean only that she hoped soon to get her guest brought amenable to her existing household economy.

Yet another conjecture seemed to suit the case better. If Marion knew little of what is commonly called love, there was no one who knew more of the tenderness of compassion than she, and it was not possible someone might be wanting to marry her, to whom she could not give herself away?

This at least covered the facts in my possession. But who was there to dare offer love to my saint? Roger? Pooh! Pooh! Mr. Blackstone? Ah! I had seen him lately looking at her with an expression of more than ordinary admiration. But what man who knew anything of her could help looking at her with such admiration? If it was Mr. Blackstone why—*he* might dare—yes, why should he not dare to love her? Especially if he couldn't help it, as, of course, he couldn't. Was he not one whose love, simply because he was a *true* man from the heart to the hands, would honor any woman, even Saint Clare—as she must become when the church has learned to do its business without the pope?

If it were Mr. Blackstone, certainly I knew no man who could understand her better, or whose modes of thinking and working would more thoroughly fall in with her own. True, he was peculiar—that is, he had kept the angles of his individuality, for all the grinding of the social mill. His manners were too abrupt, and drove at the heart of things too directly, seldom suggesting a by-your-leave to those whose prejudices he overturned. True also that

his person, though dignified, was somewhat ungainly, with an un-
gainliness, however, which I could well imagine a wife learning
absolutely to love. On the whole, the thing was reasonable. Only
what would become of her friends? There, I could hardly doubt,
there lay the difficulty!

Let no one think, when I say we went to Mr. Blackstone's
church, that it had anything to do with these speculations. We
often went there on the first Sunday of the month.

"What's the matter with Blackstone?" said my husband as we
came home.

"What do *you* think is the matter with him?" I returned.

"I don't know. He wasn't himself."

"I thought he was more than himself," I rejoined, "for I never
heard even *him* read the litany with such fervor."

"In some of the petitions," said Percivale, "it amounted to a
suppressed agony of supplication. I am certain he is in trouble."

I told him my suspicions.

"Likely—very likely," he answered, and became thoughtful.

"But you don't think she refused him?" he said at length.

"If he ever asked her," I returned, "I fear she did, for she is
plainly in trouble too."

"She'll never stick to it," he said.

"You mustn't judge Marion by ordinary standards," I replied.
"You must remember she has not only found her vocation, but for
many years has proved it. I never knew her to turn aside from
what she made up her mind to. I can hardly imagine her forsaking
her friends to keep house for any man, even if she loved him with
all her heart. She is dedicated as irrevocably as any nun, and will,
with St. Paul, cling to the right of self-denial."

"Yet what great difficulty would there be in combining the two
sets of duties, especially with such a man as Blackstone? Of all the
men I know, he comes the nearest to her in his devotion to the
well-being of humanity, especially of the poor. Did you ever know
a man with such a plentiful lack of condescension?"

"That may be. He is the same all through and—I had almost
said—worthy of Saint Clare. Well, they must settle it for themselves. We can do nothing."

"We can do nothing," he assented, and, although we repeatedly
reverted to the subject on the way home, we carried no conclusions
to a different result.

Toward evening, Roger came to accompany us, as I thought, to

Marion's gathering. But, as it turned out, he only told me he couldn't go. I expressed my regret, and asked him why. He gave me no answer, and his lip trembled. A sudden conviction seized me. I laid my hand on his arm, but could only say, "Dear Roger!" He turned his head aside and, sitting down on the sofa, laid his forehead on his hand.

"I'm so sorry!" I said.

"She has told you then?" he murmured.

"No one has told me anything."

He was silent. I sat down beside him. It was all I could do. After a moment he rose, saying, "There's no good whining about it, only she might have made a man of me. But she's quite right. It's a comfort to think I'm so unworthy of her. That's all the consolation left me, but there's more in that than you think."

He attempted to laugh, but made a miserable failure of it, then rose and caught up his hat to go. I rose also.

"Roger," I said, "I can't leave you miserable. We'll go somewhere else—anywhere you please, only you mustn't leave us."

"I don't want to go somewhere else. I don't know the place," he added, with a feeble attempt at his usual gaiety.

"Stop at home, then, and tell me all about it. It will do you good to talk. You shall have your pipe, and you shall tell me just as much as you like, and keep the rest to yourself."

I ran to Percivale, gave him a hint of how it was, and demanded his pipe, telling him he must be content with a cigar.

I returned to Roger, who took it and began to fill it mechanically, but not uncarefully. I sat down, laid my hands in my lap, and looked at him without a word. When the pipe was filled I rose and got him a light. Having whiffed a good many whiffs in silence, he took his pipe from his mouth, and said, "I've made a fool of myself, Wynnie."

"Not more than a gentleman had a right to do, I will pledge myself," I returned.

"She *has* told you, then?" he said once more, looking rather disappointed than annoyed.

"No one has mentioned your name to me, Roger. I only guessed it from what Marion said when I questioned her about her sad looks."

"Her sad looks?"

"Yes."

"What did she say?"

"She only confessed she had had something to trouble her, and said she hoped it would soon be over."

"I dare say!" returned Roger dryly, looking gratified however, for a moment.

"You see, Wynnie," he said, with pauses, and puffs at his pipe, "I don't mean I'm a fool for falling in love with Marion. Not to have fallen in love with her would have argued me a beast. Being a man, it was impossible for me to help it, after what she's been to me. But I was worse than a fool to open my mouth on the subject to an angel like her. Only there again, I couldn't, that is, I hadn't the strength to help it. I beg, however, you won't think me such a downright idiot as to fancy myself worth her. In that case, I should have deserved as much scorn as she gave me kindness. If you ask me how it was, then, that I dared to speak to her on the subject, I can only answer that I yielded to the impulse common to all kinds of love to make itself known. If you love God, you are not content with His knowing it even, but you must tell Him as if He didn't know it. You may think from this cool talk of mine that I am very philosophical about it; but there are lulls in every storm, and I am in one, else I shouldn't be sitting here with you."

"Dear Roger!" I said, "I am very sorry for your disappointment. I can't be sorry you should love Marion. That can do you nothing but good, and in itself must raise you above yourself. And how could I blame you that you wanted her to know it? But come, now, if you can trust me, tell me all about it, and especially what she said to you. I dare not give you any hope, for I am not in her confidence in this matter. It is well that I am not, for then I might not be able to talk to you about it with any freedom. To confess the real truth, I do not see much likelihood, knowing her as I do, that she will recall her decision."

"It could hardly be called a decision," said Roger. "You would have thought, from the way she took it, there was nothing to decide about. No more there was, and I thought I knew it, only I couldn't be quiet. To *think* you know a thing and to *know* it are two very different matters, however."

I was not moved by sympathetic curiosity alone, but also by the vague desire of rendering some help beyond comfort. What he had now said greatly heightened my opinion of him, and thereby, in my thoughts, lessened the distance between him and Marion.

And he did tell me the whole, and I learned more afterward from Marion.

THIRTY
ROGER AND MARION

During an all but sleepless night, Roger had made up his mind to go and see Marion—not, certainly, for the first time, for he had again and again ventured to call upon her. But hitherto he had always had some pretext sufficient to veil his deeper reason; and sufficient also to prevent her, in her more ordinary simplicity with regard to such matters, from suspecting one under it.

She was at home, and received him with her usual kindness. Feeling that he must not let an awkward silence intervene, he spoke at once.

"I want to tell you something, Miss Clare," he said as lightly as he could.

"Well?" she returned, with the sweet smile which graced her every approach to communication.

"Did my sister-in-law ever tell you what an idle fellow I used to be?"

"Certainly not. I never heard her say one word of you that wasn't kind."

"That I am sure of. But there would have been no unkindness in saying that, for an idle fellow I was, and idle because I was conceited enough to believe I could do anything. I actually thought at one time I could play the violin. I made an impertinent attempt in your presence one evening, years and years ago. I wonder if you remember it. Anyhow, I caught a look on your face that cured me of that conceit. I have never touched the creature since."

"I am very sorry, indeed I am. I don't remember—do you think you could have played a false note?"

"Nothing more likely."

"Then, I dare say I made an ugly face. One can't always help it, you know, when something unexpected happens. Do forgive me."

"Forgive *you*, you angel!" cried Roger, but instantly checked himself, afraid of reaching his mark before he had gathered sufficient momentum to pierce it. "I thought you would see what a good thing it was for me. I wanted to thank you for it."

"It's such a pity you didn't go on, though. Progress is the real cure for an overestimate of ourselves."

"The fact is, I was beginning to see what small praise there is in doing many things ill and nothing well. I wish you would take my violin. I could teach you the ABC's—how you would make it talk! That *would* be something to live for, to hear *you* play the violin."

"I have no time. I should have been delighted to be your pupil, but I am sorry to say it is out of the question."

"Of course it is. Only I wish—well, never mind. I only wanted to tell you something. I was leading a life then that wasn't worth leading, for where's the good of being just what happens—one time full of right feeling and impulse, and the next a prey to all wrong judgments and falsehoods? It was you who made me see it. I've been trying to get put right for a long time now. You and your Sunday evenings have waked me up to know what I am, and what I ought to be. I *am* a little better. I work hard now. I used to work only by fits and starts. Ask Wynnie."

"Dear Mr. Roger, I don't need to ask Wynnie about anything you tell me. I can take your word for it just as well as hers. I am very glad if I have been of any use to you. It is a great honor to me."

"But the worst of it is, I couldn't be content without letting you know, and making myself miserable."

"I don't understand you. Surely there can be no harm in letting me know what makes me very happy! How it should make you miserable, I can't imagine."

"Because I can't stop there. I'm driven to say what may offend you. I can't help loving you—dreadfully—and it's such impudence! To think of you and me in one thought! And yet I can't help it. O Miss Clare, don't drive me away from you."

He fell on his knees as he spoke, and laid his head on her lap,

sobbing like a child who had offended his mother. Marion started
to her feet in confusion—almost in terror, for she had never seen
such emotion in a man—but the divine compassion of her nature
conquered, and she sat down again, took his head in her hands,
and began stroking his hair as if she were indeed a mother seeking
to soothe and comfort her troubled child. She was the first to speak
again, for Roger could not command himself.

"I'm very sorry, Roger," she said. "I must be to blame
somehow."

"To blame!" he cried, lifting up his head. *"You* to blame! It
would be downright stupidity not to love you with all my soul."

"Hush! Hush!" said Marion. "You *couldn't* love me with all your
soul if you would. God *only* can be loved with all the power of the
human soul."

"If I love Him at all, Marion, it is you who have taught me. Do
not drive me from you."

"I will not drive you from me. Why should I?"

"Then I may come and see you again?"

"Yes, when you please."

"You *don't* mean I may come as often as I like?"

"Roger," said Marion, pale as death, and rising also—for, alas!
The sunshine of her kindness had caused hopes to blossom whose
buds she had taken only for leaves. "I thought you understood me!
I am not my own to keep or to give away. I belong to these
people—my friends. To take personal and private duties upon me
would be to abandon them. You don't know what it would result
in, or you would not dream of it. Were I to do such a thing, I
should hate and despise and condemn myself with utter reproba-
tion. And then what a prize you would have, my poor Roger!"

But even these were such precious words to hear from her lips!
He fell again on his knees before her as she stood, caught her
hands and, hiding his face in them, poured forth in a torrent,
"Marion, do not think me so selfish as not to have thought about
that. It should be only the better for them all. I can earn quite
enough for you and me too, and so you would have the more time
to give to them. I should never have dreamed of asking you to
leave them."

Deeply moved by the unselfishness of his love, Marion could not
help a pressure of her hands against the face which had sought
refuge within them. Roger fell to kissing them wildly.

But Marion was a woman—and women, I think, look forward

and round about, more than men do, and therefore Marion saw other things. Marion saw that as a married woman, she might be compelled to forsake her friends more or less, for there might arise other and paramount claims on her self-devotion. If she were to have children, she would have no choice in respect to whose welfare should constitute the main business of her life, and it even became a question whether she would have a right to place them in circumstances so unfavorable for growth and education. Therefore, to marry might be tantamount to forsaking her friends.

But where was the need of any such mental parley? Of course, she couldn't marry Roger. How could she marry a man she couldn't look up to? And look up to him she certainly did not, and could not.

"No, Roger," she said, this last thought large in her mind, and withdrew her hands. "It mustn't be. It is out of the question. I can't look up to you," she added, as simply as a child.

"I should think not," he burst out. "That *would* be a fine thing! If you looked up to a fellow like me, I think it would almost cure me of looking up to you, and what I want is to look up to you, only I can do that whether you let me or not."

"But I don't choose to have a—a friend to whom I can't look up."

"Then I shall never be even a friend," he returned sadly. "But I would have tried hard to be less unworthy of you."

At this precise moment, Marion caught sight of a pair of great round blue eyes, wide open under a shock of red hair, about three feet from the floor, staring as if they had not winked for the last ten minutes. The child looked so comical that Marion, reading perhaps in her looks the reflex of her own position, could not help laughing. Roger started up in dismay but, beholding the apparition, laughed also.

"Please, Grannie," said the urchin, "Mother's took bad and wants ye."

"Run and tell your mother I shall be with her directly," answered Marion, and the child departed.

"You told me I might come again," pleaded Roger.

"Better not. I didn't know what it would mean to you when I said it."

"Let it mean what you meant by it, only let me come."

"But I see now it can't mean that. No, but I will write to you. At all events, you must go now, for I can't stop with you—"

"Don't make me wretched, Marion. If you can't love me, don't kill me. Don't say I'm not to come and see you. I *will* come on Sundays, anyhow."

The next day he received the following letter:

"Dear Mr. Roger—

"I am very sorry, both for your sake and my own, that I did not speak more plainly yesterday. I was so distressed for you, and my heart was so friendly toward you that I could hardly think of anything at first but how to comfort you. I fear I allowed you, after all, to go away with the idea that what you wished was not altogether impossible. But indeed it is. If even I loved you in the way you love me, I should yet make everything yield to the duties I have undertaken. In listening to you, I should be undermining the whole of my past labors, and the idea of becoming less of a friend to my friends is horrible to me.

"But as much as I esteem you, and as much pleasure as your society gives me, the idea you brought before me yesterday was absolutely startling. The peculiarities of my position should convince you that it could never become a familiar one to me. All that friendship can do or yield, you may ever claim of me, and I thank God if I have been of the smallest service to you. But I should be quite unworthy of that honor, were I even to think of abandoning the work which has been growing up around me for so many years, and is so peculiarly mine that it could be transferred to no one else.

"Believe me yours most truly,
Marion Clare"

That same Sunday evening as we sat together, after telling me the greater part of the story, Roger handed me this very letter.

I read it and returned it to him. "It seems final, Roger?"

"Of course it is," he replied. "How could any honest man urge his suit after that, after she says that to grant it would be to destroy the whole of her previous life, and ruin her self-respect? But I'm not so miserable as you may think me, Wynnie. Though I couldn't quite bring myself to go tonight, I don't feel cut off from her. She's not likely, if I know her, to listen to anybody else so long as the same reasons hold which wouldn't give me a chance. She can't help me loving her, and I'm sure she'll let me help her when I've the luck to find a chance. You may be sure I shall keep a sharp lookout. If I can be her servant, that will be something. Though she won't give herself to me, she can't prevent me from giving myself to her. So long as I may love her, and see her as often as I don't doubt I may, and things continue as they are, I shan't be downhearted."

Here he started, and hurriedly pulled out his watch. "I declare, there's time yet!" he cried, and sprung to his feet. "Let's go and hear what she's got to say tonight."

"Should you? Won't you put her out?"

"If I understand her at all," he said, "she will be more put out by my absence, for she will fear I am wretched, caring only for herself, and not what she has taught me. You may come or stay— *I'm* off. You've done me so much good, Wynnie!" he added, looking back in the doorway. "Thank you a thousand times. There's no comforter like a sister."

Percivale and I followed as quickly as we could. When we reached Lime Court, there was Roger sitting in the midst, intent on her words, and Marion speaking with all her natural composure.

When she shook hands with him after the service, a slight flush washed the white of her face with a delicate warmth, nothing more. I said to myself, however, as we went home, and afterward to my husband, that his case was not a desperate one.

"But what's to become of Blackstone?" asked Percivale.

I know how afterward Mr. Blackstone seemed to me to have fared, but I have no information concerning his supposed connection with this part of my story. I cannot even be sure that he was in love with Marion. Troubled he certainly was, at this time, and Marion continued so for a while—more troubled, I think, than her words with Roger will quite account for. If, however, she had to make two men miserable in one week, that might well cover the case.

Before the week was over, my husband received a note from Mr. Blackstone, informing him that he was just about to start for a few weeks on the Continent. When he returned I was satisfied from his appearance that a notable change had passed upon him: a certain indescribable serenity seemed to have taken possession of his whole being, and every look and tone indicated a mind that knew more than tongue could utter—a heart that had had glimpses into a region of content. I thought of the words, "He that dwelleth in the secret place of the Most High," and my heart was at rest about him. He had fared, I thought, as the child who has had a hurt, but is taken up in his mother's arms and comforted. What hurt would not such comforting outweigh to the child? And who but he that has had the worst hurt man can receive, and the best comfort God can give, can tell what either is?

I was present the first time he met Marion after his return. She was a little embarrassed: he showed a tender dignity, a respect as if from above, like the love of a wise angel for such a woman. For the moment I felt as if Mr. Blackstone were a step above Marion. Plainly, I had no occasion to be troubled about either of them.

On the supposition that Marion had refused him, I argued with myself that it could not have been on the ground that she was unable to look up to him. And I was satisfied that anyone she felt she could help to be a nobler creature must have a greatly better chance of rousing all the woman in her, than one whom she must regard as needing no aid from her. All her life had been spent in serving and sheltering human beings whose condition she regarded with hopeful compassion. Could she now help adding Roger to her number of such? If she once looked upon him thus tenderly, was it not at least possible that, in some softer mood, a feeling hitherto unknown to her might surprise her consciousness with its presence, floating to the surface of her sea from its strange depths, and leaning toward him with the outstretched arms of embrace?

But I dared not think what might become of Roger should his divine resolves fail—should the frequent society of Marion prove insufficient for the solace and quiet of his heart.

As the days went on, though, I saw no sign of failure or change in Roger. He was steady at his work, and came to see us as constantly as before. He never missed a chance of meeting Marion, and at every treat she gave her friends, Roger was always at hand for service and help. Still, I was uneasy, for might there not come a collapse, especially if some new event were to destroy the hope which he still cherished, and which I feared was his main support? Would his religion then prove of a quality and power sufficient to keep him from drifting away with the receding tide of his hopes and imaginations? In this anxiety perhaps I regarded too exclusively the faith of Roger, and thought too little about the faith of God. However this may be, I could not rest, but thought and thought, until at last I made up my mind to go and tell Lady Bernard all about it.

THIRTY-ONE

SOME FINAL WORDS

"And you think Marion likes him?" asked Lady Bernard, when she had in silence heard my story.

"I am sure she *likes* him. But you know he is so far inferior to her in every way."

"How do you know that? Questions are involved there which no one but God can determine. You must remember that both are growing. What matter if any two are unequal at a given moment, seeing their relative positions may be reversed twenty times in a thousand years? Besides, I doubt very much if any one who brought his favors with him would have the least chance with Marion. Poverty, to turn into wealth, is the one irresistible attraction for her—and, however duty may compel her to act, my impression is that she will not escape *loving* Roger."

I was gratified to find Lady Bernard's conclusion from Marion's character running parallel with my own.

"But what can come of it?" I said.

"Why, marriage, I hope."

"But Marion would as soon think of falling down and worshiping Baal and Ashtoreth as of forsaking her grandchildren."

"Doubtless. But there would be no occasion for that. Where two things are both of God, it is not likely they will be found mutually obstructive."

"Roger does declare himself quite ready to go and live amongst her friends, and do his best to help her."

"That is all as it should be, so far as he—as both of them are

212

concerned, but there are contingencies: how would that do in regard of their children?"

"If I could imagine Marion consenting," I said, "I know what she would answer to that question. She would ask why her children should be better off than the children about them? She would say that the children must share the life and work of their parents."

"And I think she would be right, though the obvious rejoinder would be, 'You may waive your own social privileges, and sacrifice yourselves to the good of others, but have you a right to sacrifice your children, and heap disadvantages on their future?' "

"Now give us the answer on the other side, seeing you think Marion would be right after all."

"Marion's answer would be, I think, that their children would be God's children, and He couldn't desire better for them than to be born in lowly conditions, and trained from the first to give themselves to the service of their fellows, seeing that in so far their history would resemble that of His own Son, our Saviour In sacrificing their earthly future, as men would call it, their parents would but be furthering their eternal good."

"But how would her new position affect her ministrations?"

"There can be no doubt," Lady Bernard replied, "that what her friends would lose thereby—I mean, what amount of her personal ministrations would be turned aside from them by the necessities of her new position—would be far more than made up to them by the presence among them of a whole well-ordered and growing family, instead of a single woman only. But all this yet leaves something for her more personal friends to consider, as regards their duty in the matter. I will turn the thing over in my mind, and let you know what comes of it."

The result of Lady Bernard's cogitations is, so far, to be seen in the rapid rise of a block of houses at no great distance from London on the Northwestern railway, planned under the instructions of Marion Clare. The design provides accommodation for all Marion's friends, with room to add largely to their number. Lady Bernard has also secured ground sufficient for great extension of the present building, should it prove desirable. Each family is to have the same amount of accommodation it has now—only far better—at the same rent it pays now, with the privilege of taking an additional room or rooms at a much lower rate. Marion has undertaken to collect the rents, and believes that she will thus in time gain an additional hold of the people for their good, although the plan may at first expose her to misunderstanding. From thorough calculation she is satisfied she can pay Lady Bernard five per cent for her money, lay out all that is necessary for keeping the property in thorough repair, and accumulate a fund besides to be spent on building more houses. The removal of so many will also make a little room for the accommodation of the multitudes constantly driven from their homes by the wickedness of those who, either for the sake of railways or fine streets, pull down crowded houses, and drive into other courts and alleys their poor inhabitants, to double the wretchedness already there from overcrowding.

In the center of the building is a house for Marion, where she will have her own private advantage in the inclusion of large space primarily for the entertainment of her friends. I believe Lady Bernard intends to give her a hint that a married couple would, in her opinion, be far more useful in such a position than a single woman.

If the scheme should answer, what a strange reversion it will be to something like a right reading of the feudal system!

Of course, it will be objected that, should it succeed ever so well, it will all go to pieces at Marion's death. But such a work as hers can never be lost, for the world can never be the same as if she had not lived, while in any case there will be more room for her brothers and sisters who are now being crowded out of the world by the stronger and richer. It would be sufficient answer, however, that the work is worth doing for its own sake and its immediate result. Surely it will receive a "Well Done" from the Judge of us all. And while His idea of right remains above hers, as high as the heavens are above the earth, His approbation will be all that either Lady Bernard or Marion will seek.

If but a small proportion of those who love the right and have means to spare would, like Lady Bernard, use their wealth to make up to the poor for the wrongs they receive at the hands of the rich—let me say, to defend the Saviour in their persons from the tyranny of Mammon—how many of the poor might they not lead with them into the joy of the Lord!

There are many more things to say, of my own family and those of my friends, but words have already multiplied too abundantly, and there is no time left to say it all. And what better thing, in the end, can I say except that we all live in hope of the glory of God!

EDITOR'S AFTERWORD

Good stories endure. Styles and fashions fade.

The second statement explains why George MacDonald's novels have not been widely read in the last sixty years. The first statement explains why they are once more coming to public attention.

While reading *The Vicar's Daughter*, one should remember that it was not written as an historical novel—it was a *contemporary* work when published in 1872. MacDonald's works were written from life, and reflect his deep insight into the nature of God, fallen man, and redeemed man. The places and people were taken from places and people near at hand, from all that he knew best.

The Marshmallows of *A Quiet Neighborhood* and *The Vicar's Daughter* is MacDonald's name for the village of Arundel, situated directly south of London and only a few miles north of the English Channel. Arundel was the scene of MacDonald's first pastorate, from 1850 to 1853. He served a small Congregational assembly, whose chapel still stands, though disused, in the heart of tiny Arundel.

London is accurately portrayed in *The Vicar's Daughter* as well. The Tottenham Court area of London (where Percivale and Wynnie lived) still contains traces and memories of MacDonald's world.

MacDonald and his family lived briefly at 18 Queen Square, a short walk northeast of the British Museum; the house was soon after torn down for the construction of a children's hospital. This house presumably served as the model for the house of Marion Clare's memories. The square is still there with its statue, labeled now as Queen Charlotte, with a notice that in the previous century it had been thought to be Queen Anne.

The Blue Posts Pub is still there, though greatly modernized, southwest of the British Museum on Tottenham Court Road.

And Lady Bernard is based upon a very real person and dear friend of the MacDonalds—Lady Noel Byron, widow of Lord Byron, the poet. The generosity and warmth of Lady Bernard reflect Lady Byron's generosity and warmth to the MacDonald family.

The Vicar's Daughter (along with *A Quiet Neighborhood* and *The Seaboard Parish*), was reprinted in numerous editions throughout MacDonald's lifetime. But after he died in Surrey in 1905, his novels began a slow fade from the public eye. Old copies of the books traded hands quietly over the ensuing years, but no major attempt was made to reprint them.

My desire to obtain, read, and finally edit for republication *The Vicar's Daughter* led to the Wade Collection at Wheaton College, Wheaton, Illinois, one of the finest collections of MacDonald's works on this side of the Atlantic. Dr. Lyle Dorsett and Brenda Phillips of the Collection kindly supplied a copy of this virtually unobtainable volume for the purpose of preparing this abridgement.

As in the previous two volumes, the aim of the editing process has been to achieve a balance between brevity and breadth that will be economical to print, interesting to the reader of the 1980s, and faithful to the heart of MacDonald's vision. We do not pretend that this version is *better* than the original, merely shorter and easier to read. Wherever an original copy of *The Vicar's Daughter* may come to hand, it will be well worth the effort to acquire and read it in its entirety.

Dan Hamilton
Indianapolis, Indiana
November 1984